Lord of
the Forest

Lord of
the Forest

Dawn Thompson

APHRODISIA
KENSINGTON BOOKS
http://www.kensingtonbooks.com

APHRODISIA BOOKS are published by

Kensington Publishing Corp.
850 Third Avenue
New York, NY 10022

All Kensington Titles, Imprints, and Distributed Lines are available at special quantity discounts for bulk purchases for sales promotions, premiums, fund-raising, and educational or institutional use.

Special book excerpts or customized printings can also be created to fit specific needs. For details, write or phone the office of the Kensington special sales manager: Kensington Publishing Corp., 850 Third Avenue, New York, NY 10022, attn: Special Sales Department, Phone: 1-800-221-2647.

Aphrodisia and the A logo U.S. Pat & TM Off.

ISBN-13: 978-0-7582-2709-6
ISBN-10: 0-7582-2709-4

First Kensington Trade Paperback Printing: January 2009

10 9 8 7 6 5 4 3 2 1

Printed in the United States of America

Lord of
the Forest

1

---

*The Forest Isle, Archipelago of Arcus,
the Summer Solstice*

Marius, Lord of the Forest, Prince of the Green, moved through the wood. It was nearly time. All was in readiness for the Midsummer festival. He dreaded it more and more each year, putting up with giddy nymphs and sylphs and dryads from the astral and playing host to curious mortals carrying on like cretins for three days and nights.

He passed the ancestral oak in the clearing that had been chosen to serve as the Midsummer tree. All through the day, wood nymphs had decorated its branches with garlands of honeysuckle, silkworm's gauze, and summer berries. Come midnight, women would dance naked around it, chanting the fertility descants and raising the sexual consciousness of the revelers, for that's what Midsummer was, after all—a three-day orgiastic celebration meant to bring bounty to all the hemispheres of Arcus.

During the rituals, he would be expected to perform, to have coitus with fay and humans alike, if any possessed the prowess to catch him. He would be pursued—at their mercy—hunted down and captured like an animal for three steamy days and nights of bed sport with one of them. That part of the ritual would ensure a fruitful harvest.

Marius sighed. He must be getting old. Normally he would have enjoyed the sensual Midsummer rituals. He used to look forward to the chase—to the thrill of the capture and the turn-about, when the conquered became conqueror and ravished the fair maiden, who had pursued him and become Lady of the Feast—but this time he dreaded it. This time the solstice did not fall during the full moon or any of the safe phases. This time the moon-dark threatened; and at the dark of the moon, Marius, Prince of the Green, became the centaur until the new sickle moon appeared in the indigo vault, canceling the phenomenon, allowing him to return to his human form.

In all the eons since he'd been cursed to share his body with the centaur, the movable feast had only come at moon-dark once. He didn't want to think about that, not now, on the brink of what could well be another catastrophe of like proportions.

But there was still a little time yet before the festivities began, before he would have to strip naked and run masked through the forest until some skilled huntress swifter than the rest took him down and claimed his cock. All that would commence at midnight. What was wanted was a soaking in the hidden pool beforehand, and Marius headed for it like a man possessed.

Following the mineral spring deep in the wood, he passed through the invisible portal that cloaked the rock pool it fed into, scarcely aware of a rustling noise behind. It came again and he hesitated at the edge of the grotto, giving ear. The hidden pool was his secret hideaway. No one else knew it existed, and none could enter save a creature like himself because of the invisible force field around it. Except for the Sage Tree, a sprawling willow that stood beside the pool, its wispy foliage skimming the water. A venerable spirit lived inside its silvery trunk, but it was unlike the Ancient Ones that lived in the trees of the forest. The gods had gifted the willow with the power of extraordinary intelligence and speech, and Marius availed himself of its wisdom often.

Still listening, he called upon his extraordinary hearing, but all was quiet except for the echo of gently lapping water. He glanced at the willow. It seemed to be sleeping. Surely it would have warned him if something untoward was about to happen. He shrugged, tugged off his boots, stripped off his buckskins, and plunged naked into the pool.

Rich mineral steam scented with herbs rose around him, and he tore off the braided vine that held his long hair at the nape of his neck and ducked his head beneath the water. He groaned as he broke the surface again. If only he could stay hidden here in the pool until the solstice was over, but that could not be. Marius pressed the water from his hair, then seized a cake of pine tar soap from a scallop-shell dish at the edge of the pool and began to lather his body.

Rich thick suds slid down his sun-bronzed chest, parted by the dark oval nipples so sensitive to touch. It sheeted down his hard roped torso, collecting in his navel, and wreathed his hips like a garland. Reaching beneath the water, he took hold of his penis and lathered it roughly. Soon enough the transformation would take place, turning him into the creature he loathed, and that shaft, magnificent though it was, would become a gargantuan appendage three times the size it was now, a force to be reckoned with, demanding release where there could be none. As the centaur, he was of a size no woman could take inside her. Few avenues would be open to him for sexual gratification until the new moon freed him from the curse again, which, he bitterly believed, was a cruel trick of the gods. His climax as the centaur was unlike any other, and in that form, his anatomy was such that he couldn't even reach his cock to relieve himself.

Yet it was only for three days each month. Quite bearable ordinarily, though the gods made sure he was always tempted and tortured with lust during those three grueling days. And there was always the chance that passion in any form, be it rage or sexual, might bring the centaur out. That, however, was a rare occurrence.

Either would be dreaded now. This was the Summer Solstice, when he was commanded to call upon his legendary virility and perform, to bless the land with abundance. With the change to a centaur looming, and no way to predict the precise moment when the transformation would take place, it did not bode well.

Marius loosed a string of expletives under his breath. His handling of his cock with the satiny lather had made him hard. He dared not waste his seed in the pool as he had so many times before. Not this night. Soon he would be caught up in the pageantry of Midsummer, set upon and run to ground in mock captivity by a beautiful maiden, one of many who would compete to take him down and possess his body throughout the celebration. There could be only one winner. Her sexual appetites would be insatiable, and he must save his stamina for that. But, oh, how his loins ached for the release a few rough tugs on his throbbing penis would bring. He had but to rub the mushroom tip with his thumb, massaging the rich, creamy lather over the ridged head ever so gently to come. Instead, he ducked his head beneath the water and shook himself fiercely, as if that would shake off the arousal. It didn't work.

When he broke the surface again, it was to pull up short. *Pop!* went his hope of calm. He wasn't alone. On the brink of the pool stood an exquisite creature, so fair she seemed golden, as though her skin had been kissed by the sun.

Marius's jaw fell slack. There wasn't a stitch on her. Caught by surprise, he was unable to take his eyes from the perfect breasts, their hard nipples, tawny pink, poking through a curtain of honey-colored waves of hair that teased her waist. His gaze slid lower, to her pubic mound and hairless sex, her nether lips like the center of an exquisite orchid. He couldn't see her face. It was hidden behind a Midsummer mask in the image of an antelope, its spiral horns glistening with faery dust. There was no moon in the darkening sky. No rush lights had been lit beside the pool or torches around the grotto, and yet she shone with an ethereal glow, as if she were lit from within.

"H-how did you get in here?" he stammered, clearing his parched throat. "Who are you?"

But she neither moved nor spoke, and he surged out of the water and scrambled up onto the edge of the pool without a second thought for his own nakedness. He spun back toward her, but all that remained was the feminine echo of her musical laughter, like gently pealing bells.

Had he dreamed her? Had she vanished into thin air, or had she slipped behind one of the grotto trees? "Who are you?" he called out, his head turning in all directions as he searched the twilight for some sign of motion, but there was none. He continued to call out to her while he circled the pool, unwilling to concede that he had imagined her.

Most troublesome was that she had found her way into his secret retreat—the last bastion of his peace of mind, body, and spirit. Of all the supernatural isles in the Arcan Archipelago, the Forest Isle was the most enchanted. It formed a natural bridge between the astral and human planes, accessible to both mortals and the fay. Few from the mainland frequented the isle, but nymphs, dryads, sylphs, as well as their male counterparts came and went often. Otherworldly creatures of all descriptions used the Forest Isle as a holiday retreat. It had become a place where they could come to revel in the wood for both their spiritual and sexual enlightenment among the Ancient Ones, the eons-old tree spirits that lived within the ancestral oaks, pines, rowan, ash, and whitethorns, to name but a few. But the hidden pool was *his*—all his, and he wasn't about to share it no matter how exquisite a creature she was.

Behind him, the sound of a sigh spun him around to face the

Sage Tree that had lifted its branches, yawning awake. Arms akimbo, Marius addressed the venerable willow, his voice like a whip. "Outstanding, Philonous!" he seethed. "Now you wake! Who was that? How did she get in here? I know you see all, waking and sleeping. Why didn't you warn me?"

The tree gave another yawn. "You were in no danger." It reached with one of its long, lacy branches and pointed toward the obvious. "I thought you might appreciate something sweet and private to relieve *that* before the Midsummer madness begins. You know what will happen if the moon does not rise tonight and you enter into your other body. I wouldn't want to be you if they crowned me King of the Fay when that pack of lusty women finds out there will be no coupling with the legendary Lord of the Forest this Midsummer."

Marius gave his stiff cock a ruthless tug with his fist and roared, "Do not remind me!"

"She is quite comely, your little intruder, is she not?" the tree drawled on. "And very enterprising, sneaking in behind you that way. No other has managed it in all these years. What harm to—"

"This is my private place, Philonous," Marius interrupted. "*Mine!* In all my eons, I have never brought a woman here." Enlightenment struck and he stiffened as if he'd been shot. "You *let* her in, didn't you? *Didn't you!*" he shouted.

"How could I have done that?"

Marius laughed without humor. "You have your ways," he accused the tree.

"Yes, well, not this time. I was asleep, remember?"

"How did she get in here, then?" Marius demanded.

The tree sketched the closest thing to a shrug it could and gestured toward a stand of young saplings behind him. "Don't know," it said. "Why don't you ask her?"

Marius spun around so fast he almost fell back into the pool. Slip-sliding and teetering on the slippery brink, he muttered curses at the image he must be presenting, naked and aroused, floundering—arms flailing in the air—as he fought to regain his balance.

A sound from behind turned him back momentarily. Was that snoring? It was. Philonous had fallen back to sleep, and Marius cursed again as more peals of musical laughter assailed his ears. Spinning back around again, his eyes blazing green fire, he stalked toward the mysterious masked creature peeking through the saplings' branches.

"How in the name of Mica did you get in here?" he demanded. He seldom invoked the name of the God of All. He knew firsthand how dangerous that could be, but he was beyond incensed. He wanted no memories—sexual or otherwise—connected with his little oasis.

She made no move to back away but stepped out in the open and sauntered closer, stopping him in his tracks as if she'd struck him. Instead, she raised her hand, laid a finger across his lips, which had formed a hard rigid line, and looked deep into his eyes. His green fire jousted with the most alluring shade of amber he had ever seen. Her eyes shone like gold.

"Does it really matter how I came here?" she murmured.

Her voice was sultry, with a cool undertone, like water rushing over pebbles in a sparkling brook and held some of the irresistible music of her laughter. He suppressed a groan. She'd made him harder. Who was she? If only he could see her face. For all he knew, she could be an odious crone working some spell of entrapment. He'd seen enough of such creatures over the years. Still, if that was the case, Philonous would not have been so complacent . . . would he? Even a Sage Tree could make mistakes.

"I shan't tell anyone of your secret place if that's what you fear," she crooned, jarring him out of his thoughts. "I want you all to myself. Take the gift, Lord of the Forest. Time grows short . . ."

She crowded closer until the head of his erect penis touched the soft swell of her naked belly. She smelled of the exotic vanilla orchid, laced with the musk of arousal, and he was undone.

His arms flew around her. Her skin was like warm satin. He could feel its heat beneath her hair, like spider silk, as he ran his fingers through it. His hands slid lower, inching down the length of her spine, then cupped her firm, round buttocks and traced the fissure between until she shuddered.

"Remove the mask," he said, his voice husky with desire. "I would see your face. For all I know, I could be about to couple with a banshee . . . or a succubus."

"I assure you I am neither," she murmured, her honey-sweet breath puffing against his moist face through the air holes in the mask.

Marius groaned. There was no turning back. It was the solstice, after all, and he was on the verge of becoming something with a cock so enormous it would break a woman in half. It had to be now, while he was still a man, before the centaur robbed him of the offering. Else he would suffer in a perpetual state of arousal until the new moon freed him once again from the curse that turned him from man to beast whenever the heavens went dark.

"Take the gift," she murmured again, fondling his thick shaft, fingering the distended veins standing out in bold relief as hot blood rushed to the mushroom tip. *Ahhh.*

Her delicate touch—as light as the kiss of a butterfly's wing—was like a lightning strike. It was too late now for anything but being inside this mysterious creature's willing flesh, peeling back the petals of that exquisite orchidlike flower between her hot, silken thighs and pounding into her in a frenzy of carnal oblivion. Midsummer madness! Nothing short of coming until he'd emptied himself in her would slake the lust she'd ignited in him. He wrapped her legs around his waist, rushed her against the sturdy back of an ivy-covered whitethorn, and plunged into her to the root of his sex, grinding it against the flushed bud of her female erection, as hard as steel boring into him.

Huzzah for the solstice!

One by one, her thick folds seized his shaft as he entered her inner chambers until the hard ridged head of his penis nudged her womb. Crying out, she laced her fingers together behind his neck, arched her body, and took him deeper. Her head swayed until her long honeyed hair grazed his thighs.

"Mica's beard!" he cried. "Who are you—*what* are you to make my cock sing so?"

"I am spirit," she murmured.

Marius loosed a gravelly chuckle. "No spirit ever gripped my cock like this!" he scoffed.

"I am spirit of the antelope, the *Bovidae*. We are . . . what we are, Prince of the Green."

Marius had no idea what she meant. Spirit—flesh—whatever incarnation, she was about to make him come. Just gazing toward her upturned breasts, his hooded eyes feasting upon the tawny buds so hard and tall, sent shockwaves of liquid fire racing through his groin. And when his thumbs grazed her nipples, she seemed to melt in his arms.

Marius moaned. Had passion taken over? His need was unstoppable, his appetite insatiable when the change began—the white-hot spiral of excruciating agony that swept him in a blinding streak of mercurial energy from man to beast. He could feel his body shifting, stretching—straining to become the centaur. He pulled out of her without climaxing, a string of curses on his lips, and spun away just in time. He was the centaur. Fully aroused. Hooves pawing the ground.

Prancing in a circle, Marius reared, searching the darkness in all directions with frantic eyes, but there was no sign of the mysterious creature who had loved him so well. She had vanished before his eyes without telling him her name. He didn't know if she was even real or Midsummer magic his split self had dreamed up to drive him mad. He was clearly on the verge of that as he galloped off, still aroused, voicing his discomfort like a wounded beast as he crashed through the undergrowth and disappeared into the copse that surrounded the pool.

2

Marius heard the Sage Tree calling. He was just too distraught to answer. Revelers would be arriving now, but he'd calculated correctly that there would be no moon. He would have to face a horde of rampaging females hungry for sex, which he could not give them in his present incarnation, despite being aroused to the point of pain. Dark of the moon could not have been more uncertain or ill timed.

The tree's gruff voice came again. What was it saying? Something about the sky . . . Marius pricked up his ears and listened. The hidden pool with its grotto and copse of saplings was at the center of the Forest Isle. It was the entrance and first link in the chain of subterranean ways out that joined it to Lord Vane's Isle of Fire by an underwater passage.

Gifted with extraordinary hearing, Marius could hear a feather fall anywhere on his isle, for he was neither human nor fay, though he resembled both in many ways and treated them as brethren. He was an immortal elemental of the land, of nature and the forest, cursed by the gods to live out his lonely existence for all eternity, sharing the body of a creature he had once killed. He was endowed with many supernatural gifts, but not one among them could overcome the curse, for he had disturbed his bond with Nature—shattered it—when he killed the beast he had been duty-bound to protect, a most grievous crime. Oddly, it wasn't the crime itself that cursed him. He could have repented with a word. It was his lack of remorse for the beast's death to this very day, though the offense had occurred eons ago, back during the great cataclysm when the archipelago was formed. He never spoke of it, but what was happening to him now harkened back to the day of the curse, brought it all rushing to the fore of his mind. It was unbearable.

The willow tree's hoarse voice assailed his ears again, and he streaked through the little copse and confronted it, rearing back on his hind legs, forefeet flying. "What? *What*?" he trumpeted. "Spit it out, you lazy good-for-nothing voyeur!"

"Impetuous fool!" Philonous cried. "Look! Look to the sky. What do you see?"

Marius squinted toward the indigo heavens. Even though the pool was cloaked, the same sky stretched above. The moon *had* risen. Granted, it wasn't much of one, but the slim sliver shining down should have been enough to keep the centaur at bay. Why hadn't it?

"Did I miscalculate? I don't understand," Marius said, scowling toward the heavens. "If that moon hanging there is real, how am I thus?"

"These things are the gods' doing," the tree said. "You were not so very wrong, but it appears that the phases are not yet complete. It is not quite moon-dark. With all your worrying about what might be, you've lost sight of what is. You will be able to make your run tonight after all, possibly even on the morrow as well. By the looks of that moon, I wouldn't think you'll be fortunate enough to manage the whole three-day celebration, but it shan't be a total loss. Now, calm yourself, then go and make ready. It is nearly time."

Marius pounded his flanks with white-knuckled fists. "How can I, like this? And you haven't answered me—why am I in this body if the moon hasn't quite gone dark yet?"

"*She* brought the centaur out, young fool. The passion you felt for that exquisite creature's embrace is what's done it."

Marius had to admit that Philonous was right.

"If what occurred here before has made me thus, what is to keep it from happening again if I do make my Midsummer run?"

The tree sketched another shrug, lifting a long, feathery branch. "Nothing," it said, "except perhaps your willpower, now that you are aware. You are being tested, Marius, Lord of the Forest, by the look of it. These things occur for a purpose. We are never enlightened without one. Do not fly in the face of destiny. You are shown this now to prepare yourself, because you will have need of the knowledge at some point. Now, calm down and let Marius, the man, emerge."

"Who was she, Philonous?" Marius asked. "Will I ever see her again? No one has ever made me feel like that!"

"She told you who she was."

"What, that business about her being spirit? Midsummer nonsense. They all have their tall tales to tell. You don't expect me to believe that?"

Philonous sighed. "In all the eons that you've roamed the realm of Arcus, one would think you'd have found the time to read its lore, young Marius."

"You are saying she told me the truth? If that is so, tell me how is it that 'in all the eons' I have never seen her before?"

"Linnea shows herself to whom she will when she will. Evidently, you have finally gained her favor. At the very least, you have definitely caught her notice."

Marius's jaw dropped. "L-Linnea? *The Huntress*?"

The sage tree nodded its foliage. "They say she is the daughter of the Great White Stag that protects the forests of this isle and all the forests of Arcus."

Marius's mind reeled back to his latest encounter with the legendary stag, when it drove the demon lord Ravelle back into Outer Darkness, saving the forest and liberating Marius, Lord of the Dark. Gooseflesh crawled the length of his spine just thinking about it.

The blood-chilling recollection triggered deeper thoughts, and the legend of the huntress ghosted across his memory. Linnea was one of the most well-guarded secrets in Nature. She was reputed to be the offspring of the Great Stag himself, and Ria, a Nature elemental of mixed human blood who possessed the spirit of the antelope. Linnea was an enigma of myth so far removed from worldly and otherworldly lore that she had become lost in the mists of time. It was said she did not give her favors lightly or often . . . and she had favored *him.* He could not wrap his mind around how incredible that was.

All at once, a shock to his middle doubled him over. The change back was occurring, and he groaned, for it was always painful when bones stretched and muscles expanded and contracted. Falling to his knees, he let the transformation take him, and in a blinding, pulsating streak of silver-white light, he returned to his human form, naked, his body running with sweat from the ordeal. Staggering erect, he dove into the pool to let the mineral salts soothe his sore skin and penetrate his aching muscles. It was a quick purge, for it was nearly midnight, and the rituals were about to begin. He would wear no costume. The race was run naked. He would, however, be masked, just as Linnea had been. He blinked and saw his headdress in Philonous's branches. The tree offered it with reverence.

"Stag of the chase," the tree said. "You are safe from the centaur for this night at least, but you must steel yourself against passion, or you will call him back again, which is why you had this little test."

"I will try," Marius said dourly. It did not bode well.

"You will succeed," the tree corrected him. "Do not trouble

yourself overmuch with things beyond your comprehension. Enlightenment comes in its own time—not yours."

Marius didn't need the lecture. He was hardly a novice. He'd done this since time out of mind.

"Indeed," Philonous said, answering Marius's thoughts, "but you've never had a visit from the goddess of the hunt on Solstice Eve before. Now go! The celebration has begun!"

Marius made no reply. He took the elaborate headdress and slipped it on. It completely covered his head, but the eye and nostril holes were well placed, giving him ample air and a wide field of vision. He glanced behind him. The willow sighed and settled back into sleep mode. A quick glance toward the star-studded vault overhead reassured him that the tiny slice of moon still hung there. All was well. Why, then, were the fine hairs on the back of his neck standing on end? Why was cold sweat running over his brow beneath the stag mask? And why was his heart racing like a runaway stallion?

Marius heaved a sigh, and another, deep and cleansing, as if to purge whatever unease his extraordinary powers of perception had set loose in him. Then moving his head from side to side, he flexed every muscle in a ritualistic limbering exercise and stepped back through the invisible portal into the forest.

The hidden pool was situated deep in the wood. Few ventured this far, for it was a dismal place, where beings who had aged to a point of nearly perpetual slumber awaited their final journey to the afterlife. While they were immortal just as he was, they celebrated their lives at different plateaus of existence. Only fools disturbed their slumber.

Moving stealthily, Marius padded from tree to tree, following the brook fed by the mineral spring until he came to the clearing that separated that desolate quarter from the rest of the forest. There was no way to breach the distance and reach the dense forest except by sprinting across.

The bonfires had been lit in the clearing, the only place they were allowed since a past holocaust had cost many Ancient Ones their lives, for they were vulnerable to fire. Already, female revelers were dancing naked to the music of flute and lyre around the Midsummer tree, their lithe bodies tinted golden in the firelight. The trick would be passing them unnoticed if he was to gain a head start in the chase. This would not be easy. He'd seen his image in the brook, and it was a breathtaking one, his lean, muscular body burnished to a bronze patina, his erection standing out in bold relief against the night. Every muscle, every corded sinew of his powerful frame was at the ready for the ritual to come. Crowned with the traditional stag's head, his magnificence would be hard to miss, but the disadvantage was all part of the game.

Best to have the whole thing over with. He took a bold step into the open and began the run.

All around, the forest was alive with milling bodies, some in pursuit, some engaged in orgiastic rituals that would go on through the night. The days were reserved for sleeping, when not sampling the endless array of food and drink set out in colorful tents. Here, mead and May wine overflowed from fountains, and solstice cakes bursting with unborn grains and slathered with honey were heaped on trenchers, alongside platters of summer fruits. No meat was eaten. No animal was sacrificed.

What he gave, he would get.

Pursuit was instantaneous, but Marius was a skilled runner. He would prolong the chase as long as possible before he let himself be caught by some comely maiden anxious to forfeit her virginity to the stag of the feast. But it wasn't for the sake of the ritual that he prolonged the sport. Truth be told, he was hoping for a glimpse of Linnea again—hoping to have her catch him and finish what she'd started with him earlier, the centaur be damned!

With the help of the Ancient Ones' lush foliage, it was easy to evade the pursuers from time to time, just long enough to confuse and scatter them throughout the wood to be further misled by the tree spirits. It was all part of the chase. Then, after a time, he would emerge from the woods again, and the chase would recommence. Sometimes the reprieves were brief, and sometimes a clever young maiden would best him and claim her conjugal right as queen of the solstice feast. At that point, they would pair off and the rest would seek their pleasures among the other revelers until the dawn.

Marius was in the midst of the second such reprieve, when he saw an image through the trees that stopped him in his tracks. Moving stealthily among the Ancient Ones was another naked runner wearing a stag mask identical to his own. He could have been gazing in a looking glass. Gooseflesh puckered his scalp beneath the headdress. What was this? There was supposed to be only one Lord of the Feast.

Ravelle! It was the first thought that came to mind was the demon. The appearance of the great satyr boded ill. Ravelle, the Lord of Outer Darkness, had nearly decimated the Forest Isle with his projected image in an attempt to destroy Marius, Lord of the Dark, Marius's friend and fellow Arcan prince. While that plot had failed, the demon had old and bitter scores to settle with Marius, and it would stand to reason that the lord of the Arcan netherworld would next turn his wrath upon the Prince of the Green. What better time than the Solstice for the demon to exact his current revenge? No other entity—human or fay—would dare to make so bold an intrusion upon the Midsummer rituals.

That the demon had taken on human form was not unusual. Ravelle was a skilled shapeshifter, able to move about in any body, whether it be in the flesh or merely his projected image. Which was Marius seeing now? It was nearly impossible to tell from this distance. Even at close range it would be difficult. That was what made Ravelle such a formidable adversary.

Concentrating upon where the mystery stag was going, Marius didn't see the net until he'd been caught in it. Thrown off balance, he crashed to the ground and landed hard in a heap of mulch, the net cinched in so close around him, the antlers on his headgear became hopelessly tangled in it. It looked as if spiders had spun the delicate mesh, and yet it was as strong as steel.

He'd been caught fairly, and he made no protest as his captor came into view, her image thus far having been restricted by the awkward angle Marius found himself trapped in—his own fault for losing focus.

How fair she was, seen by fire glow, flushed from the chase. How long and slender her legs were. No wonder she'd taken him down so easily. She moved with an ethereal grace that defied description, and took his breath away as she set about the business of freeing him from the net.

Her movements were lithe as she glided around him, freeing his antlers. She did not speak as she worked, nor did she meet his gaze, though Marius never took his eyes from her beautiful face. She smiled, and dawn broke over his soul like thunder, or was that his runaway heart? It was racing, thudding against his ribs—but not from the chase. He had never seen anything so exquisite as this golden maiden bending over him, her firm breasts, with their rose-tawny nipples so close to his hungry eyes. It was all he could do to restrain himself from capturing one between his lips.

And her hair! Cascading over her shoulders from a center part, it was like a silken stream of honey, starred with pinpoints of reflected light from the bonfires, her oval face framed in wispy tendrils. His fingers ached to touch it, to run through its gossamer silkiness—ah, he couldn't remember when he'd been so taken by any female, human or fay, in all his years roaming the planet.

All thoughts of Ravelle evaporated when at last she gazed

directly at him. Those eyes, those incredible golden eyes, were all he'd glimpsed of her lovely face, concealed behind the elaborate antelope mask, when she'd appeared by the hidden pool. This was Linnea; there was no question. He would know those eyes, that body, anywhere.

Kneeling, she lifted the stag mask from his head and set it aside, according to the ritual custom, the gesture signifying capture. It was hardly necessary. She had captured him at the hidden pool. He'd thought of nothing else since—until he'd spied Ravelle. He beat that image back, crowded it right out of his thoughts. There was no place for it now, while this exquisite goddess was bending over him, her sparkling eyes revealing her arousal.

Her scent hypnotized him. The exotic vanilla orchid blended with her own feral musk, racy and evocative, overwhelmed him. Delicate, irresistible, it wafted through his nostrils, paralyzing his senses, reducing the shadow of the demon to nothing but an annoying pin prick at the back of his mind. He was as drunk on the intoxicating scents drifting from her golden skin as a knave in his cups.

Swarms of revelers had gathered around them. Beguiled, Marius hadn't noticed them until they were practically on top of him. The Ancient Ones crowded closer too, bending their boughs to form a canopy above them for the ritual mating, a verdant bower cocooning them, and keeping the others at bay. The rest soon paired off and settled into their own carnal pursuits. Though the coupling of the lord and lady of the solstice feast was private, the mating of the masses was a very public thing.

"Why have I never been favored before?" Marius murmured. It was a perfectly natural question, since they had both roamed the hemisphere since time out of mind, and he had only heard of Linnea, Goddess of the Hunt, in legends.

Straddling him where he reclined in a bed of moss and

mulch, she put a finger over his lips. "Take the gift, my lord," she whispered.

"Oh, I will." He gave a guttural chuckle. "I just need to understand—"

Her deep, searching kiss swallowed whatever he was going to say. She had the most extraordinary effect upon him. Her touch numbed all else. Her sweet breath against his heated skin was like an aphrodisiac, seeping into every pore. She was one with Nature just as he was, as if sprung from the earth beneath them. The sighing of the Ancient Ones surrounding them seemed a mantra, for it had an erotic rhythm that joined with their pulse until it beat as one. What was happening between them was more spiritual than physical, heightening awareness in a way Marius had never known before.

His hips jerked forward. His penis, already hard, surged against her belly at its full magnificence, calling her hand to fondle it. Marius groaned. How cool her delicate fingers were riding the hot length of his shaft.

"You have a light touch, my lady," he said through gritted teeth. Maybe talking was the charm. The centaur was lurking just under the surface of his skin. He could feel it straining against his awkward attempt at resistance. He hadn't had to resist before. Shapeshifting into the centaur had its own rhythm, had been something that had occurred as a matter of course. He had already transformed once in this exquisite creature's arms. The last thing he wanted was to do so again now, when he was on the brink of finishing what had begun by the hidden pool. Surely she knew he was struggling. Every muscle in his dynamic body was hard. She didn't seem overly concerned. Rubbing her groin against the hard, thick root of his penis, she rode the length of his shaft in slow, circular revolutions that brought him just shy of penetration.

Above, the uppermost branches of the surrounding oaks and whitethorns had knitted together, making a solid canopy that blocked out most of the fractured light from the bonfires. The lower branches had begun to stroke their naked bodies, their leafy boughs and tender shoots seeking every crevice, every orifice and fissure as they explored. All at once, Linnea raised her arms above her head and began to caress the lush foliage. Did the trees sigh? On the verge of carnal abandon just watching the strange ritualistic dance, Marius was caught up in the rapture of the moment. She swayed and undulated against his sex while fondling the branches, guiding the shuddering leaves to her beautiful nipples.

Moaning with pleasure, she threw back her head until her long, silken tresses tickled his thighs. He could bear no more. Seizing her about the waist in a surge of unstoppable frenzy, he rolled her over in the cool moss bed and straddled her.

Talking be damned!

Penetration was swift and deep. Groaning, Linnea arched her back as he parted her folds one by one until the head of his penis nudged her womb. Gliding on her wetness, he pistoned in and out of her, coaxing her legs up his chest until her heels rested upon his rock-hard shoulders. Cupping her perfect buttocks, he took her deeper still, until the tender nub of her clitoris against his sex sent delicious fire roaring through his loins. His racing heart felt as if it would burst through his breast.

There was no stopping now, no turning back. He could sense the centaur within growing stronger—feel its pulse, for now two shuddering heartbeats rumbled inside him. He could smell its musk and taste its essence, bestial, feral—deeply rooted in the land and in the mystery of its creation. Was it possible to control the beast now? He could not when the phases of the moon ruled the curse and he had no control. Marius hadn't expected the transformation earlier at the hidden pool, and he hadn't tried to beat the creature back.

Underneath him, Linnea writhed to his rhythm, her fingers laced together behind his neck. Marius swept the leaves away from her breasts, where they had been fondling her nipples, and feasted upon the tawny peaks with his eyes. Swooping down, he took one of the hardened buds in his mouth, sucking it lasciviously, and felt her shudder with delight as his tongue traced the pebbled areola. He felt the warm rush of her female ejaculation and the pulse of her climax as her deep folds gripped him, her involuntary spasms milking him until she drained him of every drop.

All the while, the oak trees swayed above them, fanning the fever in their skin, while the whitethorns grouped around and treated them to more intimate caresses in their turn. The Ancient Ones were gentle lovers. Marius had known their erotic embrace many times over the ages, for it was in their nature to serve the Lord of the Forest thus, and it was a great honor to be chosen by the tree spirits to receive their sexual attentions. Their ministrations tonight were somewhat subdued. Marius scarcely needed to rely upon them for carnal pleasure with Linnea, Goddess of the Hunt, Lady of the Feast, in his arms.

The Ancient Ones knew their place, though there had been that odd occasion when one of the more zealous saplings had forgotten himself and run amok. But Marius wouldn't think about that now, nor would he revisit the sinister image of Ravelle. In only moments, he'd convinced himself that the other stag was only his imagination. With the beautiful Linnea in his arms, he was invulnerable. She would be his and no others for the three days of the solstice feast. The night was young. Lost to all else in her naked embrace, he was soon hard again. The magical celebration had only just begun.

3

Marius woke alone in a hammock woven of honeysuckle vines. The heavenly scent of their creamy blooms bruised beneath his body rushed up his nostrils, intoxicating him. The heady scent of pine, ash, rowan, and whitethorn joined the mix. Their combined essence was a perfume Marius loved. This the Ancient Ones knew, and they rewarded him with it often. He inhaled deeply, a soft moan escaping. It beat through his senses like blood pulsing through his veins, grounding him—binding him to the green, to the forest, where he was lord.

The hammock was suspended between two ancestral oaks, whose branches fanned him with the cool dawn breeze. All around, the rest of the nearby trees leaned their boughs close, protecting him in their lush foliage. All at once, they moved apart admitting Linnea, laden with a skin of mead and a silver tray heaped with delectable-looking fare. The tantalizing aroma of nut-sweet cheese, grapes, apples, succulent pomegranates, Midsummer cakes, and honey reached him before she did. He swung his feet to the ground as she knelt in the moss and set the tray before him. How beautiful she was in the glow of dawn, her golden skin kissed by the sun. She had woven a circlet of wildflowers still wet with the morning dew and wore it like a crown.

"You should have woken me," he said, taking a morsel of the offered cheese.

"There was no need," she replied, selecting a fruit to offer.

"I have reason to believe there is danger abroad this Solstice," Marius said. "I saw something earlier." He hated to talk of it, but his reason had returned. And his sense of rightness. "It was only a brief glimpse, but I believe it was Ravelle disguised as I am, wearing the Lord of the Feast headdress."

Linnea paused, a ripe pomegranate in her hand. She had just raised it to her nose to inhale its fragrance, and he could see the moist shine her warm breath had left on the skin of the bloodred fruit. "Why would the Lord of Outer Darkness invade our revels?" she asked. "They are nothing compared to his in the netherworld."

"Believe me, he has his reasons," Marius said. "It goes much deeper than that. The Great Stag drove him from this isle not a fortnight ago. I've been expecting some sort of retaliation." The mention of her sire struck home.

He saw a brief tremor in Linnea's golden eyes.

"Let us not spoil the feast with dark thoughts," she said finally, easing him back in the hammock. "Rest and eat. You must keep up your strength, Lord of the Forest. There are still two days to come."

"Nonetheless, be careful. I needn't tell you what a clever shapeshifter Ravelle is. That he has taken on my form troubles me. His vengeance against the Great White Stag. That puts you at great risk. Don't be alone. And be sure when we're together that it's really me. My every instinct tells me to be wary, and I never question those."

"I can take care of myself, my lord," she said pertly.

Did she not understand how dangerous the demon was?

Marius was about to repeat his warning when a rush of black feathers streaked through the trees and landed upon the rim of the tray, where it stole a juicy grape before hopping upon Marius's shoulder to devour it with its sharp beak.

Linnea giggled musically. How he loved her laugh—not just the bell-like sound but the way it brought out the little dimples in her cheeks and twinkled in her eyes. He loved the way they sparkled, the way she seemed to glow with an inner light like the rays of the sun. That glorious smile broke over his soul.

"And who is this?" she said, hand-feeding the bird another grape.

"This is Esau, my magpie," Marius said. "He has no manners. Some call him my familiar. I call him friend."

"He's a clever little thief."

"He's an excellent judge of character. He seems quite taken with you. He's never let anyone but me hand-feed him before."

Linnea stroked the bird and took him in hand. "Well, Esau," she cooed. "I am quite taken with you also, but you must allow me to tend to your master." Breaking off a small cluster of grapes, she set it and Esau down upon a nearby clump of bracken and returned to Marius. Taking up the ripe pomegranate she had chosen earlier, she bit into the skin until it split and then the juicy pips. The sweet juice colored her lips. Breaking the fruit open, she picked out more and popped them into his mouth. The tart nectar reacted on his tongue. It made his heart race, and he seized her in strong arms and pulled her into the hammock.

"What are you, little vixen—angel, devil, sorceress?" he panted. "You have bewitched me!"

"I have told you," she murmured. "I am spirit."

"That I believe," Marius said. "You have haunted me since we met."

His hands slid the satiny length of her spine. Inching lower, they cupped the globes of her buttocks, and he groaned. She was irresistibly soft, warm and willing in his arms, yielding to his touch, to his voice, to his will. The maidens of midsummer were submissive, but she was *his*. Not just her body, but her spirit, her mind, the very beat of her heart raced for him.

He'd grown hard, his thick shaft leaning against her belly as she lay atop him in the gently swaying hammock. He moved underneath her, spreading the scent of honeysuckle as his body crushed more of the delicate flowers. She tasted of the tart pomegranate juice. He licked it from the soft lips so eager for his kiss. When she took his face in her hands, he drew her thumb into his mouth and sucked and teased it with his tongue until his hips jerked forward.

Having made short work of the grapes Linnea had given him, Esau hopped down from the ferns and flew back into the hammock, where he began pecking at the discarded pomegranate, plucking out the fleshy pips one by one while making loving little pleasure clucks. Tenacious in his attack, he persisted until he'd knocked the fruit to the ground, where he pounced upon it, tossing back his sleek black head to devour it in bits and catch every succulent drop of juice trickling down his white breast and distinctly marked sides.

"Esau has stolen your breakfast," Linnea said, her tender lips against his.

"Magpies are shameless thieves," Marius said. "Esau is no exception, I'm afraid. Leave him to his pleasure while we take ours, my beauty."

"Should we not be resting now, like the others?" she inquired. Her hands, cool and soft, traced the outline of his broad chest and narrow waist and inched ever closer to the throbbing hardness flattened against the soft swell of her belly. It was almost beyond bearing.

"We are not like the others," he murmured. "You have already seen me at my worst. Soon the moon will go entirely dark, and it will happen again. The change depends upon it. I do not want the beast to spoil the magic. There is so little time."

"How did it happen before if the moon is not yet dark?" she asked.

"Lately, the beast has been emerging when I am agitated or aroused—or taken by surprise, Linnea." She only laughed. "I have no control over the transformation when the moon goes dark."

"What did you do to anger the gods so greatly that they have punished you thus?" she asked. Her innocent curiosity overwhelmed him. What a strange, complex creature she was, possessed of an awestruck innocence, yet smoldering with sultry passion that defied description. She was at best an enigma, and he longed to peel away the mysterious layers of her psyche and solve what lay hidden behind the veil.

Marius hesitated. It was a fair question. "We lords of the green who tend the forests of the world are duty-bound to protect the land and creatures in our charge," he said. "I killed a centaur, and the gods punished me by making me live in the body of one during the dark of the moon."

"But, if it was an accident—"

"What happened was deliberate, and I am punished because I will not repent of it."

"Whatever provoked you?" she breathed, incredulous.

"Surely you have heard the tales," he began.

"I do not listen to tales, only truths."

"My tale is that," Marius shot back. "But why darken the day with it, when our bodies are so in tune with Midsummer revelry and our appetites are so eager to be slaked?"

"Because," she insisted, "you have piqued my curiosity now, and I would hear of this terrible thing from your own lips, Marius, Lord of the Forest. And why is there no Lady of the Forest at your side?"

She had shifted slightly so she could fondle his cock. What made her think he could concentrate with that going on? A man would have to be carved of stone to remain clearheaded with such a soft, skilled hand manipulating his sex.

Idly, but not without intent, he reached for her breast and began working her hard, tall nipple between his thumb and forefinger. "I wasn't always alone here," he began. "Eons ago, I had a mate—a wood nymph of remarkable beauty. Our union was to be celebrated during a Midsummer feast. There was a centaur in the forest in those days. Overcome with lust, it chased her. And raped her . . ." He fell silent.

"And she died," Linnea said, answering her own question as his words trailed off.

He nodded. "Centaurs take their pleasures where they will. They are mindless creatures that have neither intelligence nor scruples. And they are created beings—immortal. There is no female of their species. They are ardent seducers. Few can resist their prowess, but a centaur's cock would break a human woman, nymph, or sprite in two. Yes, she died, and yes, I killed the creature who killed her, and no, I will never repent of it. For that I was cursed."

"I understand," she murmured, her voice tinged with sorrow.

"How could you possibly?"

Linnea smiled sadly. "I do," she said. "Someday I will tell you how, but this is not that day, Lord of the Forest. Now is our time, yours and mine, but there is something more, I think, than that which curses you burdening your soul. . . ."

Marius gave a cryptic laugh. "I do not have good luck with women," he confessed. "Eons later, I tried again to find a willing mate, but the greatest seducer of all, Ravelle, Lord of Outer Darkness, lured her into the netherworld, where she became his concubine. And now . . . there is you."

"Hm. You do not trust me," she said.

"That is neither here nor there," Marius replied.

Having nearly pecked the pomegranate clean, Esau hopped close, taking an interest in one of the wildflowers in Linnea's garland, pecking at it with his sticky beak until he'd plucked it free. "Your bird trusts me," she said, "and he seems not to be the sort easily fooled. Take the gift, my lord. Take it without question. That is the first step."

She straddled him then, grinding herself against him as she took his lips with a hungry mouth. Riveting shock waves ripped through his loins as she deepened the kiss, her tongue curling around his, teasing the sensitive depths of his mouth, flitting like a hummingbird, releasing her sweet honey essence. Again he was undone. Seizing her hips, he raised her up and glided into her in one long slow, tantalizing thrust, riding her wetness. He wanted to feel each of her lush folds open to him as he took her deeper, wanted to savor each welcoming embrace as his shaft penetrated her vagina. He wanted to respond to every contraction, every pulsating involuntary spasm, every deliberate tug bringing him closer and closer to orgasm.

His heart hammered in his chest. Nothing existed but that suspended moment. Nothing mattered—not the curse, or the past, or Ravelle and whatever retaliation the satyr was planning. The moment was theirs alone. Marius embraced it greedily.

Clasping her slender waist, he raised her up and down upon his penis. Rapturous agony! He could barely stand the sensations ripping through his loins, could barely control his runaway need long enough to prolong his climax. His loins were on fire. It felt as if his bones were melting from the inside out.

Something he only felt with the approach of moon-dark, when all his senses were heightened. Then he could smell scents reserved for the gods, divine attars and sacred oils. He could hear and feel the restless movement of the Ancient Ones' roots beneath the ground, though others treading the same ground might sense nothing but the crunch of fallen leaves underfoot.

He could hear bees humming in hives and skeps on the opposite side of the isle, and he could listen to the litany of ancestral voices carried on the wind and intuit threatening storms in the air when they were still days off. He could see into the hidden corners of this world and into other worlds as well, and sometimes into the future. But most startling of all was what occurred when moon-dark approached and he became aroused. Then his sense of touch, his ability to feel, and his sexual appetites became so acute, it was almost beyond enduring—a frenzy so rapturous it blurred the edges between pleasure and pain, a euphoria meant only to be experienced by the greatest of gods. That was happening now. There wasn't much time.

Linnea arched her back, swinging her long hair like a horse's mane until its golden splendor teased his thighs. Marius could see the spirit of the antelope in her, in the way she moved. There was a delicacy to her gait, indeed, in every motion. The centaur in him recognized the nervous sideways and backward motions that took her now and then—and when they were not in sexual congress—the long-legged stride for speed. She could have possessed the spirit of a gazelle, a lithe, fleet-footed creature, she certainly had the lustrous eyes of that animal—or she could indeed be the spirit of the great curly horned antelope her Midsummer mask depicted, or any bovid for that matter. This enigmatic female goddess of the hunt riding his cock had taken his mind, his body, and his own spirit by storm.

Marius gave a deep-throated groan as the orgasm took him. She knew just how to take him deep into sexual magic than any other female had ever done. That and pre-moon-dark ecstasy triggered a surrender that threatened his reason.

He wanted to come again and again in that exquisite body. He wanted to keep her. What would happen when Midsummer madness was done? Would she stay with him? He couldn't imagine it, a goddess like her remaining with the likes of him. He was cursed, both man and beast. He was only an attendant of the Ancient Ones, keeper of a primitive little spit of verdant land in an enchanted archipelago. What had he to offer that would entice her to stay? Worst of all, the great demon of the Outer Darkness wanted his hide—he could not put Linnea in danger—

Her climax gripped him suddenly, triggering another groan. He felt her release, felt her potent pleasure in it. The scent of her musky-sweet essence rushed up his nostrils. He inhaled her, filling his lungs with her honeyed fragrance, a soft moan escaping as he found her lips and tasted her deeply. He couldn't drink his fill, and when their lips finally parted, his came away from hers reluctantly, thirsting for more.

Slowly, the madness in him was yielding to his rational side. The Midsummer fever raging in his blood would not be slaked, for the passion beat in him like the throb of a pulse—his own and that of the land. He could feel it in the forest floor beneath his feet as he swung them to the ground—a restless thrumming through the Ancient Ones' roots. It was highly charged with pure sexual energy, just as it always was during the Midsummer revels, but this time there was something more.

Something that reeked of death.

The Otherworld would not be denied.

"No more," he said, rising. He reached for her hand, pulling her up alongside him. "We need to make an appearance." What he really meant was that he needed to see if Ravelle would make an appearance. There was no need to alarm her, but his instincts were screaming now, silent but too clear to be ignored. "A brief stroll among the revelers, and then perhaps a refreshing bath," he went on. "The hidden pool where we first met is not far. The mineral springs that feed it possess many powers besides the obvious. I go to it often."

"Like a babe to its mother's breast?"

"Yes. You could say that."

His reply was tame but his thoughts were not. The centaur

was lurking just beneath the surface then. What Marius wanted was one more time in her before the appearance of the beast robbed him of pleasures he might never know again. Cloaked and guarded by trees older than time, whose powers not even he had ever tapped, the hidden pool was the perfect place for such a tryst.

Linnea waved her arm and a garment appeared, a gossamer robe spun of spider silk spangled with the morning dew. She swirled it around her, and Marius wondered why. It hid nothing. It was as transparent as the air, the dewdrops like a million prisms giving birth to rainbows as the sunlight filtered down through the uppermost branches. It sparkled even more brilliantly once they'd left the sanctuary of the trees, catching the eyes of the revelers lazing about and taking advantage of the delectable fare in the colorful striped tents at the edge of the wood. A strolling circus had joined them, half-clad performers singing bawdy songs as they set up for their entertainments.

The music of dulcimer, lyre, and flute surrounded them, though no musicians showed themselves. Marius had forgotten how hypnotic the ethereal Midsummer music could be. It resonated through his body, erotic and evocative. He couldn't remember it ever having such an effect upon him before. Sounds, smells, images, like the dazzling gossamer wrap Linnea flaunted in the sunlight had increased in intensity a hundredfold. Yes, the centaur was near. There was no time to lose if he was to have her one more time before the beast within—the beast he abhorred—took possession of him once again.

Linnea began to sway to the music, her long hair whipping the air, spreading her scent as she danced wildly, her tiny feet scarcely disturbing the sweet grass carpeting the forest floor in that sector. Mesmerized, Marius could do naught but stand and stare, his member swelling at the mere sight of her. She was feral then, his enigmatic antelope goddess, whose other self—like his centaur—lurked just beneath her golden skin. It was almost as if she were drawing his centaur out, challenging it—at the very least flirting with it. Did she not know what fire she played with? Still, he couldn't bring himself to look away from her undulating movements. She was pure sex, a shimmering vision of seduction. All eyes were upon her as she whirled and spun and seduced the sun streaming through the clearing. It made love to her in turn.

Reaching out, she beckoned him to join the dance. A gasp rumbled through the spectators that had gathered. It took a moment before Marius realized his naked arousal had caused it. Lords of the green had no modesty. Naked or clothed, their sexuality was not a private matter. Fertility was their purpose, and nudity was as natural to them as breathing. He gave their awestruck appreciation only passing notice, for he had eyes only for Linnea. Her shapely figure beneath the sheer robe had his full and fierce attention. She was exquisite, and she was his for the taking, at least until the Solstice revels ended.

"Come," he said, taking her hand. "Our bath awaits, my lady."

Linnea's eyes held a playful glint filled with mystery and promise. Marius was thrilled by it but she avoided his hand and darted past him, her laughter like silver bells pealing.

"I will race you there, my lord!" she cried out, streaking past him. "Catch me if you can!"

Her words were like a caress riding the breeze as Marius raced after her. He dared not let her out of his sight, not with the threat he feared still looming. But he'd forgotten how swiftly an antelope could move. His own strong legs were carrying him at a good pace through a mist that had suddenly risen. He could no longer see her ahead, though he could hear her laughter. His heart began to pound, not from the exertion of the race but rather from a shadow of fear he could taste as her laughter grew more distant and finally was no more.

4

Linnea heard Marius following her but at some distance, calling her name as he thrashed through the undergrowth. Dear Goddess, neither man nor centaur could move with her subtlety. She laughed inside at the frustration in his voice, letting her slender feet carry her ahead with scarcely a sound, feeling wonderfully giddy. May wine was deceptive. Still, she'd not had so much that she stumbled as she ran. No doe could go more lightly.

Of a sudden she saw one.

The animal looked out wonderingly from the thicket that concealed her, straight at Linnea but only for a second. Did the creature have a fawn nearby? Linnea paused, looking into the doe's eyes. The soft-eyed doe simply stared back at her and then . . . she was joined by not one but two fawns, spotted and spindly-legged. She looked to each of her children as if admonishing them for coming forward, until Linnea reached out to stroke her slender neck.

The doe seemed fragile, Linnea knew. But she was capable of rearing and lashing out with her split hooves to protect her young. Both fawns nestled close to their mother, trembling ever so slightly. It would not do to have Marius, foolish with lust, burst through the branches that concealed them all and frighten the little group.

"Well met," she whispered to the beautiful animal, "but you must dash away. The forest is full of men." She gave the creature a final caress and stepped away.

Then the doe trembled too of a sudden, her brown eyes sparking with fear as she looked over Linnea's shoulder. Filled with instant apprehension, Linnea whirled around to see what stood behind her.

A man—Marius? So it seemed, but . . . A prickling uneasiness took hold of her. He stood in the shadows, his outline familiar, not saying a word. Linnea chided herself for her skittishness and tried to catch his elusive gaze. No mask—his head was bare—but then Marius had not worn the antlered headdress a moment longer than he had to. Why did he not speak? She peered through the rustling leaves that partly hid him, trying to see more. The male figure took a step back.

Something in the sensual movement of his body almost convinced her that it was indeed her solstice-spelled lover. But not quite.

She would scare the doe and fawns half to death if she spoke, so Linnea held her tongue, willing him to step forth and come to her.

Did he understand? She was not at all sure if she had reached him.

Half in light, half in darkness, he stood looking at her, his gaze impenetrable. She must have made him angry by running away. Bah. He had no right to control her—during Midsummer, she was his equal.

Ah. Her thoughts had gotten through to him. Her lips parted a little as she observed an aura begin to emanate from his body. Soon enough it reached her, enfolding her in a curious warmth that addled her mind a bit.

She felt the doe move closer and nuzzle the shimmering gossamer of her gown. Linnea raised her arm as if to let the animal under but all the doe did was nip at her gown and tear off a piece.

"Oh!" Linnea cried. "Why?"

The doe's ears twitched, then lay back against its slender neck. She looked questioningly at the woman and then at the man, as if she was unable to understand the ways of humans. She shook her head, the scrap of gossamer still held in her teeth.

"Do not be afraid, little sister," Linnea said, looking at the doe and fawns as they turned as one, ready to bound away. "He is not unlike you and me. Scarcely more than human, after all."

The doe shuddered and looked one last time at Marius, who had withdrawn back into the woods. Then she vanished with her fawns. The leaves closed behind them as if they had never been there at all.

But Marius was very much there. His enfolding aura said what he would not—he wanted her—but was he sulking? His eyes gleamed at Linnea and she felt more drawn to him than before. The seductive power of his masterful embrace had pleased her greatly—and his readiness to give her even more pleasure was something she was willing to exploit.

"Come to me," she said softly.

Without saying a word, Marius moved closer. The aura around him changed and the strange magnetic power of it intensified. She heard a faint hum . . . then it grew louder. His lips moved as if he was speaking but she could hear nothing. A darkness surrounded him now, moving with him, falling upon the leaves his body brushed through, turning them from green to an unearthly, iridescent black.

But inside the dark aura he was still Marius, wasn't he? Warmly alive, radiant and sexual. Oh, how she wanted him— her ability to reason was beginning to desert her entirely.

As he pushed away the branches, a few of the blackened leaves turned to ash, the pattern of their skeletons threaded with the red of burning incense. Traces of smoke rose in curlicues from them and wafted to her through the air.

Linnea could not help but breathe it. Sweet but heavy, it clouded her mind. Fantasies as potent as the fragrance permeated her mind.

Sexual fantasies. Of a sweet submission to his will. He had satisfied her every desire, true, but the incense that rose from the leaves he burned made her crave more. He did not touch her or speak. Willingly, wonderingly, she dropped to her knees as he came closer and closer still.

Marius reached out and closed her eyes with a brushing touch of her fingers. Acquiescent, enthralled by some unknown art of his, she parted her lips when he touched his fingertips to them.

Ahhh.

Was the low moan that echoed through the forest from her throat or his? Linnea had no way of knowing. Her tongue licked his finger as his hand stroked her cheek.

"Suck, my sweet one," he said. There was something different about his voice, but precisely what the difference was, she could not say. Linnea had no desire whatsoever to talk—her only wish at this second was to bow to him, and humbly offer herself as his sexual slave. Had her wrists been enchained, she could not have been more bound to him. The sudden and silent reversal of their solstice play was deeply exciting. Eyes closed, she felt his hugely stiff cock brush against her cheek. The touch sent a thrill through her, and her nether lips grew plump with desire.

Linnea squirmed a little, then told herself to be calm. She opened her eyes and looked at him with equanimity.

But she would not obey his terse command. If he wanted to play this odd game for a while, the rules of it would be improvised by both of them. He only shrugged when she shook her head, stroking his cock slowly with one hand while the other played with her silky waterfall of hair.

Linnea looked both virginal and utterly wanton on her knees in the diaphanous gown. Marius positioned himself so that she could see his splendid shaft, pumped to hardness with pulsing veins, and the heavy balls beneath it.

She sighed with pleasure, not wanting to see anything else, and made as if to touch the head—there was the evidence of his excitement, two drops, slick and pearly. No doubt he was expecting her to eagerly wrap her soft lips around the head and lick it up. He had not commanded her to do so, but he made no comment on her stillness. She still held a measure of control. He was hotter now—devilishly hot. Her mouth could not cool him.

Marius sighed, encircling his cock in his big hand, making it rise higher from the springy hair of his groin. She watched closely, aroused by his self-pleasuring but biding her time. Even this close, she caught no trace of her own smell, though they had not bathed in the pond, let alone found it. Both of them were sweating slightly from running to this anonymous place—she wondered for a moment how she'd eluded him.

Had another woman intercepted him?

Marius was fair game during the solstice. Nonetheless, not much time had elapsed since her laughing dash away from him. No, he'd not been taken captive a second time—she might as well let herself believe that he wanted only her. And he'd allowed her to get a head start, though he could have taken time to recoup as well. But he was too much man to ever admit it. She'd ridden him so hard, pressing her throbbing flesh down against his strong body, aided by the strong hands that held first her hips and then her waist.

Again she thought it odd that she smelled nothing feminine on him now. But the change that had come over him, the inner heat that had burned the leaves that touched his body, must have scorched away all traces of her own scent and silky moisture.

It was as if he was coming to her for the first time, as if their bodies had never entwined in sensual bliss. Ah, to be new to him each time would be the greatest pleasure of all, Linnea thought dreamily.

Still on her knees, she gripped his strong thighs and made a move to rise. She wanted to kiss his mouth and be held by him. But he made himself clear without saying a word—she gasped faintly when he pushed her back down. "Marius?"

She caught his gaze and felt a frisson of fear. His eyes had changed too. For a moment, only a moment, he did not look like himself. His natural masterfulness turned fierce. In the depths of his green gaze was a dull red that glowed and his curved mouth was pressed in a hard line.

He was too aroused, perhaps—Linnea kept her grip on him as his hands fisted in her hair and forced her toward him.

"Take my balls in your mouth," he said roughly. He moved one hand to the side of her chin and made her part her lips again.

"Marius—no—" Her surprise made her breath catch. He made her crouch lower with one firm hand. Linnea obeyed but murmured in protest when he pulled her hair. The sound seemed to please him.

"Then I will play with myself. I don't want to punish you."

What had he said? Was this the gentle but passionate lover who had treated her body with worshipful regard? The enfolding warmth of his odd aura kept her from thinking and the strange hum filled her ears again, blocking out the sounds of the forest.

She had indeed been humbled and would be made to watch without being given permission to touch. His large balls tightened as he applied himself to their stimulation, cupping one and then the other, fondling them far more roughly than she ever would have done.

His vigorous handling was stimulating to observe. She found herself as intoxicated by his male scent as she was by the faint trace of smoke that lingered from the burning leaves.

He held her head more tightly, fully dominant, watching her watch him.

Linnea stroked the massive columns of his thighs as she watched—that much he would allow—thinking of the centaur inside.

His cock was not *that* long. No, he was a man still, if a changed one.

A sensual mischievousness made her want to grasp his cock instead, but she didn't, held back by an instinctive wariness. She wanted her solstice lover to return, the strong fellow who thought of her pleasure before his own. When he grew calmer, she might take his cock into her mouth with voluptuous care.

He seemed unusually tense, perhaps on the verge of ejaculation—ah, yes. Marius, standing tall above her, gave a low cry.

His thighs were iron-hard and he stepped his legs apart, working on his flesh with both hands now, rod jutting out and balls drawn up so tightly she could see just a little of his muscular buttocks. Heat radiated from his genitals in waves, intensifying the aura that still surrounded his naked body. He had not been this scorchingly aroused with her, she thought, feeling slightly piqued.

Now, he was a man possessed, showing off a sensuality of demonic strength. An answering wildness surged within her, and Linnea's caressing fingers dug in and held on, forcing him this time to stay close to her. She had never seen a man take himself to this point of arousal alone, had never been told to stay on her knees and watch.

His groin tightened too, the muscles there tensing to rock hardness. The deep grooves that delineated the lower half of his belly resembled the horns of some mythical beast. Fitting for the solstice.

Marius gave a growl that made his entire body shudder. He reached out and grabbed her hair so strongly that it made her cry out. She slapped his hand away and scrambled back. A sudden rage sprang into his eyes.

Had she gone too far? Linnea did not understand what animal impulse had possessed her. Her other self was a gentle creature, except when danger was present.

He glowed darkly, on fire with arousal. She was both fascinated and repelled by the strange sight. Marius let go of his hot flesh and closed the distance between them, seeming gentle once more.

She did not recoil when his fingertips brushed her eyes, closing them for a second time. As if by magic they stayed closed. She might as well have been blindfolded as she knelt before him. Then he brushed her lips. She could neither part them nor speak. And then she found that she could not move. She had been enspelled. But why?

What in the name of the Goddess of All was he going to do?

Then she heard a snap and a rip, the sound of a green branch being taken from a tree. One swift step forward by Marius, and a firm push had her on all fours, her body trapped between his thighs. Linnea wanted to claw at him, unbalance him somehow and wriggle free but she could not move, could not protest. She could only feel and what she felt was fear. Laced with sexual arousal, to be sure, but that was only the response of the flesh.

Was that what he wanted her to feel? He kept her motionless as he bent over and lifted her delicate gown. Hot as his body was, she felt a chill race over her skin. Suddenly bared, her soft behind trembled.

Snap. The green switch in his hand came down, a light stroke that stung. Then another. And another. He was giving her a whipping—*that* she had not expected. A flush of heat suffusing the skin of her buttocks as he continued, and she experienced a mingled sensation of delicate pain and intense pleasure that was indescribable. Even the sound of the chastising switch, swishing down and snapping at the end of the stroke, was breathtakingly erotic.

Her slap could not have caused him pain, but he did want to punish her despite what he'd said. Trapped between his legs, there was nothing to do but surrender and let him lash her.

The sensation was incredible.

Overcome with intense desire, Linnea regained her ability to move, but only a little. Struggling—it seemed to excite him, he breathed so harshly—she pushed her bare bottom up as far as she could and as much as she dared. She wanted to cry out, beg for more, but the magic touch to her lips kept her silent. He misunderstood. Marius set the switch aside. His large, warm hands soothed the buttocks he had whipped with such consideration, stroking and caressing her flesh over and over like a man warming his hands on some glazed vessel filled with hot liquid.

The inside of her thighs were wet from her excitement. Keeping her trapped between his thighs, Marius thrust two thick fingers into her sex without ceremony or warning, penetrating her very deeply from behind. The spell that had kept her silent dissolved in her moan.

But he would not touch her clitoris, which throbbed and ached as if it too had been whipped. All she wanted was to touch herself, relieve her pent-up sexual frustration, and she reached backward with one hand as best she could.

"No." Marius stepped his feet apart and freed her from the prison of his legs, though he captured her wrists with one hand and held them. Her hands were weak. Startled, gasping, he gave her a slight push and she sat back on her haunches, her gown swirling about her.

He let go of her wrists and she rubbed at her eyes, releasing that spell that had closed them with fierce determination, even though it hurt. She wanted to see. She had to see. What had just happened and why she had done it, she was unable to understand.

You did not do it. It was done to you. The huntress became the prey. My prey.

That was decidedly not her voice she heard in her head. Or Marius's. Suddenly afraid, Linnea looked up at the man above her. The dull red spark in his eyes glowed with infernal fire . . .

and to her horror, the handsome face of the Lord of the Green began to change.

Deep furrows seamed it and a lurid scar cleaved one cheek. Marius-who-was-no-longer-Marius had grown immeasurably old and wicked, his skin like black leather, except for the scar, which pulsed in a thin line of bloody red. Leathern wings with cruel claws at the joints sprang from his shoulders and twisted horns sprang from his long, goatlike head. A rank smell came from the lips that parted in an evil smile.

"So you enjoy a whipping. I will have to do that to you again."

"N-no." Her gasping reply was barely audible. "Who are you?"

"You don't know my name? Can't you guess?"

Mutely she shook her head.

"I know yours, Linnea. And I am beginning to know you. You think far too highly of yourself. Next time I will whip you harder. Your eyes will be wide open. Mouth too. I will let you cry as much as you like."

"No!" She gathered her gown about her, as if the fragile folds could protect her from the violence in his gaze. She tried to rise. A gesture from his clawed hand pinned her to the spot. More vile magic. Tears sprang to her eyes as she struggled to rise and flee. One rolled down her cheek.

He flicked it away with a claw. "You are easy to fool," the creature growled. "And ashamed, I see. You gave in very quickly."

She was ashamed, profoundly so. But the demon had tricked her first and trapped her second. It had all happened so fast and her desire for him—not this unspeakable beast, but Marius—had been so strong that she had been completely vulnerable to a dangerous illusion. Frantically she cast her mind back, trying to remember every detail.

His curious silence—the growing aura—the unholy odor of the leaves burning against his scorching skin—his strange moodiness and the change in him—

She had been defenseless.

He cackled with glee. "What if the real Marius was watching? I expect he would have been excited to see you whipped. How your bottom glowed! Hot and red! Not a mark on you, though. Count yourself lucky."

Too late she remembered Marius's words of warning. *Make sure it really is me, Linnea.* She was too dizzy, too humiliated to remember the name of *it* . . . oh, what was his name? The demon's wicked magic had brought her to her knees all unawares. She had humbly worshipped him, tricked into submission, passively watching, exciting the vicious joy that shone in his eyes now.

At least she had not touched him or taken his cock in her mouth. She averted her gaze from it. Hideous to her eyes, it had grown longer.

"Wh-where is Marius?"

"Bah. Your mighty steed is crashing around in circles. His anger made him transform too quickly to think and I tied his tail to a tree." The demon raised his clawed hand and a strand of scarlet liquid shot from it, arcing in the air and hitting the ground with a hiss.

The strand cooled to a red color as dull as his eyes and then to gray. He reeled it in and wound it up. "With a rope of iron like this, forged by a blacker magic than you can imagine. Such bonds cannot be broken. A centaur with no tail is an ugly sight. Marius will have to rip his own flesh to free himself."

He was preoccupied by his own cleverness and cruelty. Linnea tried to creep backwards, still on her knees, but she could not.

"Stop wriggling," he sneered. "You will move when I tell you. In fact, you will do everything when I tell you." He set the coiled strand on a rock, studying her for a long moment. "But not willingly."

"Never."

"It doesn't matter. You are exactly the bait I need to catch that idiot Marius. He will hear your screams and get loose eventually."

Unable to help herself, she cowered as she watched him spin several more strands. "If you can capture him so easily, why do you need me as bait?"

He snorted and a blue plume of smoke issued from his nostrils. "For the fun of tying him up again and tormenting him, of course. He is very strong, Linnea. He can endure the pain I would inflict on him. But I suspect he could not stand to see you hurt. Sentimental fool."

She was silent.

"I have planned his humiliation for some time. He is proud but he will kneel before me in the end. And die a miserable death. You get to watch that too."

There was no reply she could make to his vicious boasts. But a flicker of hope held steady in her deepest heart.

"I loathe all of the cursed ones of the Arcan Isles," the demon went on, "and the feeling is mutual. I will have vengeance upon them in turn. Gideon's wings ripped off and his precious Rhiannon chained in my cave—hmm, that will be amusing. And that Simeon who calls himself Lord of the Deep will fight to the death to save his Megaleen. He won't win, though."

The demon rattled on, scratching himself in an absent-minded way. The last shreds of the false skin that had made him look so like Marius fell off and shriveled. Then she heard sounds in the woods . . . rustling . . . branches breaking . . . but whoever or whatever it was, was far away.

Marius—oh, Marius. If you can free yourself, come for me.

He was her only hope. The men among the revelers would not come this far. And they were no match for this leathery monster. She fought the sudden thought that Marius might not be either. If she were free, could she outrun him? Linnea, quivering with fear, looked up at the merciless demon who had tricked her, and knew she could not.

The obscene length of the organ she'd averted her gaze from bobbed in front of her face.

"Don't want to look at it? Of course not. You hardly know me, at least in my own skin. And I did not introduce myself, did I? Do you really care? Your mind is elsewhere. On Marius."

True enough. She kept her eyes cast down and said nothing.

"Yes, you went to him straightaway. You were so eager, Linnea. Masked and tipsy on May wine and even more drunk with lust."

She gasped. Had he—?

"Yes, I saw you two fucking. You are beautiful naked or clothed. I watched you with Marius," he whispered in an ugly voice, grasping his cock in his claws. "He does not deserve you. But I want what you gave him so freely. And I will have it. That is why I became what you wanted. Him."

Linnea clapped a hand over her mouth and looked at what he was holding with horror. She saw eyes, three tiny eyes, blinking in the lumpy flesh of the grotesque head.

Goddess help her. She had *not* seen those weird little eyes when first she'd knelt before him. His cock had been exactly like that of Marius, smooth and silky and perfect. The demon was a shapeshifter of uncommon skill. The most intimate details of the manly body he'd assumed had seemed right, and the spells he'd cast had inflamed her lust and overcome her wariness.

The doe had known better. The doe had tried to warn her by tearing at her clothes. But she'd had to protect her fawns and run.

"Who are you?" Linnea asked again and wondered if he even had a name. Yes. He did. Marius had said it, even if she couldn't remember it. If she were to guess—and hit upon it—speaking his name would only increase his power.

The demon continued to stroke himself. The three tiny eyes closed with perverse pleasure. Linnea watched as the slit in the head gaped under his crude self-stimulation. In it were teeth,

sharp and small as needles. He laughed, knowing she was looking. "You almost had that inside you," he said. His claws tightened around it and the slit oozed drops of dark fluid. She jerked
back, seeing the drops fall to the ground and eat through the
fallen leaves like acid.

The foul creature that had enspelled her grunted and then
screamed with fiendish delight as he climaxed, pouring his foul
seed into the earth. "Ah! Ah! To have you watch—and be so
frightened excites me! So good—ah! I come too soon!" His
hands were as contorted as his face as he stripped out the last
poisonous drops and Linnea shrank back farther. She was only
too aware that the force he generated would keep her in his
power for however long he wished.

"Are you—the Dark One?" She choked out the question in
a whisper, even more afraid.

"Some call me that," he said angrily. "I have lived a long,
long time and have many names. Yes, I am the Lord of the
Outer Darkness. The great and wicked Ravelle. And as soon as
I catch my breath, I will ravish you. And it will be my very
great delight to hear you scream my name, not whisper it."

She shook her head in mute terror.

The demon shrugged and gathered up the strands of iron
rope. "Rise." He made the gesture that allowed her to do it.
"Walk to the tree and put your back against it."

He pointed.

The tree was not like the kindly, ancient oaks, or the supple
ashes and witch-hazels so beloved of sorceresses. No, it was
ironwood, gray and cold to the touch. She walked to it and
turned around, her spine pressed to its rough length. At the
demon's command, the lowest branches whisked around her
wrists and pulled her hands high.

"Weakling," he said with contempt. "I might not need my
ropes for you."

Linnea's breasts rose out of the diaphanous gown, bare and

vulnerable. One did not beg a demon for mercy, she thought, silently willing herself not to cry out.

Her feet barely touched the ground. He kicked them apart and her ankles were bound in turn by the low branches of lesser trees that stood near, as cold and gray as the first.

With a single swipe of his claw, he tore the gown apart in front and left a scratch on her chest. A streak of blood welled up from it.

"Ugh. An imperfection. But a necessary one. Never mind. I wish to see your sex." He snapped his fingers and was surrounded in an instant by tiny creatures—insects? They made the strange hum that she'd heard. She narrowed her eyes.

No, though they had wings, they were not insects but tiny demons, miniatures of Ravelle himself.

Two flew down and she felt infinitesimal claws seize her outer labia and pull them apart none too gently. She was lost in a hellish dream that was all too real, beset by unimaginable evil.

"All of it," he told them. One of the little demons pinched at her clitoris and pulled it out. Ravelle's gaze at her most private flesh made her feel filthy all over. His eyes widened, glowing, burning and—he let out a shriek as a flash of black and white swooped down and stabbed him in the back, again and again.

The magpie drew blood as dark as the demon's seed. It spurted from the wounds the bird made, maddening the demon, until his tiny cohorts let go of her and went after poor Esau.

The brave bird defended itself, but it was harried by many, feathers plucked from its living skin until it cawed in pain. He was losing the fight and then—the fierce imps whirled in midair when Marius, a full centaur, galloped into the stand of trees and reared. The flying imps could not stop him from coming down with a mighty blow of his hooves upon the demon. Bleeding, Ravelle was flung against a tree which bent in an arc and shot him into the clouds above.

The tiny demons shrieked and buzzed off after their master.

Flailing wildly and shrieking himself, Ravelle came down furlongs away, crashing through treetops and vanishing in a plume of smoke.

"Marius!"

In a fury, he kicked the ironwood trees that bound her into splinters, ignoring their low, agonized howls, and freed her swiftly. "Get on!" She gathered up her ripped gown and mounted him somehow, straddling his broad back and noticing dazedly that he still had a tail, though it was in tatters.

Off he went, crashing through the forest in the opposite direction from where Ravelle had landed, followed by Esau, diving and swooping through the trees. She reached out her arm to the wounded bird and he grasped desperately for her wrist, flapping unevenly with so many feathers gone. Linnea flinched as the tiny claws of his feet dug in to the marks of her bondage, but the bird held on until she could draw him close to her bosom.

She clung to Marius's mane for the rest of the wild ride, her fear pounded out of her by the jolting swiftness of the centaur's race to safety, ducking branches. Most of the trees leaned back to allow them passage, but a few did not, bending down as if to sweep her off her rescuer's back and stab out his eyes while they were at it.

The forest had its betrayers too.

He galloped on and on, and, finally winded, his sides lathered with foaming sweat, brought her to another pool. He went in circles around it, slowing his pace, gasping. The pool was untroubled and serene, though that, she now knew, could be an illusion as well. Her fear came back but it was paralyzing, slowing her thoughts to a state that felt like an opium dream. Linnea eased off Marius's back, hardly able to think. She was barely aware that she was still holding Esau.

Marius turned to look at her and smiled sadly. "Lucky magpie."

Linnea looked down at the bird nestled between her breasts and her hand supporting it. "He is safe enough. Are we?"

"For now," was all Marius said.

"What is this place? Why have you brought me hence?"

"There is healing here. You will need it."

"And you? Your tail is in bleeding tatters."

He didn't answer, but looked down at his body, willing it to change. She saw the horse's glossy hide heave, twitch, and roll back until his own flesh was revealed. It was as if he was being flayed alive—and the pain he seemed to be feeling was commensurate. Marius cried out in agony. Four legs became two. Hooves turned into feet. Linnea could only stare. He had been magnificent as a centaur, but to her, he was more so as a man.

The skin and hooves of his centaur body, shed and stepped out of, drew together in a crumpled heap of hide, flesh, and cartilage. She watched with fascinated revulsion as it got smaller and smaller and sank into the ground, remembering that the demon too had shed a skin, though she had not seen Ravelle do it.

The scratch he'd given her throbbed upon her chest, though it no longer bled. But something of his ill temper and distrust had infected her from it. She was too overcome to fight off her growing unease.

Indeed, she had no way of knowing if this Marius was any more real than the demon version. She must remain on her guard—but oh, she was weak. Dangerously so. She could not bound away into the woods like the wise little doe. Nor could she remember the words that would summon her father, the Great White Stag. She had only seen him twice in her life.

Fully himself again, Marius sat down heavily upon a rock, breathing hard, still sweating profusely. He rubbed the spot at the base of his spine where his tail had been as if it still pained him.

"You should have become a man when he left you tied by your tail."

"I would not have been able to reach you quickly. As it was, I sent Esau ahead. He could see more than I could from the air and sound the alarm."

"He took Ravelle unawares. But the poor bird was in mortal danger from the imps."

Marius looked over at Esau, his head tucked under his wing and his breast puffing out in frightened little breaths. "He too will be healed, Linnea. But you must go first."

"Go where?"

He pointed at a tree. "The being who lives in this place is a true healer. I am not."

She gazed at him with suspicion. "And where is this being?" She gestured around them at the silent trees and mirrorlike pond. "I see nothing but these damned woods and yet another pond. What if we have to run again?"

Marius looked at her steadily. "Indeed we may."

"What if we are caught?" She wanted to fly at him, whether to rain blows upon his hard body or be held in his arms, she could not say.

"It is not easy to outrun a centaur. I will change, and change again if you need me to. It is painful to make happen, but I can. Because of you, I think."

If only she had his gift of transformation. To have his strength, to be able to escape—on their desperate journey hence, she had blocked out the overwhelming power of Ravelle's malice, his delight in seeing her strung up by her wrists, her body bared again to his evil red gaze.

Even standing in the sun, Linnea felt a creeping sense of sudden despair that made her cold to her core. They might run from him or take a stand against him, but Ravelle would wait forever.

"Can you take me away from this island? Far away?"

"I will. Not yet."

"Anyway," she said slowly, "you saved my life. I should

thank you for that." But the words of gratitude did not spring to her lips. The bird gave a faint squawk from her bosom and she looked down at it. "You and Esau."

Marius was too weary to smile. "He did his best. That beak of his is sharp. He has used it on me."

Why? Linnea stared at him, searching his guileless face. Plunged by happenstance into a world where nothing at all was what it seemed for long, she would have to be mindful of everything that was done and said. And ultimately she might have to protect herself, if it came to that.

"Understand that a centaur is an unpredictable creature," he was saying. "Like a stallion, if you will. Wild, strong, and uncontrollably sexual. Esau feels obliged to remind me not to go too far from time to time, but I cannot rely on a mere bird to help me control such powerful instincts."

She was silent again, reminding herself that she was not his one and only, just a partner in lovemaking for the solstice feast. A celebration that had turned into a nightmare in the blink of a demon's red eye.

Marius sighed hugely. "Did Ravelle—"

"I will not talk of it." She lifted the bird gently from between her warm breasts and set it in a sunny spot in a low fork of a sheltering tree. Reluctant to leave her, Esau gave a complaining squawk, then fluffed out his surviving feathers and cleaned the blood from them.

"As you wish. I see no demon's mark on you."

Should she show him the scratch? He had not noticed it. To explain it would be like being strung up again, so ashamed was she of how she had bent to the demon's will. He seemed somehow to have left traces of himself in her very brain. "You came in time," she said in a measured voice. Her troubled mind was in turmoil. If this Marius really was the Marius who had loved her so well, she could never tell him of the demon's wicked dalliance with her.

She reminded herself that she had not touched the monster intimately or kissed him in the alluring guise of her solstice lover and thanked the mysterious instinct that had made her hold back.

"Linnea, I cannot let you out of my sight from now on."

"So." She walked quietly about, but her nerves were screaming. "Our idyll was not meant to last."

"No." He stayed where he was, still recovering from the mad gallop and his forced transformation, breathing deeply. "Ravelle must have sensed my abandonment to joy and seized his chance."

She nodded, rubbing her arms for warmth. "It was you he captured first."

Marius plowed a hand through his hair, which was spiking with drying sweat. "Nothing for it. Your game of hide-and-seek went awry. I was looking everywhere for you and then there he was, breathing fire and throwing ropes of iron to ensnare me. Demon or no, I might never have found you. How quickly you run, Linnea, and how quietly. It was uncanny."

She stiffened. "And what do you mean by that?"

"I felt like a fool, that's all. There is not an inch of the Forest Isle that I do not know. But you vanished like the breeze itself."

She thought of the doe and almost smiled. "Some are better at that trick than I."

"Now it is my turn to ask you what you mean."

"Before Ravelle appeared to me, I saw a doe and twin fawns. And then a man appeared who I thought was you. She knew better. She tried to warn me. But I was bedazzled."

By my desire for you. He used it to lure me and he used it against me. She didn't want to say it because just looking at him, naked, weary, and overwhelmed, made her want to comfort him. He had rescued her, for what it was worth. But she would need her wits about her to escape with her own hide intact.

"He shapeshifted, then." Marius gave a disgusted grunt. "The real Ravelle can become anything with two legs. He is a monster like no other. I saw him in all his hideous glory, but then he meant to scare me. Who was he for you? A handsome youth? An innocent girl?"

"Neither." Linnea gave him a long look. "He turned himself into a grown man, tall and strong, who resembled you perfectly in every way. But he stood in the shadows and did not speak. I thought *you* were playing some sort of game with me. And then—"

Marius rose and came to her. He reached out as if to take her in his arms, but she recoiled. "Forgive me. I don't need to know everything."

"And you never will," she said simply. It had been so easy for the demon to decipher her emotions and deceive her. What had he said to her? *I wanted you, Linnea. That is why I became what you wanted. Him.*

Ravelle could do it again.

She would stick close to Marius. Talk, she told herself, of anything but what had happened. Just talk. Do not think. But she had to know one thing. "Is there no way—" she hesitated, her voice breaking, "that I might know for certain, if we are parted, that it is you I see and not the demon?"

Marius kept a respectful distance, walking about now, his arms folded over his bare chest. He was as naked as he had been before, although at the moment she found it disturbing. The scratch on her chest throbbed like a warning not to be weak. Linnea turned away, hiding it from his gaze.

"Besides my voice, you mean? You did say that Ravelle didn't speak to you. He is a master of illusion but the voice comes from the soul. It is harder to feign than flesh and blood."

She nodded in reluctant agreement. "After a while, he spoke. Not much. He said nothing worth repeating. His voice was different, but—" She broke off, remembering the crudeness with which he bade her to suck and touch his Marius-body, and his coarse sexual display.

Marius did not seem eager to hear the details of the encounter. "You do not have to tell me. I am all too familiar with Ravelle's brand of evil. It begins with mischief and becomes mayhem. He can barely control himself."

But he is very good at controlling others. The shame of her humiliation at his hands returned sevenfold. She hoped Marius would not see it in her face.

"There was a way once," Marius said at last. "The gods who cursed me did it with an amulet of golden stone in the shape of a horse. I will tell you of it later. We must get inside."

She closed her eyes, feeling faint. There was no shelter here, unless he meant the ground under the tree he pointed to. She felt sick . . . and she for one had a feeling that the demon had just begun to wreak havoc.

"What is that mark upon your chest?" Marius asked suddenly.

"It is only a scratch. From Ravelle. To remember him by."

He gave her a grave look and shook his head. "Worse than that, Linnea. Ravelle's claws hold poison. The scratch must be opened up and the wound cleansed."

"Will you do that?" she asked softly. Would she let him? She did not want to be touched and with good reason—

"No," Marius said, interrupting the dark flow of her thoughts. "We have tarried here too long while I rested. We simply are not safe out in the open."

She smiled bitterly. "No, we are not. You gave Ravelle the kick to end all kicks. He will be looking for you."

Marius searched her face. "You are right. He is nothing to trifle with and his strength is soon regained. Anyway, come. Or I will throw you over my shoulder."

Linnea looked around. "I don't see a door. Or a house."

He waved at a tree in the near distance and this time she looked at it more intently. It was so old and so large that its massive lower branches rested upon the earth. "Look again."

She drew in her breath as the thick bark of the trunk pulled back in shaggy, peeling folds. A door appeared and some unseen force within the tree opened it from the inside.

He held out his hand. At last she noticed that it was covered with deep scratches from the branches of the treacherous trees that had whipped at him during their mad gallop. Trees that might betray them yet. How to tell the difference in a forest so ancient and so crowded with living green would be an impossible task, at least for her. His other hand, hanging at his side, looked worse. The sides of his torso bore scratches and more than one gash.

Silently she reproved herself for not seeing them right away. So he had taken a beating as well and nearly torn off his tail to come and rescue her. Though she could not, would not, tell him of Ravelle's manipulation of her mind and how he'd had his way with her—her sense of shame was far too strong—she had to acknowledge that Marius had suffered for her.

The pain of his injuries seemed to be nothing to him, compared to the agony of shifting from one form to another. His indifference to it spoke well for his toughness—she would have to rely on that at the very least. And for now, until she could get away, she had to trust him to lead her out of the unfamiliar forest. Linnea put her hand in his and let him lead her to the huge tree.

Within a few steps of the open door, she glimpsed a chamber that held a finely wrought staircase, spiraling upward until it was lost from sight and supported by nothing at all.

Linnea took a deep breath and entered.

5

He led her inside and indicated that she should go first up the spiral stairs. Linnea hesitated, one hand resting on the curving rail, smooth as silk.

"Are you afraid?" he asked.

"I ought to be. I know nothing of this place or what awaits me."

"It is a place of healing," he reassured her again. "And it is inhabited by a very strange being, but I think you will like him. Come along—I will go first if you like."

She looked at him and then up, up, and up, not seeing where the staircase ended. The perfect whorl of it reminded her of a shell, but there was light up above and the hint of a breeze. It did not end in a closed chamber that would be suffocatingly small.

She called upon her intuition to help her decide. Her nervousness gradually subsided. The inside of the great tree seemed safe somehow, although it was dark. She had never been in one like this. At the moment she fully understood why so many animals found shelter in them. The air in it gave off a healthy smell, like herbs. Besides the staircase there was nothing else in its vast, open heart.

Even so, if he went first, she would be able to escape by running down. Just in case something demonish appeared at the top.

Marius's smile was warm and without guile. He was still naked. And she—Linnea looked down at the sad remnants of her beautiful gown. She looked violated. That did not seem to have occurred to him, but then, why would it? She ran her fingers through her hair, swiftly taking out the worst of the tangles and a few twigs.

"Ready?" he asked nonchalantly. As if he was taking her to meet an old friend. She glanced once more at the open door, looking at the thicket of green outside and the leaves moving in the dappled sun. Anything could be hiding out there.

She was safer with Marius. And she did need a healer—the single scratch Ravelle had inflicted was aching in her chest.

They reached the top of the staircase in a little while, moving up through the open heart. The sides of the tree were lined with green channels in which liquid rose and fell, pulsing like great veins, splitting off into narrow tributaries.

"How can the tree live if it is hollow?" she asked.

"The inside walls are alive from the ground up. The smallest twig on the highest branch is nourished by those." He pointed to the veins. "A huge bolt of lightning devoured the center years ago. It was meant for Gideon, the Lord of the Dark, but he dodged it. The tree survived."

There were occasional openings in the trunk—and she laughed when she saw Esau sitting in one. He cawed at them, looking hopeful.

"May we bring him with us?"

"Of course." But he looked a little annoyed when the magpie fluttered to her shoulder and not his.

They ascended and at last they reached the source of the mysterious breeze. A very strange being indeed rose to greet them. Presumably male and extremely old to all appearances. His skin seemed to be made of shaggy bark, and his eyes gleamed above the pouches and infinite wrinkles of his face.

"Linnea, this is Quercus."

The being's hand clasped hers. It was surprisingly warm—and barky. She could not think of a better word for it. He had large ears that resembled tree mushrooms, and in their crevices were long hairs, the bane of all old creatures, growing in wild profusion.

"Welcome, Linnea. I saw you coming, Marius. You made enough noise to wake the dead."

"That is because we did not wish to be dead, Quercus. Thank you for taking your sweet time to open the door."

"No centaur could get up my winding stairs, my boy. No demons either. The spiral is calculated to make their heads spin and fall off."

"Really?" Marius said.

"Yes, quite gruesome. But effective. Your head will stay on, though. Come along. I was waiting for you to change."

The tree was higher than Linnea had thought. Judging by the height of the stairs she'd climbed, anyway. One could probably see for miles from its top branches.

As if the barky being had read her mind, he waved them over to a scrying pool mounted in a table of volcanic stone. "I saw you rushing here when you were in the woods. Sit down. You are clearly here for healing and I just happen to have the right herbs for poultices . . ."

Quercus chattered away, seeming pleased to have visitors, making small talk with Marius. For his part, Marius avoided the subject of precisely why they were so scratched and banged up for the present.

With Esau on her shoulder, adjusting his position with small steps every time she moved, Linnea sat at the edge of the scrying pool, marveling at its clarity.

At the moment it showed a forest very like the one they'd dashed through. There was nothing unusual about the mirrored scene. Finches and other small birds flitted through the undergrowth and beams of sunlight shot radiant light through the greenery, picking out tall trunks.

Yet, studying it a little longer, she felt a sense of menace. Linnea straightened up and looked about the room instead. The magpie on her shoulder flew off and settled on a heavy beam overhead to take another nap. Evidently he'd been here before and had his favorite spots.

The upper chamber of Quercus's dwelling was lined with shelves holding scrolls in cylindrical cases. One lay unrolled on a table, filled with beautiful drawings of medicinal plants.

"The librarian at Alexandria sent me that," he remarked. He was carrying two cups of tea on a tray and a corked bottle of something she assumed was stronger stuff. Marius could have it. She was suddenly afraid of the memories wine might set free. Her ordeal at the end had been only seconds long, but thinking of it made her shake.

She picked up the tea and sipped at it, drawing her shredded gown around her body. The tree spirit took no notice of her near-nudity or of Marius's complete nakedness. In his own shaggy, thick-skinned way, Quercus was naked as well.

Marius uncorked the bottle and poured a dark green, pungent liquid into his tea. He swallowed it down in one go and asked the spirit for more. Quercus obliged.

Marius drank that more slowly, looking curiously at Linnea over the rim. "What did you see in the scrying pool?"

"Nothing at all."

"Hm." He studied her thoughtfully.

"There is nothing there but birds and rustling leaves," she said. "The way we came has closed up."

He frowned and looked at Quercus. "Do you think the trees are joining ranks to protect us?"

"I couldn't say. You haven't told me why you were fleeing, Marius, or what from."

Marius took a deep breath and let it out. "Ravelle. He is back."

Quercus cursed in Treeish, a language Linnea didn't understand. But Marius did.

"Strong words, Querky, coming from you," he said in mock reproof.

The tree spirit shook his head and scowled. His features, except for his wise eyes, disappeared into infinitely multiplying wrinkles. He sat for some moments lost in thought.

"I had hoped he'd given up," Quercus said at last. "Why can he not stay within the bounds of the Outer Darkness? The land of the living is not meant for him."

"He loves power," Marius said bluntly. "And I and the other lords of the Arcan archipelago will not let him have it."

"Well and good. But how are we of the Forest Isle to be rid of him?—oh, never mind. It is he who attacked you both, I see, and that is why you have come."

"He attacked Linnea. Some of the trees attacked me as I ran."

Quercus raised a mushroomlike eyebrow. "Near here? Which ones?"

"I did not have time to tie a ribbon around them, my friend. We were running for our lives."

Quercus cleared his throat. "Forgive my digressions. I am neglecting my duty. Which of you wishes to be seen to first?"

Marius nodded in Linnea's direction.

"You have many more wounds than I," she protested. "Do not be gallant."

He ignored her. "Ravelle gave her a scratch."

Quercus's face scrunched up with concern. "His claws hold a lethal poison. My lady, you should have told me of this at once. There is a poultice that will draw the foulness out. But you must bare yourself."

The creature spoke as if she were not nearly naked already,

with utmost courtesy but no embarrassment. She moved the torn but still shimmering cloth aside, presenting her breasts unselfconsciously. Marius gave a faint, involuntary sigh of appreciation.

Quercus looked intently at the scratch. "The stain of it is spreading under her skin."

"Then you must hurry." Marius's voice held a note of urgent concern.

Linnea glanced his way with no show of alarm. Since they had entered the enormous oak tree, the burning pain in the scratch had ceased.

"But it feels better," she said to the spirit.

"That is because the poison in his claws acts variably. One minute it is felt, the next, not at all. The scratch itself is a minor injury but one infinitesimal drop of his filthy juice below the skin and—well, enough said. Let me grind the herbs for a poultice."

He went quickly to work with a mortar and pestle, throwing in leaves and dried things, mixing it with water and forming a wet mass. His wrinkles had settled into an expression that seemed calm enough.

When he spooned the mixture onto a linen cloth, it dripped through when he lifted it, prepared to put it on her chest. Quercus hesitated, looking again at the remnants of her gown.

"It is ruined," she hastened to assure him. "If I could burn it—"

"An excellent idea. But you will find no fire inside my tree. Not so much as a spark. Take it off, bundle it, and Marius can set fire to it someplace else."

She rose and let the gown slip from her shoulders and crumple into a puddle on the floor. Then she sat again, amused by Marius's discomfiture. It was as her mother had told her when she began to become a woman. To be nearly naked was far more exciting than to be bare.

But the look in his eyes told her that he adored her either way. The worry that shadowed his admiration made her turn quickly to Quercus, who guided her to a long bench. "Please lie down." Then he nodded toward Marius, as if giving some silent instruction to him. Marius rose and sat at the end of the bench.

When she had stretched out on the bench, Quercus placed the dripping poultice directly upon the scratch. The resinous herbs burned far worse than the scratch and she almost screamed.

"I had not expected it to hurt so. The scratch must be deeper than it seemed upon close examination," he murmured to Marius. "Soothe her as best you can. My dear, forgive me."

"Ah!" she cried through clenched teeth. "How long?"

"Until the poison is drawn. See—it bubbles through."

She lifted her head and looked down. Bubbles had appeared on the linen, breaking one by one. A foul, sulfurous smell filled the air and Quercus ran to an opening in the wall of the chamber and opened shutters made of thickly woven leaves.

The miasma wafted out—but not before she remembered every second of what had happened with Ravelle.

Linnea burst into bitter tears.

That night, encircled in Marius's arms, she told him everything. His response was to cover her with kisses that were at once chaste and kind. His thoughts of revenge were anything but.

They sat together in the morning. Quercus busied himself with some project of his and left them alone.

"You were going to tell me about the gods—what they did to you," she said, sipping a restorative tea the healer had made for her. "Was it a punishment?"

"No, I had committed no crime. They did it for sport. My brother and I were stable boys. They took both of us on a whim. My father tried to grab my ankle as I was born aloft but he had to let go. We served for a while as cupbearers in the court of the pantheon."

"I see." She called to mind her mother's stories of the divine ones—they were more quarrelsome than humans and much too fond of having their way. "I did not know you had a brother. Is he—like you?"

"No. Although we could be twins, so strong is the resemblance. But he is not ever a centaur. His name is Darius."

This aspect of her lover's life was entirely unexpected. She had no immediate living relatives and those of her father's kind, the Bovidae, were wont to roam far and wide. Linnea had been alone for much of her young life.

"Does he live on the Forest Isle? I would hate to mistake him for you."

Marius laughed. "Yes, he does, but he is seldom seen, even by me. And you might confuse us–but he is younger. He serves as a Watcher of the Green. There are many watchers on these islands and some are evil. I can vouch for his character." He looked her up and down in the torn gown. "You can meet him and judge for yourself, of course. But I might have to dress you in a sack first."

"If I could be invisible in the eyes of men and demons, I would," she retorted.

Marius looked chagrined and she reminded herself again that she had told him nothing, even though she suspected he had guessed some of it.

"Darius is a good man."

"How did he escape the court of the gods?"

"He was first to go," Marius returned to his story. "A divine factotum dispatched him back to earth on the wings of the old eagle who'd brought him up into the clouds. Then they showed me the amulet and asked me if I wanted it. I was very young but knew enough of their mischief to say no."

She nodded. "I doubt that it mattered. Gods do what they want."

"Indeed they do. The mortals and immortals of earth must suffer the consequences. An old one enchanted the stone and then hung it about my neck. It began to glow and sparkle. Boy that I was, I was pleased with the gift, until the transformation to the centaur began. The first time was agonizingly painful."

"So I have seen," she said with sympathy.

"The gods laughed at my dismay, then grew angry at my screams."

Linnea sighed. "Why do humans worship them and build them temples and bring them offerings? It makes no sense."

Marius raised his hands in a gesture of incomprehension. "Who can say? So that they will not be the next victim of mischief or worse? I have no faith in gods or priests."

"Nor do I," she murmured.

"When the change was complete, I stood there crying. A lesser goddess, slender and small, felt sympathy for me and wove me a halter and reins of flowers with her own hands, vowing she would be the first to ride me. I knelt before her but the strongest of the gods, her lover, fell into a jealous rage. He dragged me to the edge of the clouds and pushed me out of their lofty realm to fall to earth. He expected me to die, I think."

Linnea did not care to think about the slender little goddess who had been so kind. "What happened?"

"As I tumbled, the amulet came loose from its golden chain and fell. I grabbed at the air." He nodded up at the sleeping magpie on the beam. "That one swooped down out of nowhere and caught it."

Linnea frowned. "Did the gods fling him down too?"

Marius shook his head. "No. He was flying by. Any shining thing catches a magpie's interest. Off he flew, the amulet in his beak, just before I plunged into a forest pool. When I surfaced, he was gone."

"I see. And so was the amulet, I assume."

"He never brought it back and I have never found his nest. He may have more than one nest, for all I know, but that is Esau's secret to keep. I did try. It took me eons to tame him—that's why I was so surprised when he let you feed him."

Linnea pondered that but not for long, not thinking it significant.

"But every magpie is born a thief, Linnea. And thieves do not give up treasures easily. Besides, he is only a bird and not the kind that talks."

She smiled faintly. "Still, he is loyal if he has stayed with you all this time. And he fought the demon and the imps like a little Fury."

"Esau is not always playful."

They looked at each other, sharing a brief, glowing memory of the serenity the three of them—man, woman, bird—had shared. The juicy, ruby-colored seeds, freely shared too, eaten with abandon, had seemed a portent of fruitfulness and joy. The sexual union between Marius and Linnea had been an extraordinary experience, life-affirming and utterly sensual.

But since the appearance of Ravelle, that sweet, magic mood was irreparably shattered. His demonic malevolence was far worse than the mere mischief of careless gods. It was calculated.

Marius seemed to understand that her memories of yesterday had plunged her into sudden silence and did not press her.

"You must stay here," he said at last. "And I will call a convocation of the lords of Arcan. Not here. Old Querky needs his solitude."

Quercus looked up from the scroll he was studying. "Yes, I do."

The magpie flew down from the beam above and landed on Marius's shoulder.

"Traitor," he said affectionately. "So you are back with me."

"He goes where he is needed most," Quercus pointed out.

"So he does. When there is not anything shiny to collect or food to steal."

The magpie squawked at Quercus, who laughed and responded to it in Treeish.

"No fair keeping secrets. What did he say?" Marius asked.

The tree spirit laughed again and smoothed the bird's black-and-white feathers. "He said that an army travels on its belly. And he is not wrong about that."

Marius bent down to give Linnea a farewell kiss. They had said everything that needed to be said last night. She would stay here where Quercus could keep an eye on her and she could continue to heal. If she wished, she could conjure Marius in the scrying pool although it would not allow her to speak to him.

Once the lords were gathered, it would not take long to vanquish Ravelle and hold him at bay in the Outer Darkness. Or so Marius hoped. He had not the firepower of Vane or the ability to fly of Gideon.

Clad in a kirtle of soft leaves that were fuzzy to the touch, she rose to walk with him to the top of the staircase. He gave her another kiss and caught her up in a fervent embrace that betrayed his feelings for her. Quercus busied himself with his scroll until he had done, humming absently.

"I think it is best that you do not venture outside the tree for now, dearest," Marius said softly. "Everything you might need is here. And Quercus says that you can climb out on the bigger limbs if you wish. Tuck your kirtle up and use your hands." He gave her one last kiss on the nose. "I wish I could be below to see you do it."

"Hush, Marius."

His hands slid down from her waist but he hesitated before going further. Linnea pressed herself against him and at last he stroked all of her that he could reach. Their lovemaking last night had been gentle in the extreme—and the ultimate climax shared at the same instant. She felt healed. Caressed from head to toe, tongued to full release, and rocked beneath him, his lusty tenderness had erased the demon's vile touch from her body and mind.

"Look for me in the pool tonight, Linnea. I must return to Philonous."

"The old willow must be worried about you," she murmured. "I know that I shall be." Her uneasiness about him had vanished, drawn out with the poison from her wound.

He held her close. "I hate to let you go."

She sighed and nuzzled the side of his neck, then pressed her lips to the skin over his strongly beating heart. "There. Take that with you. I would give you a token of my favor to wear, but as you have no clothes and no pockets, you will have to make do with a kiss."

Marius cupped her breasts and brought his mouth down over hers. "And there is one for you," he whispered when he stopped. "Wait for me."

"I will," she said as he turned to dash down the spiral staircase and go back to his green realm. A final look upward at her and he was gone.

6

Lord Vane, the ruler of the Isle of Fire, sat enthroned before a blaze that threatened to consume his ancestral hall. The massive stones of which it was built were black as coal, a flat black that reflected nothing.

He was lost in contemplation of the blue flames that licked around the wood in the fireplace. Marius had sent over a raft of logs moons ago, seeing that the fallen giants of his domain were gathered once their remains had dried to whiteness. That brother of his supervised the gangs of men that got them rolled to the sea and tied to a raft, but Darius himself never left the island.

The brothers were fearless, to be sure, but the Isle of Fire was not loved by those from the forest. He rose and looked out an archer's narrow window at the setting sun. The volcano—his foundry, as he thought of it—belched smoke and ash. The spew tinted the sky in lurid tones of purple and black that seemed to hover in the air. The sun's red rays pierced it like flaming arrows.

Just as he liked it.

The same disturbing gloom prevailed in his grandiose dwelling. He looked again into the roaring blaze, wishing the fire nymphs would appear. They came and went as they pleased, and he could not control them.

Which was, in a way, the best part.

A singular flame rolled around the giant log and then separated itself from the others. It shot higher, its undulating contours becoming the shape of a woman.

Hella was here. His favorite.

Vane propped his head on one hand and watched her play in the flame. The fireplace was so high that a full-grown mortal could stand upright in it. Hella, beautiful Hella, had all the room she wanted.

She was naked, of course. Her fiery blue breasts were tipped with red, and a juicy slash of red showed between her legs every time she bent over and spread her legs.

He could watch her for hours.

Right now she was straddling the giant log and pressing her cunt to it with lascivious little cries. No matter how hot it got, Hella wanted it hotter.

A smooth branch had escaped the devouring intensity of the flames and she grabbed it to keep her balance. Then she looked over her shoulder wickedly at her one-man audience.

They had the same idea. The branch was rounded on top, broken off so long ago that the weather or waves had smoothed to the size and shape of a cock's head. As for its length—he looked down at his lap—his rod was comparable. "Go ahead, Hella."

The fire nymph laughed and rose up from the log, sticking a slender blue finger into her scarlet labia. The fire within her made them pulse color that was deeper still. Extending her leg high in the air to give him a good show, she lay back on the log and spread her cunny apart.

Look your fill.

He did. He noted with more than passing interest that her clitoris was an incandescent blue amidst the scarlet of her innermost lips. The contrast was enchanting. Her blue finger parting those pretty petals, exciting herself as she thrust it dreamily in and out—my, my. The fire nymph was sin-scorchingly hot.

"The branch," Lord Vane said to her encouragingly. "Smooth and shapely, is it not? As if it was made to penetrate your hot cunt. Move up on the log."

Hella obeyed. She turned her bottom to him, swaying and dipping.

She was maddeningly delicious. Her new pose was even better. Lord Vane undid his breeches and pulled out his cock. "Spread for me, my dear. Show me everything."

The fire nymph reached around and clasped her beautiful buttocks, pulling the shapely blue globes apart for his delectation. She gave him an impertinent grin over her shoulder again.

Wanton as she wanted to be. Like a temple whore, she danced in place, showing off what the gods had given her: a tightly folded pussy framed by a sweetly curved ass that was punctuated with a barely visible anus in deeper blue. Her flawless skin shimmered as her own arousal increased.

He wanted to bury his face in her, have her push back, back, back. She liked to enfold his face with her buttocks, and allow him to take a taste of her fiery pussy, slipping in his tongue whenever she stopped. Knowing what was coming, Hella sang to herself, her voice flickering in pitch, changeable as the flames she'd stepped out of. Then she rose and positioned herself over the round tip of the branch.

This was going to be hotter than . . . Hella. Lord Vane straightened on his throne.

Hella put the tip between her labia, its unburned whiteness a startling contrast to the scarlet flesh that would soon take it deep. With erotic slowness, she eased her body down upon it, twisting and turning, riding the thick prong that seemed to have been made for her alone.

He got up and came closer, standing by the fire, much taller than Hella, who stayed inside the blackened frame, looking up at him as if she too were glad to have company.

Then he saw the reason she seemed to be experiencing even more pleasure this time. The round-tipped branch had a bump at its base, just as smooth. The perfect thing for clitoral pressure.

Rubbing, rubbing, she was shameless. Gripping the top of the burning log, her slender fingers started new little blue fires all over it. The log itself creaked and moaned, coming to a final burst of life under her.

Indeed, his Hella could raise a dead demon with what she was doing. She let go with one hand and reached between her legs, fingering the incandescent blue bud as she pleasured herself on the white wood branch.

What magic kept it from bursting into flame inside her, he knew not. But the fire nymph would not have minded. She twisted and bounced, boneless and utterly free to move however she wanted.

In her ephemeral way, she was an immortal. Yes, she vanished when the fire burned down to gray ashes, but she reappeared when the next one was lit. If she wanted to.

What few visitors he had seemed to suffer from the heat of the constant blazes, but that was just too bad for them. Lord Vane preferred to be alone. Hella was worth waiting for.

He stroked his heated shaft, moving his hand around and down and up again. The increasing length of his cock made the fire nymph's eyes spark with lust.

"Do you want that in your pretty mouth?" he asked her in a low growl.

Every inch.

She turned halfway around so that her face was turned up, and smiled wantonly, licking her lips, waiting for a taste of him. Like her labia, the inside of her mouth was pulsing scarlet. Her tongue was pure fire, flicking, changing color.

He knew only too well how eagerly it licked. The narrow tip could lengthen and wrap around his aching cock, pulling the head more deeply into the scorching recesses of her mouth, setting *him* on fire, swallowing every inch just how she'd said.

And that tongue of hers could soften and lap him tenderly until he cried out her name and begged to be sucked to orgasm.

Yes, the great lord of the Isle of Fire knew how to beg. She seemed to take a particular pleasure in seeing him do it. She'd had him on his knees more than once, his craving for her was so strong. But not tonight.

Come over me, my lord.

Her extraordinary flexibility made fellatio effortless. Arching her back, she met him halfway but stayed within the blackened walls of the enormous fireplace. He leaned, impervious to the flames. The pulsing mouth that took his cock had learned the art of fellatio well. She never, ever gagged, and she sucked hard, even if she was as insubstantial as air.

Ah, the heat . . . Lord Vane felt a sensation of melting mindlessness that was equaled only by the stiffness of his member. Naughty bitch that she was, Hella played with his balls, showing him no mercy, spanking the swollen sac between his legs, knowing it was filled to bursting with her favorite treat: lava.

She loved the blazing spurts he produced without fail, reveled in leaning back when he wanted to cover her blue breasts with shot after shot of fiery ejaculate, putting out her tongue to catch any wayward drops that missed her body.

Tonight he wanted to come in her mouth. She craved that too, voraciously swallowing the urgent scarlet rush as it pulsed from his cock hole, milking him with flame-fingers to get more and more.

His fire girl. How he loved her.

Hella wrapped her lips around the base of his excruciatingly sensitive member and fluttered her tongue against the underside of it.

He was damned if he would give in so quickly. But damnation was exactly what he wanted. Her fingers explored farther, pressing on the ridge of flesh in back of his scrotum, forcing him faster and faster to an explosive new high.

He groaned and shuddered, letting his cock disappear into her mouth and down her snug throat. She had no need to breathe—the only air she required came through her bare, blue skin.

His excitement reached fever pitch. Tiny new flames, delicate as jewelry, sprang up here and there on her nude body. She was infinitely combustible, she was his, he was hers—oh! By the gods of all that was unholy!

She stopped what she was doing and used her tongue to ease out his cock.

Controlling himself and knowing she played the trick to make the pleasure last, he methodically pumped his agonizingly hot rod while she smiled in an enchantingly wicked way. He had forgotten that the smooth, round-tipped branch was still inside her, in part because she'd twisted at the waist as no mortal female could ever do. She rode it for a while, gripping the log as before without looking at him.

I like to make you wait.

"But am I not your lord? Do I not command you, Hella?"

When I want you to.

She began to press her clitoris against the bud at the bottom and he noticed burn marks upon its whiteness each time she pulled away. Hella enjoyed more intense stimulation in the moments before her climax and she was giving it to herself now, ignoring him.

It was not to be endured.

Lord Vane reached into the fire and hauled his blue lady out. His masterful action brought out the bitch in her again and she tried to get away, but he was too fast for her. There was no need to hold her prisoner. None whatsoever.

All he had to do was clasp each of her nipples and he did, employing finger and thumb in a slow, firm roll that melted her for a change. Writhing with erotic joy, Hella surrendered, raising her breasts in her flaming hands, offering her nipples up for his teasing, highly sensual control.

Ahhh, my lord. You know exactly what I like.

"Then why do you make it difficult for me to give it to you?"

Harder!

More firm rolls of tight nipples, standing out scarlet from her hot blue breasts. More moans. How he loved to see her like this, at his command, at least for a minute or two.

To his surprise, Hella cried out his name. Once, then twice. She leaned against, twining her arms around his neck and murmuring in his ear.

That was good . . . so good.

"Did I make you come?"

Yes.

Well, then. She was in for the ride of her flaming life. He turned her around, bent her over, and penetrated her to the hilt. Hella moaned with the echoing pleasure of her own stealthy orgasm as his hit him full force. He pounded against her soft bottom, increasing the sensitivity of his overhard cock with ever deeper thrusts, craving her heat, excited to new heights by the intensity of their lovemaking, something only Hella truly inspired in him.

He came in gigantic spurts, the lava in his balls filling up a quim already so tight and lusciously hot that he wanted to scream.

She knew it, took him higher still with sensual undulations

of her hips and buttocks, making him moan. He was weak, but he was in heaven. With her.

"Hella . . ."

She didn't speak, enjoying the last reverberations of his mighty climax more than her own, until finally he heard her one-word reply.

Yes?

"I think I—"

No, you don't. Besides, I don't really exist. You can't love a woman made of fire.

"Why not?" His question came too late. She slipped out of his grasp and went back into her element, indistinguishable from the other flames that leapt and danced and made men dream.

Several nights later, sprawled in his black-sheeted bed, the Lord of Fire could not sleep for wanting her. She hadn't come back. His restlessness was new and it upset him. Why did he feel this way? They'd had incandescent sex before—many times. Hella knew a thousand variations on the theme of a truly hot night.

It was true that sometimes he dallied with another nymph of lesser talent—come to think of it, a naughty cousin of hers had been carrying a torch for him for a while and begged him to satisfy her curiosity about him as a lover. They had parted on good terms. Had Hella heard of it? She prided herself on not being jealous.

Or . . . this thought was truly alarming . . . had she taken a different lover? Someone more potent than the Lord of Fire?

He scowled and flung back the covers, too troubled to bother with masturbating himself to sleep. He would only think of her and become more agitated.

He rose from the bed, tying back the black hair that fell to his waist with a piece of silk. Red, of course. A souvenir of his first encounter with Hella and something he kept always by his bed. She'd taken the ends of it, stepped between them, and pulled up the taut, soft silk into her swollen labia, soaking it just for him after he had given her a magnificent fucking with only his long, hot tongue. The material was still supple and it still smelled of her.

Where was she? Beautiful blue bitch that she was, he missed her dreadfully.

He went to his personal scrying pool, a smallish one he'd had installed in his bedchamber. It was filled with volatile oil that sometimes caught fire when a spark got that far. Tonight it seemed sluggish and dull. He saw nothing and moved away from it toward the window that looked out onto the other Arcan islands in the archipelago.

The full moon was brilliant in the clear dark sky, and it was possible to discern fires along the shorelines of the Forest Isle. Had the revelers attending the Midsummer solstice stayed on?

The event always caused trouble for Marius of one kind or another. But Vane knew better than to go over. The Lord of the Forest's talking trees had fainting fits the second the Lord of Fire stepped foot onto the island. In any case, he had not been summoned.

He looked elsewhere, to Gideon's island, the Island of Mists. The lair of the Lord of the Dark was shrouded in it. Vane supposed that the winged one was safe inside his labyrinth of caverns, lying with his love, Rhiannon.

How nice for them both, he thought bitterly.

His heated blood raced in his veins. Late as it was, he could do with a dip. Would Marius mind if he swam over through the subterranean tunnels that connected one isle to the next?

The shady pools in which the tunnels ended were delightful places to loll and there was always a chance of a tryst with a naked naiad. Of course, a water spirit could never set him on fire like the incomparable Hella, but they were fun to catch, squirming deliciously and pretending to protest as they took full advantage of his famously long shaft. All he had to do was sit down naked, spread his muscular thighs, and beckon. They were happy to sit down right on his lap, their sinuously curved backs and napes presented for his kisses. His shaft filled the smaller ones to the limits of their tight cunnies. Feeling cool, moist buttocks against his thighs while abundant breasts filled his enormous hands would assuredly calm him down.

He would pull the excited naiad off before the hot lava in his balls shot out, letting her wriggle in the air and marvel as his scarlet, scorching ejaculate arced over the water of the pool and formed pretty drops of volcanic glass in its depths for her to dive for.

His own arid domain afforded him no such amusements.

Vane resolved to swim over then and there.

Deep underwater, his fire banked by his leathery skin, he counted the twists and turns, figuring out where he was and popping up in a pool that seemed familiar. An aged willow draped its feathery leaves over one side of it, murmuring to it-self in Treeish. Vane couldn't make it out and didn't care.

The moon hung above, heavy and full and glowing white. Vane dipped back down again when he heard a rustle but saw nothing. It was even more fun to get a naiad by her slender ankles and make her fall upon his naked, dripping body. He knew and they knew that they came to the pools for the same reason, especially during a full moon: to indulge their sensual appetites.

He rose again, squeezing the cool water out of his long black hair, and realized he'd lost the scrap of silk from Hella.

Somehow it seemed like a bad omen. He began to walk out of the water, not making a single splash as he did. He saw not a soul, female or male. A sense of fiery frustration made his body steam faintly in the moonlight. Had the lusty female spirits of the forest all moved to a vestal nunnery? The thought was infi-nitely depressing.

Bah. His long swim had been a waste of time.

And then he saw her. She was a glow of white that he had at first assumed was moonlight on a wet rock, so still did she lie. She took no notice of his presence, paying homage with her naked body to the heavenly sphere that hung in the night sky.

The most beautiful naiad he had ever seen was about to mate with the moon. Its shimmering reflection in the water pointed directly between her opened legs. In a little while, when it had reached the highest point of its rise in the sky, its changeable light would penetrate her to her core.

Her orgasm would be as changeable and subtle. How eagerly she must be anticipating the moment. Thighs of pure white parted as he watched—no, they were pressed apart by her hands, spread wide and welcoming. She touched a fingertip to pink labia fringed with jet curls, as black as the wealth of wet hair that straggled over the rock underneath her.

Then she touched her clitoris and a shudder ran through her entire body. Demurely she withdrew her exploring finger and moved her hands to her breasts. Above her plump quim was a rounded belly that begged to be squeezed, and, instantly erect, he watched avidly as she strained upward, playing with her pink, high nipples. The solitary naiad was as round and full as the moon itself. All in all, a succulent offering.

He would not dream of disturbing her. He had only been looking for some slap-and-tickle, and an uncomplicated mutual release. This unknown naiad was a vision of unearthly sexuality. Vane had heard of moon-mating but never seen it.

The reflection on the water inched closer to the apex of her thighs. She reached out her arms as if she would embrace the mighty moon and hold it to her heart. That heavenly orb seemed to loom lower, to his amazement.

He could not blame the moon. He himself was so aroused that he forgot to take his cock in hand. Vane wanted to watch.

The advancing moonlight touched the plump undercurves of her behind, pressed into the rock. She gave a little moan and moved her hands down, leaving her nipples in an astonishing state of erection. Had another naiad wantonly straddled her and positioned her own private parts over one of those full, soft breasts—Vane had also heard that they played with each other in every way imaginable, man or no man—the nipple would have felt like a tiny cock.

Never mind that. This naiad's hands gently stretched her labia open. The moonlight touched her there a moment later. It seemed to pour down from the sky, into her, filling her—the beautiful naiad raised her legs high and clasped her ankles, offering her tender, most secret parts with shameless abandon and crying out with joy as the moon lit her up from the inside out.

The moon moved higher, caressing all of her and bathing her voluptuous body in white light. The naiad was brightness itself, helpless with pleasure, lost in a rapturous dream that he wished he could share.

Vane stayed where he was until the last of her whimpering cries died away on the evening breeze. He was a lucky man indeed to have witnessed her intimacy with the moon, and she would never know she had been watched.

He waited, expecting her to rise from the rock and scamper off to sleep with the others. But the naiad stayed exactly where she was . . . if not exactly in the same shape. Her body seemed to diminish as the moon began to move on, beginning the downward phase of its night's journey.

He was on fire again but with curiosity this time. Slowly, with utmost stealth, Vane moved through the water toward the rock. He stopped several feet away, studying the white apparition once more. The gorgeous naiad had vanished utterly. The top of the rock where she had lain sparkled silver, outlining the shape of her voluptuous body, a shape filled with a celestial light that would come and go with the phases of the moon but never fade. That was all that was left of her.

Full of wonder and a little regret, Lord Vane sank slowly

into the water and went back home through the subterranean passageways, vowing to ease his cock with Hella. If he could find her.

The stairs of his stone castle were warm underfoot—the walls radiated heat, as usual. Usually he found it pleasant but not now. His body retained the coolness of the flowing water he'd swum through but his damned mind was on fire again. It was going to be a long, long night.

Finding a towel, he scrubbed at his damp skin, feeling out of sorts, willing away the memory of the moon-drunk naiad. Was there wine in the ewer his manservant had left? He poked his nose into it—the fire in his bedchamber had gone out and he could not see whether the liquid it held was water or wine.

A whiff of grapes reassured him. Excellent. He would have a little wine—no, a lot—and look for Hella in the scrying pool again. He would not, however, tell her about watching the voluptuous naiad, so white and so cool and so very different from the slender fire nymph. He tipped the ewer up over his head, expertly filling his mouth with the thin stream that poured from it like a peasant imbibing from a leather wine sack. The rich and powerful Lord Vane knew exactly how to get stinking drunk.

An hour later, he sat staring into the pool of volatile oil. The serenity of the night had been troubled by events he could not understand.

To begin with, Marius had appeared on the scrying surface, tears running down his handsome face. He was saying something about fire . . . and an ancient tree . . . Yes, yes, get on with it, Lord Vane said mentally. When did lightning *not* strike lonely, sea-girt realms and did it not always aim for the *highest* point?

Vane had picked up the astral projection with a reverse turn of the calendrical adjuster, an invention of his own. The other

Arcan lords relied on mumbled spells and that bitch of bitches, luck, to scry. But he was a practical man. And at the moment, a very, very frustrated one. He had finished the wine in the ewer a while ago and rung for more. He was deep in his cups and irritable. No Hella. He could swear that the lava in his balls was backing up into his brain.

He reached out and turned the calendrical adjuster the other way.

"Vane? Is that you?"

He belched with surprise. The damn thing worked better than he'd thought.

"Yesh."

"Are you drunk?"

Vane's reply was obscene and to the point.

"Ravelle has returned."

That bit of news brightened his mood. Let the others dodge the demon. Lord Vane wanted to fight him.

"I can take him."

"Together, we will be stronger, Vane."

The Lord of the Fire belched again, pure sulfur this time. "Hand him over if you have him. What kind of trouble is he making now?"

Marius swiped a hand over his face and mixed dirt with the drying tears on his face. "He torched Philonous. I came in time to save him, but he might not live. I was hoping that you—that there is an antidote to fire."

"There isn't. It burns and it kills. Powerful stuff. Why I like to play with it." Foggy as he was, Lord Vane had a feeling he was supposed to be sympathetic. "Philo—who? I don't remember that name."

"The most ancient tree of all. He's watched out for me since I was cast down to the Forest Isle."

"Oh, that Philonous," Vane said with a notable lack of conviction. He did feel sorry for Marius in his drunken way.

"Can you get here quickly? Isn't there anything you could bring to help heal him?"

"I have a salve for scorches. But I just came from there." He touched a finger to the surface of the oil, wishing he could make the Lord of the Forest go away.

Marius's pleading look changed to one of suspicion. "You did? Where were you?"

"I came up in a pool I'd never seen. Nothing going on," he lied, just in case Marius knew the moon-loving naiad. "I came back and started to drink. I was looking for a fuck, but a fight will do."

Marius shook his head. "The Arcan lords must meet as soon as possible. I signaled Gideon with bonfires on the beach—"

"Saw them," Vane said indifferently.

"And someone got a message to Simeon underwater using Pio."

"That swordfish? One of these days I'm going to have him for dinner."

Marius shook his head. "Vane, listen to me. Ravelle will not stay in the Outer Darkness and the islands and their inhabitants are in danger."

"I can take Ravelle with no help from you three. Stupid horned bastard. High time someone put him in his place." Marius hesitated before he spoke again, and the Lord of Fire gave in to a mad, wine-fueled impulse. "All right, green man. I'm coming. How many subterranean turns before I get to where you are?"

"Eleven. Hurry."

For the second time that night Lord Vane hoped that cold water would calm him down and sober him up. He looked for the jar of salve that he kept by the fireplace, tied on a half-assed breechcloth, and came up in the right pool with a banging headache.

* * *

Gideon, Lord of the Dark, was already there, but then he could fly, Vane thought sourly. And Simeon had evidently just come—he was talking to Marius. The Lord of Fire spat out the water he'd swallowed, and went to join the other three Arcans. To his surprise, Rhiannon was with them.

He pulled up his breechcloth and smoothed down his drenched, tangled hair. Whatever they were kneeled around had been badly burned. He could smell it from here.

He looked down at the tree spirit on the damask cloth— from Gideon's banquet table, by his guess. Vane brought out the jar of salve and tapped Marius on the shoulder with it. "It won't do him much good, but here it is."

"Don't talk like that," Rhiannon said softly. She soothed Philonous's narrow leaves—there weren't many left—and took one of his branches in her hand.

Vane felt ashamed of himself and kneeled beside her. "Can he hear us?"

"Yes," Marius replied. "When he's conscious."

Vane winced when he saw the tree spirit struggle to open its burned eyelids, moaning with pain. He gave the jar to Rhiannon. "You put it on. A fingertip's worth on each lid. And give him water to drink. A drop at a time."

She glanced at him, forgiveness in her gaze, and Vane stood up again. He had caught a whiff of something that he recognized—something sulfurous and nasty. Hella would have attributed it to him, but he knew it wasn't him because he'd bathed twice in one night.

Marius rose and joined him a little ways off. "I smell Ravelle," Vane said immediately, keeping his voice low.

"I told you that he—"

"He's right here, very near. We can kill him now!"

"I cannot leave Philonous," was all Marius said. "But Ravelle is not long for this world or any world. Not if I can help it."

* * *

Philonous lived through the night, even though they had to move him a very great distance for fear of the demon's return. His eyelids fluttered open when the first soft rays of dawn sprang from the sun hidden below the horizon. Rhiannon leaned over the bed.

"Can you see me, Philonous?" she asked anxiously.

The tree spirit took a long time to answer, working parched lips and breathing with difficulty. He rasped out a yes. The single word took enormous effort.

"Good. That's one good thing."

Philonous was silent. His leaves plucked feebly at the soft blanket that covered him. He asked his next question just by looking at her.

She understood. "You are in Gideon's pavilion—our pavilion, I mean. You will be safe here. You can rest and begin to heal."

His old, old eyes filled with tears. He blinked them away. It would hurt too much to cry. But he had to tell them which way the demon had flown and what he'd threatened to do to Marius and his new love, Linnea. He opened his mouth but no sound came out. Philonous died at the moment the sun appeared in glory over the horizon. They buried him the next day.

7

Linnea awaited Marius at the base of the great oak inside the door, which was ajar. He'd told her to stay on with Quercus as soon as both of them knew what had happened, and that he would come as soon as he was able. Philonous's terrible injuries meant that his swift death had been a mercy of sorts.

Her own demon-wound had healed when the poison was fully drawn but the scratch had left a ridged scar. A memento of Ravelle that she would carry for life. At least she still had a life to live, unlike the poor willow tree that Marius had loved so much. If only she could fly to Marius instead of waiting, take him in her arms, and comfort him as he had comforted her.

Her strange encounter with the demon had been only the beginning.

Ravelle's malice was indeed a force to be reckoned with. He had brought her to her knees as his sexual servitor by his foul trickery and he had burned a helpless willow tree too ancient to pull up its deep roots and struggle away. Yet he would let her live. Marius was the ultimate object of his insane wrath, because she, Linnea, had chosen the centaur to be her lover. The demon's bizarre mind had taken that as an insult to be avenged.

I want you, Linnea. The insinuating horror of Ravelle's voice echoed in her mind even now.

She heard the sound of trampling hooves and a vigorous crashing in the undergrowth. They'd sent Esau with a message for him when Quercus explained that a demon as powerful as Ravelle could conjure up the scrying pools of good folk in a shallow bowl of water and spy to his heart's content. The magpie's distinctive black-and-white plumage had been dyed by her with a brush to make him less noticeable, and he'd flown far and wide until he returned with a tiny scroll secured around his neck with a red thread.

Marius wrote back that he would travel in centaur form to reach her more quickly and carry her away to a place that was safer still, no matter the stage of the moon. Then he burst out of the woods, wheeling, rearing, looking for her, until he saw her step out of the door in the tree.

She picked up the skirts of her soft kirtle and ran to him. "Marius!"

His hooves slammed into the earth with a thunderous noise and his muscular arms enfolded her. She was unimaginably happy to see him. He kissed her over and over, the top of her head, the lips she turned up to him, her cheeks, as if she was more dear to him than life.

Quercus, biding his time until the centaur calmed down, came out at last from the tree.

"Thank you, my friend, for keeping her safe," Marius said, deep feeling in his voice. "For all we know, Linnea might have met the fate of Philonous."

The wise, wrinkled face showed both grief and understanding, but Quercus said nothing except something that sounded like a blessing on them both in Treeish.

Marius turned to her again. "Are you ready, Linnea?"

She nodded and he swept her up, nearly throwing her bodily over his shoulder in his haste to depart. He flipped his healing tail as he wheeled toward the woods and Linnea managed to right herself and find her seat on the broad back, leaning forward to grasp his mane.

"Good-bye, Quercus! And thank you!"

The little old spirit watched them go with a look of sad resignation, then ducked when Esau, black as coal, swooped out of the door in the tree and flew after them.

The Arcan lords gathered once more, in Simeon's stronghold by the sea this time. Ravelle, filthy beast that he was, was known to be finicky about getting his cloven hooves wet.

A raw wind from the east, sent their way by prior arrangement with Quercus. He liked to meddle with the weather from his nice, dry tree and had whipped the waves between the isles to high, dangerous peaks after all had arrived. They were safe enough.

"I say we kill him as soon as possible by fair means or foul," Gideon began. His wings were folded about his shoulders against the cold draft, as his eelskin suit was insufficient protection from the damp, which he hated. "What think you, Simeon?"

The selkie lord's answer was far more thoughtful. "How will we be sure that it is him?"

"We stick a knife into him," said Lord Vane. "If it is Ravelle, he will turn back into his real self."

"And if it isn't, we have harmed an innocent," Megaleen said.

Vane scowled. "Who cares?"

"Philonous would not ask us to take a life for his," Marius said. "We would dishonor his memory if we did, even by accident."

"Ravelle has gone too far," the Lord of Fire spat out. "He will not stop at the life of one old tree." The discussion seemed to bore him. His long black hair spilled over his shoulders and he pushed it back irritably.

Linnea studied him from where she sat with Rhiannon

across the great hall of the stronghold. They had risen from the table to oversee the sea-maids preparing the sleeping chambers for them and had just returned.

That look in his eyes—for all his gruffness, she had the oddest feeling that he was missing someone. It would be going too far to say that the lord of the Fire Isle might be in love—he seemed too fierce and too selfish for that tender emotion. But she sensed an essential loneliness that seemed to weigh on him. He sprawled in his seat, tapping his fingers on the table, his long legs wide apart, and she immediately looked elsewhere.

Rhiannon smiled at her. "What do you think of him?"

Linnea paused to consider Vane once more. "I think the lord of fire is as wild as he is wily."

The other woman gave a low laugh. "It is hard to believe that you have only just met him. Precisely right. But he may be our best hope against the demon, if he is not distracted by his, ah, urges."

"Urges. I see." Linnea glanced his way again, feeling disloyal to her impulsive, hard-charging, good-hearted Marius. But Vane had sexual magnetism that seemed hard for him to contain.

Perhaps he saw no need to.

Responding instinctively to feminine scrutiny, Lord Vane returned it in an extremely bold way, as if he were imagining a threesome. Annoyed by his behavior, Linnea rose from her seat and extended a hand to Rhiannon. "Let us sit with our men," she said in a low voice. "I do not care to be stared at like that."

Rhiannon nodded and came with her. "Do not take it personally. He is who he is. He has been in a bad temper of late, but that is nothing new."

"Reason will not save the day," Linnea pointed out. "The demon is not going to negotiate."

"I think you should bring that up when we rejoin the others."

Linnea looked again at Lord Vane, whose air of genial menace reminded her in some ways of Ravelle himself. "He may be the man, as you say."

"Yes, he is more than a match for the demon. They share a willingness to fight to the death, though Vane is not unkind. Just uncivilized. And cursed with a fiery temper."

They came closer to the table where Megaleen was still seated next to Simeon. Marius and Gideon each had an arm draped over the empty chair next to them, as if they had been patiently waiting for Linnea and Rhiannon.

Linnea hung back a moment longer. "Has Lord Vane a lady?"

"Of a sort. When he is drunk, he tells stories of her. His beauty bare and all that. She is, I believe, made of fire."

"Then they will be happy. But I wish he would stop staring at us."

Rhiannon took her hand. "Pay no attention."

They took their places by the men they loved, and the discussion continued far into the night.

Lord Vane banged his fist on the table. He'd gone down to the kitchen during a lull in the talk and from thence to Simeon's cellars, where he'd found several small bottles of kelp brandy and smuggled them back up to the hall concealed in his tunic. He was quite drunk. There was nothing the others could do about it.

"I tell you," he growled, "Ravelle is a rank amateur. I can match him fire for fire, dirty trick for dirty trick."

"I don't doubt it," Gideon said as calmly as he could. "But—"

"But nothing. Why will you three not let me fight him one on one?"

"We are six. Seven, counting you. And we are stronger together," Rhiannon said. She glanced at Linnea, whose drowsy head rested on Marius's shoulder. She was still awake, though, observing the proceedings through heavy-lidded eyes but Marius was in dreamland, even though he was sitting in a straight chair. Must be the horse in him, she reflected. Rhiannon envied him the ability to fall asleep in an upright position. The discussion had dragged on for hours and, thanks to Vane's boorish behavior, was deteriorating into masculine showing off on his part.

For the moment, he had shut up. He too was looking at Linnea, Rhiannon noticed. As a newcomer among them, Linnea had said little, sticking close to Marius. There was a love story in the making, Rhiannon thought with an inward smile.

From the windows outside, the first light of dawn was barely visible over the sea. Simeon rose. "We have talked until sunrise and come to no useful conclusions. Let us retire."

"You can." Vane uncorked the last little bottle of kelp brandy and put it to his lips. His gorge moved rapidly as he drank it down. "I'm going."

"Where?" Gideon asked.

"That is none of your affair. Fuck off." Vane sat the bottle down so hard it cracked. Marius woke at the sound, and looked around confusedly. Then he kissed the top of Linnea's head and closed his eyes again. Vane stared at the two of them with burning eyes.

"You are spoiling for a fight, my friend," Simeon said firmly. "I think you should sleep it off."

"Yes," Megaleen said. "There is a chamber ready."

"With smooth sheets and soft pillows and rushes strewn upon the floor. Peaceful and quiet," Vane said.

"Of course," Megaleen began but Vane glared at her.

"Is there no woman who will warm my bed?" he asked rudely. "Can't you send up a strumpet?"

"No."

"Bloody hell. I'll be damned if I'll sleep alone." He only glanced at Linnea this time, but both Megaleen and Rhiannon caught it, and they exchanged a long look.

They rose from their seats, a move that prompted Linnea to lift her head and nudge Marius awake.

Half awake. Enough to stand up and follow his lady to the

chamber they would share for the night. His hand moved down from the small of her back, absently patting her buttocks.

Lord Vane, slumped in his chair, watched that with angry eyes. Rhiannon lost patience with him and urged him roughly to his feet. He grumbled at her, then remembered where he was, shooting a surly look at the two remaining lords of Arcan.

"What?" he snarled. "Why the stern faces? I didn't do anything."

In answer, Gideon and Simeon moved to the back of his chair and grabbed him together under his arms, hauling him to his feet.

"Let me go!"

His loud protest was ignored, and they half-dragged him to the stairs that led to the kitchen, bumping and shoving him down.

Megaleen and Rhiannon heard the heavy door of the stronghold groan open and the quiet voices of the men-at-arms.

"He does not deserve to be treated like a lord when he acts like a ruffian. I suspect they will bring him to the stables," Simeon's lady said. "He can sleep it off there."

"In all that straw?" Rhiannon replied. "His very breath might set it on fire. Kelp brandy is potent stuff."

Megaleen raised an eyebrow. "You have a point." She moved toward the stairs herself to follow the men. "He can sleep on stone then. Outside."

Lord Vane did not awaken for hours. The sun had set. He ached all over and there was a bitter taste of seaweed in his mouth. Some thoughtful soul had left him a jug of water, even if he had lacked bedding.

He got up and put it to his lips, rinsing out his mouth and pouring the rest of it over his head.

He must have been quite drunk. The other lords were generally more forgiving when he was in his cups. But then all the women had been present, which was unusual. He pissed next, in a splashing stream that betrayed how long and deeply he'd slept. Relieved but not feeling chipper otherwise, he looked out to sea and thought of the new lady. Linnea.

Something about her was deeply exciting. She had spirit to spare and an obvious, animal sensuality that intrigued him. He'd not been able to take his eyes off her. Doe eyes, lithe body, graceful walk—her dainty feet in pointed slippers reminded him of little hooves, like an antelope's.

Marius was no match for her. The way the centaur was always crashing around in the forest—bah. He was too clumsy for the elegant Linnea, Vane thought, yawning.

He turned around, hearing distant voices coming from the stronghold that towered above him. Some friends, he thought sourly. They'd dragged him outside to sleep it off in the cold, which was why he ached.

He listened intently. The pointless discussion of what to do about Ravelle seemed to be continuing. He didn't want to get into all that again. If they'd left him outside, then he could come and go as he pleased.

The evening torches had been lit and the windows above him glowed. In the highest one, he caught a glimpse of a female form.

The very female who'd been on his mind. Linnea. He was almost sure it was her. Vane studied the rock walls of the stronghold, not seeing a way up. But if he was careful, he could climb the rough stones themselves, row by row.

He looked down. It was a long way to fall if he lost his grip. His brains would be dashed out on the rocks below and his body swept out to sea by the foaming breakers. The silhouetted woman passed by the window again, moving quickly. He had a sudden urge to get to her before she went down the endless stairs and sat demurely at the table with the others.

Now.

It had always been his rallying cry. The Lord of Fire was not to be gainsaid.

He gripped a slab of stone with both hands and hoisted himself up to the first row. The climb was arduous but exhilarating. He'd had to cling to the building like a spider, inching up, but the effort cleared his mind and made his hot blood fizz.

He had no idea if she was still there, though. Vane's hands gripped the edge of the small terrace at the top of the tower and he pulled himself up just enough to look over. Instantly, a volcano of pure lust boiled over in his soul, not that he had one, and he almost fell, looking at her.

Linnea was bathing in an enormous tub made of wooden staves. He hadn't known there was one in the tower, but he didn't pity the maids who had to carry up the water to fill it. He would have done it himself, just to see her naked, playing by herself, pink and slippery. Her long hair was wet—she must gone under to soak it—and it lay in lovely wiggles over her back and shoulders that dripped back into the water.

He couldn't see her nipples, only the tops of what had to be perfect breasts, round and full and floating.

She was lathering sweet-smelling soap in her hands. The fragrance tickled his nostrils. Then she raised one arm to wash underneath it and straightened up, revealing her breasts, tawny-pink, erect nipples, dripping water.

He wanted to suck every drop.

Vane almost lost his grip and cursed under his breath. Much as he wanted to watch her on the sly, he didn't want to die doing it.

She was busy with her ablutions and he peered around through the jagged rock edge of the terrace. Shoved in one corner was a tall screen. A long cloth had been slung over it, for drying purposes. If he could crabwalk and then clamber over, he could hide behind it.

He did it.

Vane flexed his cramped fingers and squatted behind the screen to ease his muscles, tense and aching from the hard climb. And that wasn't all that was hard. He had a massive erection that wasn't going to go away. The leather breeches the Lord of Fire preferred to wear would hold back his throbbing cock.

Unless she wanted to see it.

He was tempted to hand her the towel when she got out. If she screamed, who would hear?

He certainly wasn't going to harm her. He would make some ridiculous excuse, ease past her and down the stairs, and plead drunkenness if anyone caught him. To hell with all of them, anyway. Except her, of course.

Linnea stood up in the tub and he gasped. The raw wind of yesterday had died down to a fresh breeze and it made the water dripping down her body sparkle in the sun. It was still cool, though. Those nipples of hers were tight and high. She was flawless, except for a thin scar in the middle of her chest that was still pink. From a fall? He didn't care. The imperfection only added to her incredible beauty.

She put one foot up on the edge of the tub and bent over. Vane moved to get the best view of juicy-wet labia. Just what he liked. A plump cunt snugged between pretty haunches. All she needed was a pert white triangular tail over it. Like a doe in heat. Taking her time about it, she ran her soapy hands into her pussy and gave it a thorough, luxurious scrub. Almost as if she were a little sore.

Marius must have had her last night. The thought didn't make Vane jealous. It only added to his excitement. She used the extra lather to wash between her buttocks, too, bending over a little more and spreading to get in there. One slender finger slipped into the tight hole. Then out.

She was innocently shameless. He was overcome with lust by that unexpected move and adjusted his position. And his aching balls. Did she like a man in there too?

Vane was no stranger to that kind of play. He reached between his legs and gave his genitals a punishing squeeze. Much more of this and he would start to spurt. The lava was impossible to control as soon as the pulsing began.

Linnea dipped down to rinse and rose again, stretching pleasurably. She bent way over to get an ewer that held more water, beautiful folds appearing in her belly as her breasts bobbed in the air.

She held the ewer over her head and poured, and rivulets trickled down her breasts. He thought immediately of Hella, covered with his hot spray, laughing with lust, rubbing his come into her hot blue skin.

He couldn't do that with Linnea, not in the same way. But he could shoot his load into the bath the way he did for the naiads, let it cool the molten drops. He could imagine her bringing them up out of the water in her cupped hands.

Smooth drops of volcano glass. Something pretty to keep in a box or fondle in her hand to remember him by. Marius didn't have to know.

Vane was getting ahead of himself. But he was extremely tempted to seduce her. Something about the way she handled her own flesh told him she hadn't been completely satisfied last night. Women always needed more fucking than they wanted to admit.

If a man took his time about exciting their sweet bodies— tongue, hands, dildos—they were crazy for it, more than ready, begging for a long, thick cock driving deep and hard.

She wouldn't have to be polite about it with him. Whatever she asked for, Vane would give, over and over again. Within the limits of the fire curse, of course. He would never, ever hurt her. He had never hurt any woman, no matter how drunk he was. The seething lava in his balls couldn't touch a woman who wasn't a fire spirit. Vane touched himself between the legs and blew on his fingertips. He was dangerously hot. He would have to ease the pressure or risk an explosion.

Linnea was rubbing foam into her dripping hair in slow circles. Her eyes were closed.

Now.

He kneeled and unfastened his breeches, rubbing his stiff cock with rapid strokes. *Unh. Unh.* He had to come. If he sprayed the rock wall with it, it would cool in a hurry and then he could go back to his leisurely observation. Intense, almost painful, his orgasm made him shake. Gripping hard, he pointed his cock at the wall, forcing it down, not seeing the scarlet spurts because he was watching Linnea.

She poured more water over her head, rinsing her hair. Her eyes were still closed. Then she turned her head rapidly from side to side, whipping the water out of her hair. The dark strands tenderly lashed her bare skin, and Vane was transfixed all over again. He squeezed out the penultimate drops of come and stuffed his throbbing organ back into his breeches.

That too. Whipping. If she liked to get rough.

He was no stranger to that either. But he would have to handle her with utmost gentleness, because Marius would notice any mark upon that perfect skin.

Linnea sighed and stepped out, standing on the flat stones of the terrace and looking around. He took a deep breath, not sure if she would come his way or what he would do about it.

A maidservant came out onto the terrace, holding a long cloth like the one that had been slung over the screen.

Was he safe? Not quite. The young woman enfolded Linnea in the cloth, rubbing her gently all over. Would this sweet torment never end? At least he'd had the presence of mind to get rid of some of his sexual heat.

But two beautiful females, one naked, one not, gentle mistress and sweet young servant occupied with the sensual routines of bathing, were almost too much for the randy Lord of the Fire.

The maid kneeled at Linnea's feet, taking a smaller cloth from her waist to dry them. Linnea sat down and extended one foot. The maid changed her position and took the foot on her lap.

As far as Vane could see, Linnea's toes were resting on the mound between the other woman's legs. But maybe not.

Carefully, the maid shook scented oil into her palm from a little bottle that had swung at her waist, and rubbed it all over Linnea's bare foot, top and bottom, moving with slow strokes over her ankle, making circles with her thumbs.

"Ah. That feels wonderful." Linnea smiled down at the maid.

Vane had no doubt she was right about that.

Each toe was treated to an individual massage as the two women chatted and laughed. Their soft voices and free companionship were shatteringly sexy to their hidden observer.

Linnea put that foot down on the stones and set the other on the maid's lap, wriggling her toes. "More, please, Narcissa. I can't get enough. Where did you learn to do this so well?"

"Mistress Megaleen taught me how." The girl continued, her skilled fingers oiling and rubbing Linnea's soft foot everywhere and sliding up the slender ankle as before. "She did my feet to show me exactly what felt best, then she let me do hers."

Oh yes. He could see it. Now there were three women to dally with in Lord Vane's overheated imagination. Linnea, Megaleen, and Narcissa.

"Would you like me to rub your legs, Mistress Linnea?"

Linnea laughed charmingly. "I am getting the royal treatment." She held onto the cloth that swaddled her at the top, but lifted the hem to reveal her legs all the way up to where her thighs met her body, taking her foot out of Narcissa's lap.

A woman with a woman. Not self-conscious and not, in her mind, thinking about sex as far as Vane could tell. Which made the sweet innocence of the encounter all the more potent for him.

The maidservant kneeled between Linnea's legs and raised the other woman's feet to her shoulders, resting them there.

"This way I can get underneath and above. Just relax. This is the best part."

Indeed. Vane saw Linnea's labia when the maidservant spread her mistress's legs. He kept his face close to the concealing screen.

Murmuring in a soothing way, she shook more oil over the top of Linnea's legs, catching the drips expertly in her palms and applying them to the undersides. Using long strokes, she rubbed it into the skin, then began to work more deeply, rubbing and sometimes squeezing.

The steady rhythm lifted Linnea's behind at the same time. Just a little. Over and over. Linnea leaned back on her arms to brace herself. The maidservant was absorbed in her task, wriggling back a bit to sit on her haunches. She was a strong peasant girl with fine, big buttocks and thighs that were shaped by hard work, in contrast to Linnea's grace and delicacy.

What he saw and what he thought mingled hotly in an irresistible fantasy. Rooted to the spot, silent, Lord Vane stripped both women in his mind.

He took it farther. Naked in his imagination, the strong young maid gave in to the temptation in front of her face and began to tongue her mistress's pussy, spreading her legs wider and pushing in with pent-up desire. Linnea threw back her head and let her do it, glancing now and then at the door of the terrace to see . . . Vane filled in that bit quickly . . . to see if Marius was coming.

In this fantasy—his fantasy, Vane reminded himself—there would be only one man. Him.

Linnea stroked the maid's hair, then lifted her face, wiping the girl's moist cheeks, laughing. Then she settled onto her back and stretched out her legs completely. Her excited pussy made a juicy noise when it stretched open too.

Narcissa slid in one finger, then two. "Do you enjoy that, dear mistress?"

Linnea whispered a reply he could just hear in his fantasy. "Use three fingers, Narcissa. I like the full feeling—oh!"

She gave a little cry in Vane's mind when the maidservant obeyed her soft command. He closed his eyes.

The women grew more excited and went head to tail, eagerly lapping at each other's pussies. They climaxed for the first time. Then Linnea played little games of obedience with her maidservant, demanding that the peasant girl tie on a leather dildo and service her vigorously indeed.

Soft giggling filled his ears as he swayed a little on his feet, still hidden, lost in his erotic dream of Sapphic play.

"Does that tickle?" Narcissa was asking in reality.

"A little," Linnea said. "What sort of oil is that? My skin is not all greasy."

"No, you will not need another bath."

How unfortunate, Vane thought groggily. Unslaked lust fogged the brain far worse than wine or brandy. He took several deep breaths. The massage seemed to be over.

The maidservant lifted Linnea's relaxed legs and put her feet on the flat stones. "How was that?"

"Wonderful."

Hear, hear. Vane squeezed his hard cock inside the leather that restrained it, forcing it to calm down.

"Thank you, Narcissa. You may go."

The maidservant made an awkward curtsey, picked her bottle of oil, and went back into the room. Linnea drew the drying cloth more tightly around her, draping the longer end of it over her bare shoulders. The breeze had gotten stronger.

A sudden gust swirled around the tower terrace and knocked over the screen. Linnea's beautiful eyes widened with shock when she saw Vane standing there. He looked directly at her, not seeming ashamed to have been caught. She wanted to smack him—then remembered how unpredictable his temper was. She stiffened her spine before she spoke, knowing that the maidservant had closed the door to her room behind her and gone down the stairs.

She was alone with the Lord of Fire.

"How did you get here?" she asked at last. "And how long where you watching?"

He shook his head. "Don't know."

That was not an answer to either of her questions. Screaming would be useless and might only provoke him. If he had a shred of nobility in him, he would not take advantage of her vulnerability—or his far superior strength.

"Go," was all she said.

To her surprise, he did. She could not help glancing down as he passed by her on his way to the terrace door. Lord Vane's breeches contained an immense erection. His balls were so large that they showed through the leather.

She hoped he was hurting. He slammed out, unseen by anyone but her. Simeon and Megaleen had seen fit to give her and Marius this secluded tower, for which they had been grateful.

Marius made love to her twice last night, with the surpassing gentleness he'd shown since he'd learned the details of her encounter with the demon. At last she had been able to comfort him in turn, caressing his strong arms and shoulders as he grieved wordlessly for his lost friend. The sexual release had brought a flood of emotions, and their sleep had been deep and dreamless.

Lord Vane must have been very drunk indeed to have scaled the tower in the night. She could not imagine how he could have done it in the daylight while she was bathing. He was a brawler and a fighter, not light on his feet.

No, he had fallen into a sot's dream and risked his life to crawl up, thinking he was scaling a mountain. Her talking to the maid had woken him up. He looked like a disreputable inhabitant of some nameless hell, to be sure.

Lashings of dark stubble along his hard jaw. Dark eyes that still glowed, despite the aftereffects of disgusting kelp brandy. Hair that looked like the wind had combed it. And that body—

ill-clothed but strong enough and skilled enough to climb a stone tower in the dark.

He didn't seem to be able to put on a look of guilt. It would have been utterly out of character if he had. Linnea went inside the bedchamber and pulled up the covers over the hollow in the tangle of sheets where she and Marius had fallen into sleep in each other's arms, bone-weary and troubled.

She sat down on the edge of the feather-stuffed mattress, plucking one that had come halfway out of the ticking and twirling it in her fingers. Ought she to tell him that Lord Vane had been behind the screen? What good would it do?

Marius and the other lords of Arcan had more than enough to worry about. Vane's penchant for roistering was well-known to them, but he hadn't harmed her or so much as set a finger on her. Nor had he said anything to upset her. He'd simply left without a backward look, standing tall and proud as ever, not slinking out.

Anybody could do something stupid when drunk.

She decided not to give him away.

Gideon, Simeon, and Marius were too deep in conversation at the table to look up when Vane traversed the wide hall. Nor did the maids, slopping the stone floors with rags, talking to each other. His steps were swift and soft, and he went out the small door set into the great one, ducking his head. Well-oiled because of the corrosive sea air, it didn't even squeak. Vane hastened away.

With luck, there would be a boat on the shore and a man to row him back to the desolate Isle of Fire. The wind blew in gusts along the rocky shore, chilling him to the bone. He leaned into it, striding faster.

He would get a roaring blaze going in the fireplace in his bedchamber when he reached his island. With luck, Hella would appear. He needed her more than ever.

8

In the loneliest part of the Forest Isle ...

Ravelle was sulking. His behind still ached from where Marius had kicked him, and it was bony to begin with, sagging in leathery wrinkles without any fat.

He lowered himself into a pool fed by a natural hot springs and groaned. Sitting down was next to impossible. No, he would stay lifted up with his arms and let his saggy behind float. He had more than one reason for taking a bath. His revenge upon Marius for that tremendous kick which had flung him into the sky had not been as easy. He still smelled of smoke, even though it had been days ago. Old Philonous had been full of resin and did not burn cleanly.

Soaking, he thought back upon the murder of the tree. He had not been quite sure Philonous *was* dead, but Ravelle had left him for dead, put it that way. He wished he hadn't tried to terrify the willow even more by telling it he would plan to sell Marius to a particularly unsavory traveling circus where he would be exhibited as a freak to ordinary men. And embellished that by threatening to shackle the centaur after that to a giant millstone, blinded and beaten, once the world was bored with looking at him.

The old tree had shrieked with rage and Ravelle had had to do his worst too quickly and wing away. Who knew who might have come to Philonous's aid?

In a little while, he felt somewhat better and eased himself up on the rock the same color as himself, stretching out to dry in the sun. A small bird flew over him and he waved it away, not wanting to be shat upon.

Next one, he vowed silently, would be grabbed out of the air and eaten raw. He was hungry too, which did not improve his mood.

Soon enough, another bird flew over him, a larger one. Black. Not a crow, though, he thought, squinting at it as it settled on a different rock, its back to him. Was he, Ravelle, camouflaged so well that he had not been noticed? He reached a long arm down into the water to splash the oblivious bird, and managed to do it, much to his malicious pleasure.

The bird was drenched, immediately preoccupied with getting rid of the water from its unexpected bath. Ravelle noticed with curiosity that the blackness was dripping off it. He saw white feathers stained with dye wearing off and some that were truly black. It was a magpie. Marius's magpie? The one that had stabbed him in the back?

Oho. He would happily crunch Esau in his jaws alive. Ravelle rolled over and flattened himself like a creeping lizard, moving over the rock he was on like a shadow. Again he reached out a long hand and grasped the bird, which turned its head to look at him at last with beady eyes, its heart pounding frantically in its breast.

It was Esau. The bird gave a despairing croak.

"What brings you here?" Ravelle asked nastily. Then he opened his mouth and displayed sharp rows of teeth.

The bird trembled in his claws.

Ravelle opened his mouth wider. "Scared? The teeth in the back are even sharper. But I am not sure whether to eat you head first or tail first."

As if in answer, Esau squirted a disgusting gray-white stream onto the demon's belly.

"Fie!"

Ravelle flung the magpie away and Esau soared off.

Back to his master, no doubt, Ravelle thought with fury. He dove into the pool and came up flapping his wings, rising straight up, cloven hooves dangling as he flew after the bird. If he kept back far enough, he could follow the magpie through the air.

Flying, Esau could not look back to see if he was being pursued. It would be interesting to see where he went. The demon's leathery wings creaked a little as he went higher. Marius's stupid bird was a dot in the sky, disappearing fast.

Ravelle flew faster, dropping when the bird did but keeping his distance when Esau finally alighted on an outcropping of rock high above the treetops.

Of course. His hidden nest. A collection of magpie junk. Bright pebbles and feathers, glittering mica, sacred to the God of All but not to this wild bird, who helped himself to it. From where he'd landed, on an uncomfortable branch with lots of leaves to hide him, Ravelle saw gold.

The magpie had indiscriminate taste. There were pebbles, gold, jewelry he'd found or stolen. Ravelle would pick through it once the bird flew away.

Esau seemed to want to rest. He scratched at his miscellaneous collection and then sat down in the middle of it, basking in the strong sun. The bird put its head over one shoulder to preen itself, fluffing out its feathers to rid itself of the pond water the demon had flung at it.

Ravelle landed on a crooked branch, keeping vigil. If he

sprang forth now, the bird would fly away and no doubt lead Marius back.

The demon was not ready to do battle again. Disgusted by the ease with which Marius had blasted their supposedly all-powerful master into the air, his ungrateful imps had deserted him, although a double-crosser among them had informed him before buzzing off that his legions in the Outer Darkness were threatening an uprising. A younger cousin of his was apparently plotting his demise.

He could not take on the powerful lords of Arcan by himself. Right now it seemed that all he could do was bide his time, and kill Marius over and over again in his bloody daydreams.

If he could really do it, then sweet Linnea might be truly his.

Ravelle settled into the crotch of the branch and chewed absently on a bitter leaf, thinking of her. She would never come to him willingly. She would have to be bound. He'd gotten off to a fine start with that before the stupid centaur showed up.

He smirked, remembering the scratch he'd given her. He was fairly sure Marius did not have the expertise to draw the slow-acting poison out of it. It might be another moon before it drove her raving mad and made her ready for to be—the demon liked to coin words—thoroughly ravelled.

A sexually insatiable madwoman, all his own. Ahh. She would never be satisfied, not by him, not by a legion of lesser demons. They would line up to fuck her, chained on all fours, screaming with rage, her mind gone forever. His three-eyed cock twitched and lengthened. The slit in the head opened and murmured obscene encouragement.

Ravelle heeded it, pumping vigorously. Aging like the rest of him, his member was not always so cooperative. A stinking spray squirted out from the leaves and fell with a patter like light rain falling from a high, passing cloud.

The dozing bird shifted at the sound and then got up. It walked about its higgledy-piggledy nest, turning over a few stones in a bored way, then looked to the far horizon. A trail of smoke from a distant fire rose into the air. Esau smoothed his dry feathers with his beak and flew off in that direction.

Resting from his masturbation, Ravelle didn't notice any of it until he heard the flap of wings. He let go of his flaccid organ and pushed the concealing leaves aside. The magpie's nest was empty.

He stood up on the branch and flapped his stiff wings to get them moving before he took to the air. Was he getting old? He had lived for millennia, expected to live for millennia to come. But even a demon had to die.

Hmph. Marius first. And to hell with the bird for the moment. Ravelle lifted off from the branch and hovered, his hooves dangling in midair. Then he flew the short distance to Esau's nest.

It had been in use for some time, judging by the quantity of stones and pebbles and other things. Ravelle sat on the edge and folded up his legs, reaching in for a gold earring.

He used his claw to pierce his earlobe and stuck it in, not minding the dark blood that flowed over his claw. He didn't mind pain, so long as he was the one inflicting it, on himself or someone else.

A flat shard of black volcanic glass gleamed in the strong sun. He could see his reflection in that. Ravelle picked it up. The earring next to his withered cheek looked anything but dashing. He *was* getting old.

Ravelle tore the earring out of his lobe and flung it back into the nest angrily. It clinked off a lump of ore and fell next to a smooth carved stone that was nearly buried.

What was that?

He scrabbled around it with his claw and picked it clean when he got it free. It had a hole at the top where a chain or a leather thong had once been. At first glance it looked like a horse, but then Ravelle saw it was a carving of a centaur. An amulet. The workmanship was incredibly fine.

As he held it in his palm, it felt warm. Then it began to glow.

Interesting. No doubt a god or a demi-god had dropped it from the clouds above. It might even have fallen from the divine court even higher in the sky, or been flung in the midst of a celestial brawl or orgy.

Ravelle found a chain in the mess of stuff eventually and threaded it through the hole in the amulet, fitting the two ends together with a bit of string. He didn't bother to check his appearance in the glass shard. The amulet was interesting and he had always wanted to own something that had belonged to the gods, who were inclined to ignore him and his kind.

He put it on. Resting upon his chest, it grew warmer still. Ravelle shifted the amulet on the chain, moving it to a different spot under his collarbone. Then something else distracted him. The nest seemed to be growing smaller. Unless he was growing bigger. Ravelle looked down at his legs, expecting to see narrow goat's hooves at the end of them.

He didn't.

He saw the broad hooves of a draft horse. He ran his claws along the massive muscles that bulged where his lean shanks were supposed to be. It suddenly became impossible to sit in the nest.

Ravelle fell out, turning head over tail.

Not his own whiplike appendage, he noticed as he somersaulted through the air. A long, flowing, horse's tail. He was becoming a centaur. Ravelle grabbed at the chain around his neck and snapped it, praying to the Lowest of the Low that he would revert to his natural shape in the remaining seconds before he hit the earth.

His thick tail got hung up in the treetops and his new centaur skin peeled off with it. Ravelle windmilled his arms and fell the rest of the way. Right on his bony ass.

He lay there, gasping. The amulet, which undoubtedly was of divine make and enchanted to boot, was gone. He had to find it. When he had recovered, Ravelle beat the bushes looking for it.

Such a transformation could be very useful. He had not been able to hold onto the shape of Marius as a man for very long; that of a centaur, never. With the amulet he could be Marius the centaur for as long as he liked.

Long enough to lure Linnea to ride on his back. Long enough to run away with her and imprison her where the real Marius could not find her. And long enough to face Marius as an equal and fight with him the way maddened stallions did: to the death.

He would have the advantage of surprise. At the moment, there was only one centaur on the Isle of the Forest and that was Marius. His brother, the seldom seen Darius, a mere man of the woods, had not been so cursed.

Thrash. Crack. He broke branches and tore off leaves in his furious search through the undergrowth. Had his last chance been lost to him? Ravelle clenched his claws and screamed with rage.

He could not find the amulet.

The magpie landed on the beach, near the source of the fire that had summoned him. He looked around, uneasy without shelter. Esau was less bold than he used to be. His plucking at the merciless claws of Ravelle's imps had made him acquainted with fear.

The bird was alone. He hopped a bit, then flapped his wings and flew up to a mangrove branch, hiding behind a wide leaf. The thin trail of smoke had nearly died down.

Marius had built it, Esau knew. He must need a messenger. In the meantime, the bird would take a nap.

He fluffed out his feathers and awoke a little while later when he heard Linnea's voice, far down the beach. She and Marius were lugging a basket.

Whatever were they thinking? Had they summoned him to carry it? A small magpie could not. On the other hand, there might be something worth stealing in it. His thoughts were muddled. Esau was still rattled from his encounter with Ravelle. His escape had been a near thing.

Linnea was smiling, although she looked pale. The bird cocked its head and listened when she talked.

"Marius, this didn't seem so heavy when I packed it. And do we dare eat out in the open like this?"

He took over the carrying of the basket from her before they reached the fire. "We cannot sit in Simeon's stronghold indefinitely, you and I."

"I suppose not."

"Gideon and Simeon cannot seem to agree on the right course of action and I was weary of listening to them jawbone."

Linnea thought of Lord Vane's dangerous boldness. He might not do right, but he knew exactly what he wanted to do. She sighed. It was best not to mention him at all. Or even think of him. "Yes, Rhiannon and Megaleen couldn't get in a word in edgewise."

"That is why they went out for a sail—and why I commandeered that disreputable craft to get us here." He looked over his shoulder at the tied-up boat. "We have a furlong's walk ahead of us, but the destination is worth it. I miss the woods, Linnea."

"So do I."

"The solstice revels are long over. No outsiders will bother us and Ravelle has not shown his ugly face since I kicked him to the skies."

"If you think it is safe . . ." she said.

"One cannot live in fear. Philonous taught me that."

Marius had not talked of his beloved old friend since the moment of his death. Linnea brushed away a sudden tear and he frowned.

"I did not mean to make you sad."

"Never mind, Marius. Philonous was right."

"He is never far from my mind, Linnea," Marius said softly. "He is the one who brought us together on the sly. Did you not know that?"

"You never told me."

He shook his head. "There was never time. He was too rooted and too old to take many chances, but he thought I should. He knew me for so long, almost as long as—ah. He is here. I have summoned a friend of yours to join us."

"Who?"

Marius looked ahead, scanning the mangroves. "The magpie. There is a pomegranate in this basket just for him."

Linnea jumped when the bird flew out right in front of them in a flash of black-and-white, startling her. "Esau!"

The bird landed on her shoulder, making a noisy fuss.

"If only he could speak a little and tell us what he sees as he flies." Esau clucked in her ear and then at Marius. "What is he saying?"

"I don't know. Telling jokes, perhaps. Hush, Esau."

The bird quieted down, although it seemed nervous. Linnea soothed it and scratched it gently under the chin, cooing at him. "Where have you been, Esau?"

Marius lugged the basket up a rough trail cut into the back of the beach. "Not where we are going, I don't think."

Linnea followed, hoisting her kirtle. "And where is that?"

"A hidden meadow in the oldest forest on the island. My old stomping grounds, if you must know."

"I see."

"You can weave chains of flowers and tie me up and do wicked things to my naked body."

Linnea giggled, making her strides longer to catch up with him. "I suppose there is no harm in that."

He took her hand and in time they came to the place via a

maze of trails that she would never remember. The branches closed after them and over them. They could not even be seen from the air as they made their way.

Here, the ancient forest still protected its own, she thought. As did her father, the Great White Stag. As infrequently as she had seen him, she felt honored to have sprung from his loins.

In this secluded place, the trees remained as they once were: uncorrupted. Here, she was sure, were no betrayers, no trees whose souls could be captured by demons or men. All around her were trees of the old stock, ancient and young. But all were true to the wisdom of their forebears.

Walking on, following Marius, Linnea felt as she had in the home of Quercus: safe. And very far from the danger they still had to face.

The meadow they came into was so idyllic she half expected to see gods and goddesses taking their leisure there. Exquisite flowers, unknown to her, nodded their heads, blooming in bursts of color in the sun. Walking through them made her dizzy—the blooms seemed to float above the thick green they rose from.

She raised her eyes. The magpie had flown from her shoulder and selected a likely tree. He hopped from twig to branch, squawking. He seemed, if not less nervous, at least resigned to an afternoon in a pleasant place. A few more hops and he disappeared into a thicket.

"He has recovered from the imps' assault very well," Linnea murmured to Marius. Just in case the bird did understand, she didn't want to remind him of it. Not on such an otherwise perfect day.

"Yes, so it seems. The dye is wearing off and new feathers are coming in where he was plucked."

He set the basket down in a place that was half in sunshine and half in shade, pulling out a woven cloth that was large enough for two to lie upon.

If they lay as one.

She guessed his intent from the ardent look in his eyes. "Are you sure no one comes here?"

He nodded. There was something in the heaviness of his head and the contrasting gracefulness of his very masculine neck that reminded her of his centaur self. She gazed into his eyes, surrendering to the passion in them for the moment.

"Not hungry?" she asked him. She wasn't.

"Only for you."

She bent to lift the hem of her kirtle, intending to draw it over her head, and found that he was kneeling worshipfully before her when she was done. Linnea flung it aside, as naked as he was.

The warm sunshine bathed them both, making her languorous, filled with a slow joy as he caressed her hips and brought her lower body closer to his sensual mouth. She ran her fingers through his hair at the first touch of his tongue to her labia, sighing with pleasure. "Will you not let me lie down?" she asked softly.

"In time." He teased her clitoris with little flicks, then slid a hand between her legs to move them apart.

Linnea looked up into the arching trees above at the exact moment his tongue thrust up into her. A supple birch reached down and held her hands in its tender branches, like a maid assisting her mistress during coitus. Another reached teasing twigs to her nipples, playing with them.

Marius spread her labia open and added a finger, then another, to her pleasuring. Stronger branches from bigger birches reached around her waist, supporting her. Linnea swayed with the trees.

He lifted his head. "Trust them. Lean into them."

She obeyed, letting the branches take her weight, feeling no more substantial than a butterfly. Her bare feet were cooled by the moist grasses beneath them, and rustling leaves stroked the sensitive skin of her bottom.

Marius gently probed and tongued her innermost folds. Linnea fell into a sexual rapture, crying out inarticulately as the trees lifted her. More strong branches encircled her thighs and held them open. The birch bark was mostly smooth, with rough bits that were stimulating to her skin as well.

Marius got to his feet, wiping his mouth, and stood between her thighs. His erection jutted out. Her cunt was swollen, well-licked, ready for him, held at precisely the right height by the trees. One push and he would glide into her.

But the birches had other ideas.

They swung Linnea back and forth, only letting her have the tip of his cock each time. Marius stood still, holding himself in position. The head had the softness of a ripe plum . . . delicious but she longed for the sleek hardness of the thick shaft it topped thrusting into her.

"Give me all of it," she whispered, "all, all."

"And I thought I was the impatient one."

He too was made to wait while the playful trees gave her bottom a sensual brushing with their delicate leaves. Others joined in, mere saplings, curious about her breasts, fondling and tickling them.

A mischievous one found two acorn caps and covered her nipples with them.

Marius laughed with joy but his huge erection did not diminish in the least. He plucked the caps off and scolded the tree. "But I want to suck her breasts!" He tossed them away and made good on his words.

Swinging easily, her wrists gently bound, Linnea experienced the sensation of being suckled in midair. Her sense of being weightless increased. Excited in their own way, the trees holding her grew a little less careful and she bumped his hard body.

Still, to her pleasurable frustration, she could not connect with the rigid member straining forward from his groin.

He lifted his head and covered her lips with his, slipping his tongue between them to give her silky-hot kisses that probed her mouth as he had probed her cunt.

Lips together. Bodies apart. The trees held them away from each other for a few moments more.

Marius looked up at the birches bending over them. "Please," he begged them, "give her to me. I cannot blame you for wanting to keep her to yourselves—I know how good it feels to hold her. You don't have to let her go. But give her to me."

A rustling sigh came from the trees. Once more Linnea's body was touched all over by their eager leaves. They made her swing again and Marius's cock went all the way in on the first stroke.

Linnea cried out, wrapping her thighs around his waist and her arms around his shoulders. He brushed the more inquisitive branches away and cupped her buttocks himself, not pulling back, staying rammed up inside her. He nuzzled her face, pushing away the hair from it with his own, leaning down to nip at her neck.

A stallion with a mare, she thought dreamily, then corrected herself. No. A centaur with his lady. Even as a man, he was longer and thicker than all others. Again she marveled at the combination of strength and gracefulness that Marius embodied.

The trees held her where she was, waiting for a cue from the Lord of the Forest. He nodded and they again began to swing Linnea, only as far as his cock was long. The mushroom tip never came out, but its engorged rim, slightly thicker than the shaft, stimulated and spread her labia as she was moved away from it.

In and out. In and out.

The deep inward thrusts excited her most hidden flesh. Her labia enfolded him, squeezed the moving shaft in plump folds, made him moan as she moaned. Moving in air, becoming one with her lover in a meadow that might well have been visited by trysting gods and goddesses, Linnea knew what sexual bliss was.

He was beginning to lose control, taking over from the trees, which rustled louder with jubilation at the sight of two such happy humans. Deeper and deeper he thrust each time, holding her buttocks tightly, working her softness to slake his passionate desire.

His balls were drawn too tight to swing, but the sensitive skin at the very bottom of her bottom could feel them at the base of his slick, pounding shaft. The trees were moving as if a storm was coming on but there wasn't a cloud in the sky.

One final ram and Marius began to shake all over. She could feel the hot pulses fill her cunt and drip down as he tensed his buttocks and held steady. "Linnea!"

The sound of her name cried with such lusty joy brought her to climax. Not just one. It multiplied into several, a cascade of sensation that made her cling to him, incredibly alive and thinking of nothing but this moment. And this man.

It was then that he knew that he loved her.

9

Marius tossed a piece of pomegranate, a chunk of cream-colored inner flesh studded with seeds, in the magpie's general direction and lolled back on the soft cloth under the birches. The bird flew down to peck at it.

"Enjoy it, Esau. We appreciate your discretion."

Linnea, lying next to him, stroked his chest. "He does seem to know when to fly away and when to come back."

Marius split off another chunk and popped a few ruby-red pips into her mouth. She bit into them, enjoying the tangy spurt of their juice. Starving after several hours of incredible sex in every position they or the trees could think of, they had gone through everything else in the basket and he had just finished the wine.

The sky was still clear, but the afternoon shadows were deep gold and getting longer. The trees rustled overhead, feeling calmer themselves. Or at least tired.

Marius, big and strong and masculine as he was, had wanted a turn in their branches too and they had hoisted him, spread his thighs, and swung him with great care into Linnea's open mouth as she kneeled to suck him. Without being asked, they had also rubbed his balls with their softest leaves as he swung. When he and Linnea collapsed happily into each other's arms he'd gasped that all of their wanton attentions felt good, but they were nothing compared to her touch and her sweet body.

His final orgasm had been given to the meadow. His seed arced out over it in long, healthy spurts when she pulled away just in time and let him swing out over the green. They had remembered and fulfilled the fertility rituals of the solstice revelry. How long ago it seemed.

Those three days had come and gone a while ago, along with the revelers themselves and, she supposed, the traveling circus and strolling players and all the rest of it. Her sense of time seemed to have evaporated. She looked up into the cloudless sky and thought of Ravelle. She and Marius had enjoyed their stolen bliss, miraculously untroubled by man or beast or bird or demon, but now, in the afterglow, she felt a prickle of nervous tension.

Bliss was fleeting. Somewhere on this island lurked a creature that hated them both. Marius's kick had not killed it; the lords of Arcan were at odds over it; it lay in wait for them all.

He rose halfway and gave her a kiss before heading off into the bushes. She heard a faint rushing, pattering sound coming from there in another minute, and strove to sound cheerful when she called out to him, "You piss like a horse, Marius!"

"Does that surprise you?" he called back.

Then, nothing. She supposed he was washing himself in the brook a little further off. He had brought water from it to wash her. Drowsy from the wine she'd consumed as well and the heat of the afternoon, she dozed for a little while.

The sound of Marius crashing back through the bushes made her wake up. He stood over her in centaur form. Unless she was still dreaming. The blue sky had softened to a deeper shade and twilight was just beginning. She had slept for a while, evidently.

"You have changed shape. Why?"

He seemed disinclined to answer. "Something came over me."

Perhaps the lateness of the day had saddened him. The glow was gone. "Oh. Well, then I will not have to walk all the way home—but where will that be tonight? Where are we sleeping?"

"Not at Simeon's stronghold. But we must go," he said.

Linnea sat up, looking for her kirtle and shaking her head to clear it. "All right, my love." She looked at him again. He was smiling down at her, pleased by her words of endearment.

She pulled the kirtle over her head but kept the hem of it lifted, ready to mount him and ride.

Marius bent down to pick her up without his usual grace. They were both tired, certainly. She straddled him, her hands in the mane that went halfway up his back, vanishing to a thin line of hair between his shoulder blades.

She pressed her thighs against his sides. His centaur hide was a little rough on the soft inside skin but like everything else that happened with him, pleasurable to her. Linnea leaned into him.

Marius took a few steps backward as if he was not sure of which way to go and then trotted out of the meadow. Either the wine had gotten to him or the ground was uneven, because his gait seemed somewhat unsure.

"Wait," she said into his ear. "What about Esau?"

"He can fly, Linnea," he chided her. "He will follow, like as not."

She could not argue with that.

The twilight sky deepened to indigo and thousands of stars came out in the vault above. Marius's pace had picked up and she had to hold tightly to his mane.

He no longer spoke to her, concentrating, she thought, on getting them to where they going.

Gideon turned to Simeon with a look of concern. "They have not returned."

Simeon's face was grave. "It is well after moonrise. Marius

told me he was coming back with Linnea. He wanted her to remain here, not on the Forest Isle. Not at night."

"Understandable. A bower of twigs and leaves is unsafe, unlike this fortress, though it may be home to him," Gideon said.

"I never should have allowed him to leave in the first place. But a centaur gets restless indoors."

"He was in man form," Gideon pointed out.

"No matter what, Marius is impetuous. He would have escaped if I had gainsaid him or had the men-at-arms stop him."

"At least he would have left Linnea behind. She is most at risk."

Simeon gave a curt nod. "Unfortunately, you are right. But I don't know what to do."

"Search for them. What else?"

"In the dark, Gideon? By torchlight?" Simeon asked. "We will be picked out immediately by Ravelle and his henchmen. Remember, demons are strongest by night. It is their natural element."

Gideon threw up his hands. "What else can we do? Rhiannon will go out herself if I do not."

"And she will take my Megaleen with her," Simeon said gloomily. "Their sail around the island did not tire them out, alas. Pio pulled them for most of the voyage. They are upstairs talking. Probably about us."

Gideon scowled. "I fear, Simeon, that we sat and talked for too long when time was of the essence."

"Vane certainly thought so. He was all for waving swords and chopping off heads."

"He was raving drunk."

Simeon nodded. "The steward of my cellars said the kelp brandy is all gone. No wonder Vane slunk away before morning. But he was right in a way. I have a feeling that our enemy has gained on us."

"There is no way we can confirm that or find them until daybreak."

Gideon folded his arms across his chest and flexed his massive wings. The movement made a rush of air move through the hall. "I have flown in the dark before. I might see them, or their signal fire, if Marius makes one in a clearing."

"Then go. I am no use in that regard."

Gideon clapped the Lord of the Deep on the shoulder. "Your stronghold has served us well. I hope to return with both of them. If I have to carry them by the scruffs of their foolish necks, I will."

Simeon laughed. "You might be able to carry Linnea. Marius will have to run home himself."

A little later, without telling Rhiannon, Gideon launched himself from the highest tower, the one where Linnea and Marius had spent the night. He soared out over the archipelago of Arcan.

He would search from above, island by island. The waning moon afforded some light.

Beyond the Arcan islands stretched the infinite sea. From far above the enormous, endless waves were no more than minute wrinkles on its silver surface, breaking white upon the isolated beaches.

He swooped and dove down through the air. He would fly low over the beaches of the forest island first, because that was where Marius had gone. Simeon's men-at-arms had found the fellow whose boat had been commandeered and extracted that much information.

From the air, the islands seemed closer together. But the ocean that separated them was rough and very deep, and going from one to other was rarely easy.

Marius, rash as usual, had taken a risk by going out upon it with only Linnea. The lords sometimes availed themselves of the subterranean tunnels. Because of her, Marius could not.

He must have been desperate to get away from Simeon's stronghold, if only for a day.

The feeling of the wind rushing through his wings energized Gideon. No longer were there watchers on high, waiting to hurl lightning bolts at him for his transgressions.

Life was precious to him now, not a torment to be endured.

He zoomed down to the first beach, flying low. There was nothing. Not a wisp of smoke or anyone upon it.

Up he flew again, over the headlands that separated this beach from the next, longer one.

He made several passes over the second one, in case he missed something. But it was as empty as the first. It took less than an hour to survey all the others and soon he was back where he started.

Gideon rose on a column of warm air above the island's center, startling a circling hawk as he went high up.

From this vantage point the forest seemed impenetrably black, as if it were made of black stone like Lord Vane's desolate foundry of an island and not thickly carpeted by green, living things. Not a pinprick of light illuminated it. Gideon reminded himself, flying a little lower, that the solstice revels had ended. There were few fires in the forest at other times because Marius did not allow them as a rule—a law that his mysterious younger brother Darius enforced in his peregrinations.

Gideon let out a gusty sigh and spiraled down, going for a closer look. The hawk was gone. He'd seen it plummet through the air like a stone after it sighted game, a running rabbit, perhaps. The birds of prey were blessed with eyesight that was unimaginably keen. Gideon wished he could say the same.

Marius and Linnea most likely were still on the forest island, but he could not find them. His diligent searching from the air had tired him, but he had no wish to return to Simeon just yet.

A distant rumble from Lord Vane's island came to his ears, and a plume of sparks shot skyward from the volcano.

Fireworks, he thought. Only fireworks. The cataclysm that had created Vane's island was not likely to repeat itself, according to the soothsayers who read the signs and portents of inner earth. The most learned among them told stories of another island that had vanished when the Isle of Fire was born, roaring upward from the sea. That one had been inhabited by a race of men who built vast temples and lived in peace with one another.

They and their city had been swallowed by the hungry sea in an instant. As he would be if he did not find somewhere to rest. He changed course and swooped off to see Vane.

He found him in front of the fireplace in his private chambers. Still aloft, Gideon had taken the liberty of looking in at the higher window and bypassing the servants altogether.

Vane was alone. Gideon hovered outside the window, not wanting to startle the fiery lord, and hallooed.

Vane didn't look up. "Is that you, Gideon? I thought I heard flapping. Come in."

He seemed to be recovered from his drunken binge, Gideon thought. "Thank you." The window was narrow for him, but he managed to get through by folding his wings tightly. Gideon jumped down from the stone sill and went to Vane.

He'd hoped to toast his wings after his long flight in the high air, but the fireplace was cold, littered with gray ash and black bits of wood.

The man who sat in front of it seemed to lack warmth as well.

"No fire tonight?" Gideon asked him.

Vane shook his head. "Too much trouble."

"Have the servants run away?" It was entirely possible, given Lord Vane's famously bad temper.

"I sent them away. What brings you here, Gideon?"

"I went out from Simeon's stronghold to look for Marius and Linnea. They went to the Forest Isle and have not yet returned."

Vane raised a thick black eyebrow and shot Gideon a quizzical look. It was the first time he had looked at him. "Marius is not a prisoner, is he? Can he not go where he pleases?"

"Of course. And he always does."

"Well, then. What do you want me to do? Send over the hounds?"

"No. Not yet." The great lord's pack of hunting hounds were a legend in their own right. They could go for days without tiring and always ran down their quarry in the end. But they were noisy and half-wild.

Until the four of them had hit upon the best way to vanquish Ravelle and keep him in the Outer Darkness where he belonged, it was best to operate in secrecy when possible.

"Let me know, then," Lord Vane said, adding, "I suppose I made an ass of myself at Simeon's table. He can be a stickler for ceremony and protocol. What a bore. How angry is he?"

Gideon chose to be tactful. "He is more concerned about Marius's disappearance."

Lord Vane ceased staring into the emptiness of his hearth, and got up, stretching as if he had been sitting there for some time, brooding. "Marius can take care of himself. A centaur acts first and thinks later. He is not one to dither like you two."

The comment was blunt. From anyone other than Vane, it would be an insult. "You and Marius have much in common," Gideon said evenly.

"Do we? I wish I had his lady. Linnea is beautiful. Wish, bah. I want her."

Vane's inner fire was suddenly visible in his dark eyes. Gideon gave him a narrow look. "She is indeed lovely, but not every woman is yours for the taking."

"Spoken like a true friend," Vane said wryly. "Of Marius. Not me."

"Your sexual appetites are unquenchable, or so I have heard."

Lord Vane laughed in a rude way. "Throw water on me and the fire will go out."

"Not for long. And speaking of that, why are you without one? I don't think I have ever flown near this island without seeing a glow in every window."

Vane scowled. "Spying?"

"Do you have something to hide?" The question held a sharp edge. The Lord of Fire's interest in Linnea was suspicious, given that she and Marius had just disappeared. He'd helped himself to many a maiden in the past. And nymphs. And naiads—no female was safe around Vane. His passionate skill was such that all went with him willingly, but they were spoiled for other lovers after him and difficult to please.

No one else measured up, or so Rhiannon had told Gideon. He studied Vane, whose air of indifference seemed put on.

"Of course not," Vane said at last. "And if you are thinking that I seduced her, think again. I didn't have the time, for one thing."

"That is hardly reassuring."

Vane strode about his chamber, kicking a limp leather boot into a corner with its mate after he almost tripped on it. "Gideon, I was joking."

"Hmph."

"That damned discussion of what to do about the demon went on forever," Vane said peevishly. "I got drunk—"

"Obnoxiously so. You were loud, you were full of yourself, and you were ogling the women."

Lord Vane didn't seem in the least deflated by that description of his behavior. He seemed proud. "So I was."

"I am not surprised that you admit it, only that you remember it."

Vane came to where Gideon stood, his arms folded across his chest and his wings tense, and jabbed a finger at him. "Bah! I also remember you and Simeon hauling me up from the table and—"

"How is it that no one saw you leave his stronghold in the morning?"

"Because I slept outside on cold stone where I was dumped by the men-at-arms! I treat my hounds better than that!"

"Don't look for pity." Gideon favored him with a contemptuous look. "No one wanted to listen to your ranting."

"Were you expecting me to come back in and say a polite good morning to all? Have a cup of tea?" Vane grumbled. "I hate tea. And I hate mornings. And it will be a long time before I go back to Simeon's hall."

"You still have not answered my question about how you left it, Vane."

The two men stood glaring at each other.

"I hired a boat and had a man row me home. Don't look at me like that. It is the truth."

"I hope so," Gideon said quietly.

"I have been here ever since. When exactly did she—they, I mean—disappear? Linnea was in the stronghold the next morning, was she not?"

"Are you asking me or telling me?"

Angry and exasperated, Vane made a move as if to shove the winged lord, but thought better of it and let his hands drop to his sides. "I have had enough of these strange questions! I never touched Linnea!"

Gideon sensed an evasiveness still, but his intuition told him that Vane's answers were essentially true. "Good. Then help us find her and Marius."

Lord Vane had fallen into a mood far blacker than he had been when Gideon entered through the window. "I see," he snarled. "I am expected to prove myself, is that it?"

"We will need your help. Whether or not you actually want to give it."

Lord Vane dragged over another chair from a corner and set

it in front of the fireplace. "Never let it be said that *I* am not a good host. Sit down. And tell me everything you know."

He stormed over to the wall and yanked on a woven belt to summon a servant.

A youth came in, glancing at Gideon for only a second, but listening intently to his lordship, who ordered wine and food sent up at once.

The servant left, and Vane went to a wrought iron rack that held firewood and began throwing logs into the fireplace with tremendous force.

Ash puffed out and Gideon coughed. Vane flung himself into a chair.

"You forgot the tinder," Gideon pointed out. "And it's not going to light itself."

Both comments earned him a furious glare from Vane, who got up again and grabbed a spiky handful of dried pine needles and little cones, squatting to shove it under the tumbled logs. He looked about for his flint.

Gideon pointed to the mantel and Vane cursed. He struggled up—he was indeed stiff and achy from his drunken slumber on the stones—and grabbed the flint and the sliver of fatwood next to it, sitting on the edge of his chair this time to strike sparks.

Once. Twice. Neither caught. But the third spark did, glowing bright red on the sliver of fatwood. Absently, Vane blew on it.

The other man watched him. There was nothing else to do at the moment. The spark turned into a tiny flame under Vane's breath.

Gideon's eyes widened with amazement. The flame stayed small but it took on the shape of a perfect little naked woman. Blue with scarlet nipples.

"Hella," Vane said with surprise. With one finger, he lifted her off the fatwood. The place where she'd perched was scorched black and a red ember glowed in its center. He threw the kindled wood into the logs to start the fire and put her in the palm of his other hand. "You're back. How nice to see you."

The fire sprite stuck out her flickering tongue at him. *You're the one who went away.*

"Did you hear that?" Vane asked Gideon, laughing.

"Yes, I did." Gideon looked from the sprite named Hella to Vane. Her brightness made the gloomy lord of fire much more cheerful.

"She gets bigger, much bigger. She is nearly my height, in fact, when she gets going. All I have to do is blow on her."

Gideon smiled and raised a hand. "Not now, Vane. We have things to talk about. Keep her small."

Vane played with the sprite for a few more moments, letting her dance on his palm. Then she strolled over to his thumb, straddled it, and bit hard on the callused tip. "Ah, Hella. You are vicious but adorable." He turned his attention back to Gideon. "All right, I will keep her small."

"Thank you. Just until I go." He could well imagine what would happen after that. He had no doubt that the sprite, full grown or blown or whatever the word was, provided Vane with supernaturally excellent sex.

The servant brought the provender and the fireplace roared up as Gideon told Vane of Marius's restlessness, and Simeon's reluctance, under the circumstances, to let him and Linnea go. And so on and so forth. He kept it brief.

The sprite in Vane's palm turned her beautiful little face up to her master. *Who is Linnea?*

"That is none of your concern, Hella. Be still," Vane said.

Gideon continued with the rest: the boat they'd commandeered, where Linnea and Marius might have landed and gone, and all the rest of it.

Vane listened thoughtfully, then set Hella on his knee and turned to him. "It will have to wait until the morning. The hour is late and dawn is not all that far way."

Gideon sighed. "Yes, that is what I thought."

"But I will help you," Vane said in a low voice. "You have my word."

All the surliness seemed to have gone out of him. Gideon was sure Hella's unexpected appearance had much to do with that.

He rose, warm and well-fed and a little drunk on Simeon's strong wine. But he was feeling more hopeful. He bid the great lord of fire and his blue concubine good-bye.

When Gideon had flown away, Vane set Hella on the flagstones in front of the fire, and watched her kick burning bits back into it for sport. He peeled off his clothes and got down on his haunches, naked.

Mischievous to a fault, the sprite ran between his legs and pushed at his balls with all her strength, making them tighten up. She was no longer than his cock at the moment but that was growing rapidly and stiffening.

She put her hands around it and swung on it. Vane looked down at her and blew a gentle breath that tossed her fiery hair.

Hella leaned her head back and let her hair hang down as she swung, enjoying a few more moments of being very small. Then she let go of his cock, a tree trunk compared to her, and ran out from under him.

He blew on her all over, making her bigger, taller, and more shapely. Her breasts swelled from the soft stimulation of his breath and she turned around so he could blow upon her legs, lengthening them, and make her buttocks round.

He blew her cunny at the very last in little puffs that excited her, then stopped to catch his breath, laughing and exhausted. "You do not usually make me work this hard, Hella!"

Punishment. You deserve it, faithless one.

"Since when are you jealous? I have done nothing!"

I don't like the way you say that woman's name. The one Gideon was talking about. She pretended not to remember.

"Linnea?"

Her eyes blazed. She gave Vane a slap that scorched his cheek and he grabbed her wrist.

"It is you that I want most!"

That is no great honor.

He swept her up in his arms, full size but weightless, and threw her on the bed. "You need what you are going to get, spitfire!"

Hella spread her legs. Her labia throbbed scarlet and the blue finger that slid between them and dipped in was phenomenally sensual to watch.

Vane stroked and pumped his cock while he observed her practiced masturbation. "Do that while I am gone. You don't need me."

I do. It isn't enough. I want you. All of you. She added a single word. *Now.*

Coming over her, he grabbed her ankles and lifted her legs until her knees were by her ears. She pushed his hands away and clasped her ankles, moving her legs so high her bottom came off the bed. She was infinitely flexible.

Without further delay, he positioned the tip between the tight folds of her scorching flesh and drove himself into her to the hilt, moving his hips so his balls pressed against her upraised bottom with each thrust all the way in, making her scream with pleasure.

His pent-up frustration from spying on Linnea, fantasizing about Linnea, exploded inside him but it didn't make him come.

He pulled out, flipped the startled Hella over, and yanked her up onto all fours, her quivering behind spread and ready, the freshly fucked cunt between them juicy and ready for his length. He mounted her like a crazed stallion, going deep, taking wild pleasure in their mutual abandonment.

Imagining Linnea. With him.

But a mere stallion wouldn't satisfy Linnea. No, he thought for a fleeting second, she needed a centaur. The image of Marius, doing to Linnea exactly what he was doing to Hella, excited Vane beyond belief. Pulsing out hot jets of lava into Hella's cunt made her wild with joy, and she came only seconds later.

Drained, gasping, he stayed on his knees, his cock still inside her, feeling not joy but sadness. Even in his fantasy Linnea belonged to Marius and not him.

He pulled out of Hella without a word and collapsed on the bed beside her. She sat up, patting out the little flames that danced along her labia, a sure sign that she had been deeply satisfied.

She gave Vane a loving look, but said nothing as she stroked his sweating chest, making it sizzle. Then Hella rose and poured water from the ewer by the bed into a dark bronze bowl. She blew it, heating the water and testing it with a fingertip, then soaked a cloth and gave him an intimate, loving whore's bath where he lay.

He ignored her and fell into a troubled sleep.

After a while, Hella dwindled down to sprite size and flitted about the room in an indecisive way. Her small blue form hovered several times inside the window that Gideon had flown from. She hesitated one last time, then soared out in the black night.

10

—————

Linnea waited where Marius had left her, not as afraid as she would have been ordinarily in the dark—not after a day of such sensual joy.

They weren't far from the beach, near a marsh as far as she could tell. The night noises seemed nothing out of the usual: musical croaks from small frogs, buzzes and chirps from the cicadas, and the swift beating of unseen wings now and then. Swallows chasing insects. Esau had left her shoulder and joined them, just for the sport of it.

She leaned back against a tree that had felt smooth to the touch and quietened her mind. Soon enough the battle against the demon would be joined. She was looking forward to spending another night in Marius's protective arms, wherever he would take her.

Linnea straightened and sat forward when she heard Marius coming back. On two feet—with so much practice, he was getting more and more skillful at transforming quickly from one to the other.

As a centaur he would have unbalanced the small boat he had borrowed—or rather, commandeered, to use his manly word.

Men. They always had to be heroes, or pirates, or rogues. Never just themselves. Not that she would have changed a thing about him. Especially not his impetuousness—she scrambled to her feet as Marius burst through a thicket, swearing under his breath.

"The boat is gone. The rope was broken."

"Cut?"

"Hard to say. I noticed the rope was frayed when I tied it up. It wasn't much of a boat to begin with, of course. I was just happy it didn't leak."

"Oh no. Who would—"

He sat down dejectedly and she sank on her knees next to him, touching a hand to his shoulder. He shrugged it away.

"A fisherman. A demon. Who knows?"

Linnea sighed and put her hands in her lap. "I hope the man you got it from doesn't need it tomorrow."

"Too bad. It is not as if I can swim back to Simeon's island and explain," Marius said crossly. "He will be wondering where we are. They all will."

"Should we light a signal fire?"

He shook his head. "That might signal someone we do not want to meet."

He hadn't said the name, but it was clear enough to Linnea that he meant Ravelle.

"Well," he said at last, blowing out a long breath, "there is no point in sitting here. It is going to be a long night."

"Let us go down to the beach and walk along it," she suggested. "The boat might have simply drifted off if the rope broke."

He didn't seem to want to argue. "Maybe. All right. There is enough moonlight to see by."

He got up and took her hand, and Linnea let him lift her to her feet. "Ready?"

"Wait a minute. The basket. I left it under the tree." She went back for it, tripping over a thick vine that clung to her ankle. For a brief, unpleasant second she thought of Ravelle's clutching claws and shuddered.

The basket was where she had left it, empty and light. She went back to Marius and followed him the short way to the beach, pushing aside the mangrove leaves and stepping carefully amidst the tangled roots.

"Stay to the high side of the beach," Marius said. He looked worriedly at the sky. The indigo vault was thickly strewn with stars. What was left of the moon was not enough to obscure them.

She walked with him in silence for some distance, not seeing a trace of the boat. Nor did she see a light upon the water of a bobbing, golden-flamed lantern on a prow. No one was coming to get them.

The others had no way of knowing where they had come in from the water on the Forest Isle, which had many beaches.

Still, the night was peaceful and she was with him. Unless a demon were to blot out the moon and howl down from the sky—she told herself not to think that way.

Marius's grip on her hand tightened.

"What is it?" she asked softly.

"I thought I saw a light."

She scanned the horizon. Only the faintest sliver of reflected moonlight separated the dark sea from the even darker sky. "Where?"

"Above us." He studied the heavens. "A flicker of blue. It's gone now."

"A shooting star?"

"No, I don't think so."

She stopped, holding on to his hand and making him stop too. "I don't see it. And I don't see the boat. If it did drift away, it's long gone."

"Then we will stay here," he said reluctantly. He let go of her hand and scanned the dark, tangled trees behind them. "Bah. The mangroves are full of biting insects and the beach is too open." He walked a few steps away and Linnea hurried to catch up.

Something flashed out of the darkness and brushed her shoulder where the kirtle had slipped down. "Ow!" she cried, clapping her hand over the spot.

He hurried back. "A bite?"

"Yes, Marius! But what bug bites so hard? It feels almost like a burn!"

He peered at her shoulder. "The damn things will devour us if we sleep in the trees. It will have to be the beach. I will dig a hole for us to give us some shelter from the wind. It always picks up during the night."

She flung the basket down, feeling the last shred of her peaceful mood evaporate. "Above the line of high tide, if you please. I don't want to drown."

He kneeled down and got to work, scooping out huge handfuls of sand without a word. Linnea regretted snapping at him. It wasn't his fault that the boat had disappeared and tomorrow they could head inland and walk to where other beings could help them.

She kneeled beside him and scooped sand too. It wasn't long before they lay together in each other's arms, cradled in sand so warm that they fell asleep.

The sun woke them early. There was no escaping it on the beach. Linnea sat up in the hole and looked around. It was a gorgeous morning.

The dawn sky looked like the pink inside of a gigantic shell, fading to white where the sun rose in majesty. There were no clouds for miles and the sea was unusually calm.

Marius was already up, coming back from down the beach, dragging pieces of driftwood in a scrap of fishing net he must have found. He had the basket slung over one shoulder, stuffed with leaves.

"What are you doing?" she called.

"Collecting herbs for tea and berries for breakfast and wood for a fire."

She laughed. "What will we boil water in?"

"A shell. Go look for a big, thick one, and smaller ones to drink out of. There is fresh water in the wine bottle. I rinsed out the dregs."

Linnea stood up, stark naked and deliciously warm, and ran into the sea to bathe. The salt water stung her shoulder where the bug had bitten her, but it was not so painful it kept her from swimming.

She floated for a while, watching Marius snap the bleached, bone-dry wood, toss it into the pit where they'd slept, and strike rock on rock to light it. After a little while a thin trail of smoke rose in the air. He kneeled by it and fiddled with the wood.

She swam in to shore, refreshed, and walked slowly toward him through the shallows, foam swirling around her knees and then ebbing to her toes.

"Good morning, goddess," he said, looking up from his fire. He had been blowing on it to keep it going. Orange and red flames, and even a few little ones that were blue and green, barely visible in the strong sunlight, licked over the white wood. The fire made snapping sounds and fought to stay alive. Marius picked up a stick and poked at it, frowning.

She bent down and gave him a kiss on top of his head. Her wet breasts touched his back.

At that instant something bit her again and Linnea straightened with a cry, waving at the air. "Ow! Another one!"

"The bugs like you," he said absently. "I can't blame them."

"Do not mock me," she said indignantly, "it hurts!"

"Let me look." Moving awkwardly in the sliding sand and careful of his fire, Marius got up. "Where is it this time?"

"The other shoulder. In the back." She wasn't going to cry or complain about a couple of bites, but the pain was intense all the same.

Marius examined both her shoulders closely, but he didn't say anything.

"Well? Is there a stinger? Why do they hurt so much?"

He came around to face her. "I will have to make you poultices. It is a good thing that I learned something of them from Quercus. The bites look more like burns. The one from last night has begun to blister."

Linnea sighed. The sun was already strong and if they did not head back into the woods soon, whatever skin was not covered by her kirtle would be scorched too.

Her spirits were lighter after their beach breakfast. They'd left a heap of berries for Esau to find and filled the basket with them, eating them as they walked into the forest, dropping one every few feet as a game for him, in case he decided to walk instead of fly.

Marius's poultices eased the blistered spots on her shoulders and she no longer thought of them. A centaur again, he found his way by the position of the sun above, and when the woods grew thicker, by smell. His nostrils flared widely, judging the way to go by the wind.

Linnea, on his back, admired his regal posture. Her steed and her lover were one and the same, an incomparable convenience. She patted his flank and kissed the back of his neck.

He tasted of sweat and salt. Delicious.

"Do not distract me, Linnea. We have far to go."

"Must we go back to Simeon's stronghold? I would rather be here with you."

"We cannot without the boat. But we must find a way to let him know where we are and as quickly as possible." His voice was tinged with guilt. "By now he has sent out searchers looking for us. They might have seen the fire I lit this morning, if it is still going. Ah me. There wasn't much wood to be found."

Linnea looked up at the little bird that flew by. Its feathers were gleaming indigo, a reminder of the beauty of last night's sky. There was still no sign of Esau. Had he startled the bird? She glanced over her shoulder to see if he'd found them.

What. . . . what was *that*? A blue flame danced in midair behind her and vanished.

Linnea shook her head and closed her eyes, then looked again.

Nothing. She must have been imagining things. They had woken at dawn and been going for some time without much food.

"When will we stop, Marius? I think I need to rest for a bit and I'm sure you do too."

"Me? I could gallop through woods like this for days. But of course you lack a centaur's stamina. We will stop in a little while. There is an old orchard not far away."

Linnea put her arms around his muscular middle and pressed her cheek to the meatiest part of his shoulder. He took good care of her, to be sure.

They supped in the orchard, Marius browsing thoughtfully on green things and Linnea eating a windfall apple from last year that was miraculously free of wriggling inhabitants—she'd split it to the seed-star at its core to make sure—and cheese and grain-rich bread.

He had stopped at the cottage of an elderly spirit, a gruagach with mixed human and bovid blood by the looks of her, the keeper of a small herd of cows. She had been happy to fill the basket to overflowing with cheese and bread and other things to eat for both of them.

Nothing was too good for the Lord of the Forest. And his lady, the gruagach had added, dropping a creaky curtsey to honor Linnea.

"I wonder where Esau is," Marius said when they had finished eating. "We could use him to send a message, though it is a long way to fly. Still, we are not yet close to any of the ponds that connect to the tunnels linking the islands."

"I looked for him as we went along," Linnea said. "I saw—" She stopped. The blue flame in midair had been a figment of her imagination and there was no point in mentioning something so trivial.

"What?" He sprawled in the grass and fallen petals of the apple blossoms, his four legs relaxed, propped on a muscular arm, looking content. He used his healed, once again magnificent tail to swat a determined fly that was bothering him.

Sqursh. He got it. She made a face at him. Marius grinned with manly triumph, as if he had personally vanquished a certain loathsome demon with one blow.

"Nothing," Linnea said in answer to his question. "He always comes, though, doesn't he? It is a pity you can't teach him to talk."

"I only know what he is saying when Quercus is around to translate. And I don't get over to his tree very often. I should. He's a good old soul."

"Yes, he is." Linnea went over to Marius, settling her back against his sprawled bulk and looking up into the clouds that drifted over the orchard. They were tinged with the deeper pink that heralded the end of the day. "Shall we spend the night here?"

"Why not? How are those bites, by the way?"

"Healed, I think. I am glad to be away from whatever made them."

With his arms, Marius lifted her away from him, ignoring her protests. "Hush. I have to make a bed for us, don't I?"

"Yes, but—"

"I need room to wallow." Looking utterly ridiculous, he began to roll on his back from side to side, crushing the fragrant grasses and petals, making a bed as wide but not as deep as the one on the beach. Linnea laughed heartily at the way he looked when he was done, his centaur hide covered with bits of broken grass, the hair on his handsome head thoroughly disheveled.

"You look like a fool!"

"That is no way to talk to a lord of the forest," he said severely.

There was a flash of black-and-white as the magpie joined them at last, cawing his agreement with Marius. He settled on a gnarled branch and looked at them with beady eyes, as good as saying *well? Anything left for me?*

She scrambled up and found a piece of grain bread, balancing it on the branch for him.

Then she went back to Marius and they were happy as two beings could be until night fell.

She woke feeling chilly. Marius had done the impossible and gotten up without waking her, no doubt for the usual middle-of-the-night reason. She missed the feeling of safety he gave her. Sleeping next to a centaur was a delicious experience—all warmth and massive muscles.

Linnea gazed dreamily at the sky through the branches and leaves of the orchard's trees. One night later, there was a little less moonlight, and because of that, the stars seemed infinite in number.

Oh. There it was. Above her. That blue flame. Bigger. It vanished when she sat up quickly, her heart racing. It was real. She had not been imagining it.

It took a while for her pulse to return to normal. She forced it to, casting her mind back her mother's tales of will-o'-the-wisps. They only harmed those who had hurt them in some way. Their power was negligible.

The flash of blue had to be one.

A cool night breeze brought mist, stealing slowly around the base of the trees. It is only mist, she told herself. The low-lying drifts of it came closer by imperceptible degrees, fragrant with night-blooming flowers and the sweet exhalation of the earth itself.

Linnea sank back down, enspelled without knowing it, and fell asleep again.

The blue flame reappeared, dancing in the breeze. It bounced along the edge of the bed of crushed grass Marius had made, growing larger as the breeze picked up. And hotter. The mist kept its distance. It was formless but sentient. It had no love of flame and this one had dragged it up from the valleys below. Fire spirits were wily creatures, seldom seen on the isle. This spirit was wilier than most, having knowledge of paralyzing spells.

The flame separated into two small arms, two little legs, flowing hair, breasts, belly, buttocks, and a curious but beautiful face. The sprite grew no bigger, because the breeze died down.

Hella, fully formed but half the size she'd been with Lord Vane, inspected Linnea from head to toe as she slept. *So this is my rival.*

The Lord of Fire was not around to hear her speak or soothe her anger. He had no way of knowing she'd flown this far or even that she could. He was used to her coming and going.

Hella herself scarcely knew what had possessed her to try and find these two. She'd been lucky to stumble against them on the beach at night, brushing Linnea's shoulder without seeing her at first.

She had not meant to burn her the first time. The second, well . . . Marius had called Linnea a goddess. She'd wanted to gag.

Tired and feeling cold, Hella gave in to the volatile rage that seethed in her fiery heart. Even the way Vane had said Linnea's name had irked her immeasurably. In their off-and-on eons together, she had never heard him speak with such tenderness in his voice of any woman. Certainly not her.

Few words, but loaded with foolish emotion that was utterly unlike him, the good-for-nothing-but-one-thing, gorgeous, black-haired, heartless bastard.

She tapped her bare foot on the grass, starting a flame. She rolled a rock over it to put it out. Stamping on it would only make the flame leap higher.

The uncrushed grass that had survived Marius's wallowing rebelled against this further mistreatment. Strong, deep-rooted stems reached out to grab her ankles. Startled, Hella kicked and stamped, triggering more small flames. She ran in a circle around Linnea and a circle of blue fire leaped up.

She could no longer control it, but she had never intended to—god of fire!

That great oaf Marius was thundering out the bushes right at her! Hella leapt into the air and spiraled upward, dodging his hooves. She looked down.

Marius trampled the burning grass around Linnea, bellowing with fury, waving his hands to dispel the encroaching mist. The formless cloud collected itself and retreated into the night. He was roaring a name she knew only from the tale Gideon had told Lord Vane.

"Ravelle! Ravelle!"

The centaur vowed vengeance upon him in words so bloodthirsty that Hella sped away. She didn't see him bend down to lift Linnea in his arms.

Unharmed. Still sleeping.

He kept vigil over her for the rest of the night, holding her in his exhausted arms away from the ground, staring into the dark trees and undergrowth until his eyes were red and strained.

First Philonous, his friend for life, and now her—neither would have been in such peril if not for him. And she was the love of his life. Something he had not told her—it scarcely seemed possible that she was indeed his, even after their enchanted coupling. Danger swiftly brought them close, and he'd foolishly thought he'd taught the demon a lesson. There was no end to Ravelle's spite or his ambition. The peaceful island of forests would serve him well as a base for conquest, its inhabitants no more than bumbling rustics, its trees and green growing things easy to cut down in vicious swaths.

Marius did not regret his attack upon Ravelle—he only regretted not finishing him off the first time he'd had a chance. To see Linnea, so beautiful and vulnerable, on the verge of violation, had pushed him over the edge. To keep her safe by his side had been his only thought ever since.

He was to blame for stepping away from her tonight. To have come back and see her lying in a circle of fire, a demon's loop to draw her to the Outer Darkness in spirit had her flesh burned, had shattered him.

There were other bursts of fire within the orchard during the night. Cruel imps, dancing for joy among twisted branches. For all he knew, the demon had drawn a larger circle around the first, preparing to take him and Linnea. His arms ached as she stirred slightly, moaning. Did she sense what he could not see? The darkness was all-encompassing.

A feeling of waiting menace pulsed in his veins, grabbed at his jugular, and took over his brain. Revenge. He would have it.

His nostrils flared, whiffing the air for demon sweat or shit or blood. Nothing. Where was the horned one? He wanted to get his hands around that leathery, stringy neck and make Ravelle's death last a long, long time.

It was odd that he could neither smell nor see any trace of him. Had one of his filthy underlings and not Ravelle started the circle of fire and dragged the lethal mist in from the netherworld to smother her? The close ranks of trees in the old orchard could hide beings that were smaller than the demon.

He dared not set Linnea down or leave this place. Fitfully, he slept standing up, conserving his strength for the dash he would make to Quercus's safe house on the morrow. If she did not wake, he would strap her to his back somehow and thunder away.

Marius was half-crazy with fatigue and rage when the sun did him the favor of coming up. He wanted to shake his fist at it. "Make her open her eyes!"

He held her up like an offering, praying for mercy on her behalf. The warm rays stole across the limp woman in his arms and Linnea tensed but did not waken. A rush of frantic love filled his heart as he thought wildly that she might not wake at all. Whatever poison had been in the mist had seeped into her brain before he'd lifted her, filled her lungs as she lay sleeping.

"My love . . . oh, speak to me!"

She murmured his name in reply. Her eyes stayed closed. He had to get her to Quercus once more—if the gruagach would help—

Linnea was still breathing. He looked at her kirtle, her skin—were there hidden burns that festered? No, the flames had not touched her. She responded, if only a little, to the sounds she heard. There might be hope.

All thoughts of rejoining the lords of the Arcan Isles fled from Marius's mind.

He bellowed in the direction of the gruagach's cottage, hoping she would understand and come quickly. Soon she appeared between the rows of trees. Her hands, strong from milking cows, clung to a cane. Did she have sufficient strength in the rest of her aged body to maneuver Linnea?

He softened his voice as she came closer. "She has been injured—it is demon's work—you must bind her to my back! Make haste!"

The old gruagach unwound a leather girdle with intricate straps from around her waist as Marius shifted Linnea's position. She lay in his arms as if the subtle poison had begun to paralyze her. Tears welling from his eyes, he pressed a desperate kiss to her forehead, hoping against hope that her eyes would open.

Linnea did not respond this time.

Quickly, together, they moved her around to Marius's back and the crone made short work of tying her securely. He would have to run with utmost care, bent forward to hold her, rolling into each stride so as not to jar her.

Without a word of farewell, he fled the orchard. The gruagach stood in the crushed grass, looking after the centaur and his burden, shaking her head sadly.

11

Quercus examined the still sleeping Linnea, grave concern in his eyes. She lay in an alcove of the oak, upon soft leaves of the plant called lamb's-ears piled as deep as a man's arm—or a centaur's. With the healer's blessing, Marius had plowed up a large section of Quercus's medicinal garden to make her a bower. Sobbing as he turned over the earth and rooted out hundreds of plants, he prayed the bed would not be her last in this world.

"Will she live?"

"I cannot say, Marius. I will try different antidotes, but without knowing what the poison is—"

"I could not capture mist in a bottle," Marius said heatedly.

The wise tree spirit laid a comforting hand on his shoulder. "I am not blaming you. And as we can both see, she breathes and she lives. There is certainly hope."

"Not for Ravelle." Marius reiterated his vow, in gruesome detail, to kill the demon on sight.

"Ssh. Do not speak so in front of an invalid," the healer chided him.

"But she cannot hear. She no longer responds to the sound of my voice."

Quercus shook his head. "We do not know for sure that she cannot hear, Marius. There may be swelling within the skull or some other unseen injury that must be treated." He added after a pause, "If I can."

Marius clenched his fists as if he was trying to keep himself from shaking the wrinkled old fellow.

Quercus shot him a stern look. "You must control yourself. Anger is no healer. There is hope, as I said." He looked again at the unconscious Linnea. His concern for her was clear in his old face. "But I will not offer false hope. Besides my herbs and my alchemical potions, I recommend a tincture of time."

A frustrated roar burst from Marius's lips.

"Hush!"

Marius hung his head. But he looked at Linnea from under his eyelashes one more time. If that roar did not make her react, it was possible that nothing would. She did not move. He wanted to roar again, with fiercer rage this time. A roar that would burst the trunk of the old oak asunder.

"It is a good thing that you are not a healer," Quercus said dryly. "Come away. She must rest quietly and I will not allow you to disturb her."

"Is she sleeping, then?" Marius asked frantically, following him away from the alcove in the oak. "Is that what you would call the—the state she is in?"

"It is not sleep, exactly. More like a form of suspended animation. She rests in a state beyond time as you and I know it."

"For how long?"

"I don't know."

The old tree spirit and the impetuous centaur, as old but eternally youthful, stared at each other until Marius quieted down, smearing away tears he was not ashamed to shed in front of Quercus. The healer went to his shelves and began to take down scrolls and treatises.

"Did you examine the injuries to her shoulders?" Marius said.

"I did. They are indeed burns, as you thought."

"She thought she'd been bitten by an insect."

Quercus selected a scroll and unrolled it, placing smooth river stones here and there to keep it open. "No, although your poultices would have served for such minor injuries as well. They were made correctly."

Marius inclined his head in a nod. "Sometimes I listen to you, Quercus."

"That is a good thing."

"If we can do nothing but wait—"

"That is the wisest course to take in these cases," Quercus informed. "I have few clues to go on, unfortunately. But as far as those, I will study my scrolls while she sleeps." He glanced at the one in front of him but Marius grew immediately restless, tapping his foot. "You are a more difficult patient than her. What's on your mind? Ask me questions if you like."

Marius hesitated, not wanting to sound foolish or fearful. But he'd held Linnea in his arms for hours last night and there had been no way to comb the remains of the circle of fire for bits and pieces that Quercus could analyze to help her now. "I did not smell Ravelle last night," he blurted out. "Because of what happened to Philonous, I assumed it was the demon. But I could be wrong. I know that there are different treatments for different evils."

"So there are." The healer clasped his hands behind his back and paced the floor for six strides exactly, three going, three coming, before answering. Marius knew it was how he composed himself before replying to a difficult question.

"Beginning with the burns," Quercus said when he stopped, "I studied my scroll on the subject while you sat with her, after you'd settled her on the bed of lamb's-ear leaves. The marks on her shoulders are small and round, like the burns of a sprite. The kind that live in fireplaces."

Marius raised his eyebrows. He could think of nothing to say to that for a moment. "But we were out in the open—well, an orchard—and had been a-wandering in the woods. She seemed to need to be amidst the green. As did I."

"Noted. But were you two near any fireplaces before that?" Quercus asked. "Perhaps Linnea was tending to one and poked too hard among the coals. She might have inadvertently hurt a hidden sprite."

"Ah," Marius said. "Let me think. No, there were no fires lit in Simeon's stronghold. When we left it, we built a small fire on the beach of this isle as a signal to Esau and another in the morning before we went back into the forest."

"Ah. Well, then, it is a puzzle as to how she got those burns."

"Ravelle's imps, I thought." Marius said.

"So you told me. I respectfully disagree."

"But they are no bigger than sprites and as evil as he is. If Ravelle did not make the circle of flame around her, they might have—"

Quercus raised an eyebrow. "Speculation, given the evidence. Tell me everything that happened from the time you set foot on the Forest Isle."

"We landed and in time I led her to the sacred meadow. You know the place."

"Of course I do. A little paradise. Primeval. Unspoiled. Some say it is where love began in the world."

Marius was almost overcome with emotion to hear him say so, even in his absent way. "Oh, Quercus—we made love for hours there—I cannot count the ways—"

"No doubt it did you both good," Quercus said thoughtfully. "Happiness is an antidote to evil, to be sure. Your lovemaking could have protected her from the poison of the mist, in fact. I will have to look it up. Your seed may be extraordinarily potent in that regard." The old healer gave him an approving look. "But tell me of the other happenings, if you please. The unusual ones."

"Well," Marius went on more slowly. "There was a blue fire that appeared very briefly once or twice near us. At night. It went away. Could that have been—"

"A fire sprite," Quercus sighed. "Just as I thought."

"The circle of fire?"

"That is new to me. I do have a scroll on demon-circles and other black magic." Quercus paced again and glanced into the alcove at Linnea. Marius went to look in too, unable to keep away for long. Her soft breasts rose and fell under the woven cloth that covered her.

"May I see the scroll? I trampled the fires so quickly—I was half-crazy with rage—but I do remember it," Marius said. He would never forget. Tongues of flame, darting upward from the crushed grass. A living noose of death for a gentle girl who had never harmed a soul.

"Of course." Quercus took an odd device from a hook on the wall, a tube of wood that had been fashioned with infinite patience and connected to a smaller tube with a hollow vine. "Let me listen to her heart."

His face was a study in wrinkles as he concentrated on what he heard, but he did seem pleased. "Steady and strong. An excellent sign."

Marius's regard for the healer shone in his eyes. "Is it?"

The tree spirit put the device back on the wall. "Yes. However, she is not out of the woods yet, as we say." He gave a chuckle, pleased with his little joke.

It broke the tension. Marius smiled. "Would it be all right if I sat with her for a while? Never mind the demon scroll for now—I just want to—"

Quercus patted him on the shoulder. "I understand."

He left Marius standing there, looking down at Linnea, lost

in slumber. Her color was better although she was still motionless. Something about the atmosphere of Quercus's home within the heart of the old oak was doing her good.

Marius perched on the edge of the bed. He smoothed the cover over her, feeling clumsy but not caring. Her motionless hands rested at her sides and he picked up one and kissed it as softly as he could. Then he set it down between her breasts, over the scar of Ravelle's wound, over her beating heart.

Steady and strong.

No words had ever made him happier.

He turned his head at the sound of Quercus returning. The tree spirit's gaze was piercing and Marius was hard put to meet it.

"She will not recover without you, Marius. If you must be a hero, think about that."

"What do you mean?"

Quercus extended a spindly arm and drew Marius away from the alcove to the other side of the space. They sat at a small table next to a window that looked out over the treetops, tossing and nodding in the balmy breeze.

"Let me explain," Quercus began. "You thirst for revenge against Ravelle, but if you lose the battle, Linnea will be alone forever."

Marius cast a yearning look back to where Linnea slept. He could not say that he would be beyond all caring after his death. His soul would always long for her. Their union on this earth was meant to last forever.

He curled his thick fingers into his palm until they hurt, thinking.

"The circle of fire injured you more than it did her."

"It was meant to kill her, Quercus!"

"Perhaps. Perhaps not. There is often more than one explanation for things and—"

"It was not done as innocent sport, you fool!" Marius had

no trust in Quercus's reliance on pure reason. "Investigate, deduce, eliminate—bah! I prefer a punch or a kick!"

"And how many times have I bandaged your knuckles and mended your split hooves?" Quercus inquired dryly.

"Often."

"But this time, my impetuous friend, you have someone else to consider besides your enemy and yourself."

"Linnea would want me to do my utmost to destroy Ravelle," he growled.

"She cannot tell you what she wants." Quercus glanced toward the alcove and back at Marius. "Your mind is enflamed with hatred. I can understand why, but—"

"Should I extend the hand of brotherhood to Ravelle?" Marius's tone was scathing. "Only if I can break his fingers one by one in the next instant. And then I would tear him limb from limb—"

Quercus sighed and gave a little shake of his head. "You told me that the other lords of Arcan had convened to decide what to do. Accept their help and do not run away from it. You are not alone in this difficult time and acting as if you are is unwise. You are too willing to risk all, Marius."

"What else can I do?" he muttered.

"Love her. Stay with her while she heals. What if she cannot walk when she awakes, Marius? Be her hero then."

Marius fell silent, his thoughts troubled.

"I cannot do it all myself if you rush off on a rampage. And if you never come back, well—enough said on that subject. There is yet time to consider the best course of action."

"You sound like Simeon," Marius scoffed. "He thinks too much, as does Gideon."

"Then you should listen to them."

"I did!" Marius said angrily.

"Then think of her. Without you, she will pine away like a flower without the sun."

"Ravelle has struck twice. There will not be a third time if I can help it," Marius said under his breath.

"So. You are determined to kill him?"

Marius's face was set in hard, stony lines. "Yes."

"Banishment to the Outer Darkness is not enough?"

"No. He doesn't stay there. It is time someone did what is necessary to rid our islands of his evil."

"And will the other Arcan lords be in your way?" Quercus inquired acidly. "You can simply kick them aside, I suppose."

"I would not do that, but Simeon and Gideon are too cautious."

"And Vane?"

Marius grunted. "The great lord of fire has his good points, although he is a sot and a rogue. He cannot be trusted, in my opinion."

Quercus made a wry face. "So that leaves you and only you, eh?"

"Yes."

"You are very sure of yourself." Marius said nothing, and the old healer heaved another sigh. "Well, I have said my piece. Ravelle is a formidable adversary."

"I will take my chances. His legions have not yet appeared on the island. For now he seems to act alone, except for his evil imps."

"Alone? Hm." Quercus fiddled absentmindedly with a second mushroom that had begun to grow where his left ear was. "I would think he would know better by now. But his powers were far greater than those of his kind and he has always ruled by force. Still, his arrogance makes him vulnerable."

Marius sensed what the healer would not say out loud. *So are you, Marius.* He only shrugged in reply.

"You have the advantage if he is old and getting careless. I suspect advancing mental deterioration. You may well win."

"I *will* win." Marius clenched his fists again. "For her. Because of her. Love comes once and I have found it with Linnea. I want to be with her for the rest of my days, here upon this island. Paradise has no meaning to me without someone to share it with."

The old healer nodded, lost in somber thought. "And if she should die?"

"I will too. By my own hand."

Quercus took down a bottle from the shelf and brushed the cobwebs from it. He pulled the cork with some difficulty and set it on the table, then plunked down two wooden goblets.

"What is that?" Marius asked.

"Elderflower wine." Quercus looked into a net bag and pulled out something folded in moist leaves. "And here is a sweet cake to eat with it. Let us talk no more of death and vengeance. As I said, there is hope. And there may be a way to do in a demon without risking your handsome hide, Marius."

"Only one bottle? I could drink five."

"There is more."

"Bring them out. Let us discuss the many ways to do in demons. I might even listen. When I am drunk, I can be talked into anything."

Quercus hesitated, then bent down to take more bottles from a hidden cupboard. "If that is the only way I can convince you, then I will take it."

12

Several hours later . . .

"Good stuff. Give me more." Marius held out his goblet. He had eaten none of the cake, but nearly all of the wine had gone down his throat.

"You have had enough. Centaurs shouldn't drink."

"Now you tell me." Marius tipped his goblet over his face to get the last drop, but he missed his mouth. The dregs went into his eye and made it sting. "Ow! Querky, make me a poultice!"

"Serves you right if it stings. Maybe it will snap you out of it—"

Marius's eyes rolled and his temper exploded. He railed at Fate, at Ravelle, at Quercus himself.

"Keep your voice down! Would you wake her?" The healer dashed to the alcove and looked in on Linnea.

"I would avenge her," Marius muttered, filled with swirling rage.

Quercus came back and leaned over him, staring into Marius's bloodshot eyes. "Your centaur nature is taking over. You must leave before the rest of the change happens. Now! Go!"

A second later Marius swept his arm across the table with impulsive anger, throwing the empty wine bottles and the scroll with Quercus's carefully outlined plans to the floor. He got up, knocking over his chair and wandering from the table to look at Linnea.

Quercus's barky chest heaved as he suppressed his own anger. A worthless emotion, in his opinion. Hard to control for him; impossible to control for Marius. He heard nothing from the alcove for several minutes but stayed where he was, hoping that the sight of Linnea would bring Marius to his senses again.

"She is the same!" came a deep, moaning voice. "Still as death!"

"Do not wake her, Marius!"

He came back to the table, his eyes glazed by tears and rage. "I must find the fiend—it is now or never, Quercus!"

The tree spirit was rolling up the damaged scroll. "Then go!" he snapped. "You will not listen to reason and neither Linnea nor I should have to listen to you!"

"You do not know what it means to love as I do!" Marius bawled. With his human foot, he pawed the floor and gave Quercus a maddened glare. Not because he was drunk, though he was, but because the change to a centaur was coming on just as the healer had said.

"She has been here but a few hours and already her condition has improved. Would you risk a relapse, you fool?"

"No—no—" Groaning with confusion, Marius stumbled down the spiraling stairs, Quercus hot on his heels. The healer pushed him outside.

Marius stopped a few paces away, breathing hard as his sides expanded and his buttocks transformed into the heavy hindquarters of a centaur.

"Go!" Quercus slammed the door and opened it again for a parting shot. "I wish you luck. Try to come back alive." He shut the door again with a polite click and the thick bark rolled rapidly over it.

Befuddled and angry, now pawing the ground with enormous hooves, Marius looked at the place where the door had been. He shook his head, but that was not enough to clear it.

Her ... on that bed ... he could not help but think of her lying helpless in the circle of fire. What if he had not come back in time to put it out? Ravelle *had* done it. Marcus would gallop over the island without stopping until he found the demon.

Trample him. Split his skull. Fling him off a cliff.

To hell with Quercus and his caution. Same for the lords of Arcan. They had no real use for an animal like him. He didn't belong in places where battle shields hung on the walls, never used.

He blew out a snorting breath that reeked of wine.

He looked to the tree and said a silent good-bye to Linnea, knowing she at least was safe. It *was* time. Marius's blood surged in his veins. He took off, head lowered, tail flying. And ran for hours.

Exhausted, his hide foamed with sweat, Marius stopped at last. Gods above. Was that a centaur in the road? Or an apparition? The mange-eaten creature was hideous.

"My brother ... help me," the centaur said in a querulous voice.

Marius circled it but only once. "Brother? I have one, but he is a man. Who are you?"

"I have no name." The centaur coughed and the carved piece of stone about its neck banged against its collarbone. Marius could not see its eyes, but was sure they were rheumy. There was an air of age and illness about it, as if it were about to collapse inside the hide that sagged upon its bones.

A bad omen, Marius thought wildly. He galloped on.

The old centaur picked up its head and looked after him. Its eyes were demon eyes, glowing red in the darkness. It took a shambling step after Marius, then another, and shuddered as its mangy hide wrinkled off the leathery skin beneath.

Ravelle followed, sometimes on the earth, sometimes in the air.

It was time to deal firmly with Marius. His return to the Outer Darkness had been worthwhile and the nascent rebellion quieted. He would not miss his troublesome cousin, who'd met a deservedly miserable death.

When that unpleasant business was over, he'd returned to the Forest Isle, looking for Marius. Not an hour ago, one of his imps had glimpsed the real centaur charging madly through the woods and flown off to notify the demon, looking for him first at the northern coast, where hell-soldiers had put in, transported at night from the Outer Darkness in galleys manned by slaves, to a narrow valley where nothing lived and they would not seen. There they waited, not patiently but silently, for Ravelle's command.

The entire island would be his in time. He had particular plans for Marius.

After Ravelle's fall from the magpie's nest, it had taken him hours to find the amulet that had fallen with him. All he had to do was wear it around his stringy neck. Warmth empowered it and the all-powerful spell of the gods who'd enchanted it was still effective.

To his chagrin, it did not turn him into a centaur like Marius. Ravelle had wanted to be entirely virile again, endowed with powerful muscle and a glossy hide. It was not to be. Each time he put himself through the transformation, he looked worse.

As for tonight, in the valley, he desired the pleasure of attacking Marius as himself. His cracked, leathery, and wicked self. His iron ropes would bind the centaur's legs this time, not just his tail. His blacksmith had fashioned an iron bridle, too. And tipped a supple whip with it.

Rising into the air again, he saw the glimmering sea beyond the valley. A swift ship was waiting there to remove Marius to his ultimate fate.

Ravelle wanted to make the agony last. Merely killing him was not enough. Forcing Linnea to watch his torment would break the centaur's heart. He did not know where she was, of course, but she would be easy enough to find when the verdant isle was set afire.

Smoked out of hiding, running for her life, screaming for Marius. The great thundering idiot would bellow for her and earn himself worse punishment.

Furlongs away, Marius picked up a cold but still foul scent of Ravelle at last. Maddened all over again, he followed it, slipping on cinders into a valley of death which opened into the pounding sea. He had been here only once—few beings ever went to this dreadful place.

An eon ago, a freakish eruption from the volcano on the Isle of Fire had been carried hence on an evil wind, contained by the valley's narrowness. Every living thing in it had been killed in a few horrifying seconds and neither Marius nor his brother had been able to sound a warning.

He caught his leg in the twisted roots of a ghost tree, downed by the blast, its last scream frozen on the face on its trunk. He had to go slowly. He could die here, a meaningless death that would leave Linnea alone to grieve unrevenged, his bones picked by vultures and worse creatures—the carrion demons, Ravelle's underlings.

The smell of him grew stronger. Marius went on, finding his way and marking his escape route in his mind. A crunching noise came to his ears. He pricked them, listening.

It was an irregular sound that sometimes matched his gait and then stopped, as if the beast that made it were walking or creeping in the cinders, then bouncing in the air.

Marius whirled around and reared, seeing nothing behind him but ash and desolation. His hooves hit the earth and he breathed deeply. The noise had to be Ravelle, for he could smell the demon's rank sweat. Ravelle would not show himself but he was not far away at all.

Fear cooled Marius's blood in a way that reason could not. His courage and his love for Linnea made him foolhardy.

The chase was on. But he could not run.

He moved sideways down the steep slope, forcing himself to look at the charred skeletons of the creatures who had not escaped. Bones of birds caught at the moment of flight, tangled in the branches of more ghost trees. Bones of bears, great jaws agape in final agony. The pitiful skeleton of a chained hound near the bones of a hunter reaching to free it. Too late.

Then, a centaur with massive bones like his. A jagged shard protruded upward through the ash. A broken leg. But for that, his unknown cousin might have survived.

The sight stopped Marius cold. He bowed his head for all who had perished in this terrible place so long ago . . . and lifted it again when a stinking whiff of demon filled his nostrils. Ravelle was very close.

Here in this place where nothing grew, it should have been easy to see him. Marius's head turned swiftly to survey the bleak terrain. Nothing. Silence. Even the stars seemed to look away from this place.

Wham.

Ravelle landed on Marius's back and the centaur staggered from the pain. Long claws closed around his throat and dug in. The white desolation around him went black.

13

Overhead, the moon had risen, cold and white and round, and stars blinked down. The first battle for the Arcan Islands had begun beneath them: centaur against demon.

Clinging to Marius with hideous strength, Ravelle could not be shaken off. He smote blow after blow upon the centaur's head, maddening him to fury.

Marius reared and screamed. In this desolate place, no one heard—or he thought for a fleeting second, no one responded. A red haze welled behind his eyes as the demon's head banged his. Again he reared, nearly toppling backward in his effort to be free of his assailant.

Through loose rock and cinders, fighting the slope of the valley to stay upright, he staggered on, not knowing where he went and dimly realizing through the pain of Ravelle's attack that he was being driven down. Each blow made fresh stars appear in his vision, and he groaned with agony. The demon on his back laughed in fiendish glee. The centaur dropped to his knees.

"I have bested you at last, Marius!"

Not yet.

With a supreme effort, Marius rose all the way up at once, arching his back and flailing his tail. Still the demon hung on, having never lost his clawing grip. A final savage blow to the back of his head felled Marius at last.

A dreadful banging brought him back to consciousness—he saw sparks first, flying in the darkness. Then the sound again. Hammer on iron.

An immense demon pounded on an anvil, naked and disgusting to look at, his skin so tough that he needed no leather apron. His assistants scurried to and fro, dodging Ravelle's kicks.

Marius understood that he was a prisoner. He felt the cruel pinch of shackles on his horse legs and noticed the handcuffs on his wrists. He lay on his side, in gritty dirt. Cinders pressed into his hide.

He could not free himself by stealth or by force. So he kept his head resting in the dirt watched through eyelids that were mostly closed. The demons and other hell-spawn about seemed to be part of an army. Ravelle's snarled commands were being carried out by the bigger fiends, whose fast whips enforced obedience from the smaller.

Just beyond the place where he was a prisoner was the glitter of the sea. In the distance he could make out the backs of more soldiers, coming out from it, heaving and jostling like a swarm of foul insects.

Little by little, he made sense of the shouted commands of the big demons and the muttered replies of the underlings. An invasion was underway of the Forest Isle and these legions were the first to land. Taking the beach had not been hard. There was no one to defend it or this tragic valley.

Marius listened, straining his ears, which were swollen and ringing from Ravelle's vicious blows. With profound guilt he heard of the ease with which the island had been captured.

His only thought for days had been for Linnea. Protecting her. Loving her. Avenging her. If Ravelle captured the whole island there would be no place for either of them to run. But the demon might allow her to live, simply to have her for his own.

What would they do with him?

The blacksmith's assistant came to him, a heavy collar of iron in his claws. This he clapped about Marius's neck, fastening the bolts that closed it with quick turns before the centaur could struggle.

He stood and kicked Marius in the ribs. "Wake up!"

Against his will, Marius groaned, but he forced his eyes open. There was a stronger stink of demon in his nose.

Ravelle had come over. "Jerk the chains to make him rise," he ordered.

Try as he might, the assistant could not do it, and the demon signaled the blacksmith.

The immense figure strode over and grabbed the iron collar, lifting Marius with one begrimed hand.

The centaur's hooves scraped for purchase in the cinders and grit. He could barely stand on his four legs, and the cuffs around his wrists kept his arms forward, unbalancing him.

"What a sight," Ravelle sneered. "The proud Marius in chains. Let's make him dance." He picked up a goad and jabbed the point of it into the centaur's hindquarters.

Marius stumbled, his movement hobbled by the short length of chain between the shackles, falling to his knees, prodded up again by the merciless goad.

Hot tears, tears of pain and fury and shame, rolled down his face. Ravelle paused long enough to smear them into the dirt and blood on Marius's skin with his filthy palm.

The centaur shook with revilement, thinking not of himself but of Linnea during her capture and bondage by this fiend. If it took every drop of blood he had, if he died in the doing, Marius vowed silently he would vanquish Ravelle once and for all.

"Do not flinch," Ravelle sneered. "I am only trying to clean you up for your new master. You are no longer the Lord of the Forest, Marius."

There was a chance that he might live. Marius made an effort to hang his head. If he was taken away, he could escape and come back.

"Who is my master, evil one?" The bitter words came out in a rush and earned him another blow from the goad.

Ravelle cackled. "Do you think that hurt? You will have worse," was all he said.

"Wh-where are you taking me?" Marius braced himself for another blow but none was forthcoming.

"To the land of men." The demon stepped back and observed Marius's entire body as the centaur shifted on his hooves, impeded by the shackles. "Don't try to change into one. I think I know how you do, though."

He held up a carved piece of stone that hung around his neck.

Marius's eyes widened with amazement. "The amulet—the one the gods used—" Too late he realized that he ought not to have spoken.

"I thought it might be," Ravelle said with satisfaction. "It still works. I turned myself into a centaur and misdirected you to this valley of death. Do you remember? Or did I beat you too hard when I rode your back?"

Marius's mind whirled with confusion. The amulet had been lost for eons, seized by the magpie long, long ago as Marius had fallen from the heavens. He'd thought it gone forever. Esau'd had no idea of its worth or its magical powers.

"How did you come by that, Ravelle?"

The demon rubbed the stone, making it glow. "I followed that stupid bird of yours to its nest."

So Esau had had the amulet all this time. Marius could not blame the bird for stealing it or for keeping it. Thousands of years had passed since he'd fallen from the sky. "When?"

"What does it matter when? That is for me to know," Ravelle said.

"The gods gave it to me. That amulet is mine," Marius said without thinking. Absurd to say that to a demon, he told himself in the next instant, as if he expected so evil a being to be a good boy and give it back.

"Is it?" the demon asked. "But it worked well on me."

Marius was silent, remembering the weak and aged creature that had stopped him in his mad dash, its mien so strangely repellent to him. His brain had been soaked in Quercus's wine, his wits further addled by his heedlong, half-crazed galloping in search of the demon.

Think of it, Marius. Your quarry was near enough to touch, near enough to kick to death. He had not looked closely enough at the aged, pathetic beast in the road, had not realized that his mortal enemy had taken yet another form to lead him astray.

He shook his battered head. The action made him dizzy and made his bruises throb with renewed pain. His own death might be imminent, he thought, but Linnea at least was safe. No torture would persuade him to reveal her whereabouts and the healer Quercus was at least as wily as a demon.

Let Ravelle brag a bit longer. "What have you done with the magpie?"

The demon smiled thinly and gnashed his teeth without answering. His meaning was clear enough. Poor Esau. Killed and eaten, feathers and all.

Was he next?

"That will not be your fate," Ravelle said. "You get to die more slowly."

Marius heard the nearly silent whoosh of something heavy swung through the air and turned his head just in time to glimpse the blacksmith's hammer coming at his head. The glancing blow knocked him out.

* * *

He awoke for the second time to a sickening sensation of pitching and rolling, and understood after a while that he'd been put on a ship and was now at sea. Through the hatch above, he could see huge sails billowing against the night sky, their corners straining against taut ropes. Dashes of spray came through the holes of the hatch, wetting his face and his chest. His hooves slipped on the water-sloshed wood.

He felt a new, agonizingly painful ache in his head, but could not explore it. He was shackled as he'd been before, the collar still around his neck. Now the chains on his legs were fastened to ringbolts in the small space below the hatch; his fetlocks painfully chafed.

Marius knew without trying to make the change that he could no longer shift his shape from a centaur to a man. He was certain that Ravelle's possession of the amulet had taken the ability away.

If the demon were to break the carved stone, Marius was doomed to be a centaur forever—unless his heart broke along with the stone. He could not remember the terms of the curse after all this time.

The strong wind died down and the sails fluttered uncertainly, until sea-demons swarmed up the rigging and furled them with raw cries. Then he heard the rhythm of ranked oars by the hundred, the galley slaves below whipped into speed. The heavy, irregular tread of a three-legged demon above made Marius step nervously, testing the limits of his iron restraints. He looked up just as a long claw came though one of the holes in the hatch cover, lifting it.

The demon squatted and its seamed face peered down at him. Not Ravelle. No horns. Its wings were furled tightly against its back.

"Hungry?" it asked. There was a gleam of sharp teeth in its visage.

Marius endeavored to press back against the walls of the small space that confined him without answering.

The demon smiled in an ugly way. "I am." Another one joined it and peered down into the hatch. Above them the night sky was dark but for the briefest second Marius saw a flash of some winged being far, far above the open sea.

He thought of Gideon. *Do not save me,* he wanted to howl to the heavens. Better that one Arcan lord should die than all.

Enshackled, he endured the demons' taunts and kicks.

The Lord of the Dark followed the black man-o'-war a while longer, evading the gaze of the lookout in the crow's-nest atop the main mast by going behind clouds. He'd been fortunate to catch a glimpse of it as he'd reconnoitered the Forest Isle, searching again for some sign of Marius from the air.

He'd seen nothing . . . then fires, small ones, at the mouth of the valley of the Great Death where a poisonous blast had killed so many so long ago. Swooping as low as he'd dared, he'd seen the demons, massed by the thousands and this ship, anchored in deep water offshore. So it had brought them.

There had been rowboats and coracles by the hundreds, also at anchor or drawn up on shore. One boat had headed for the ship, riding low in the water with heavy cargo—some chained beast had been upon it, attended by demons.

Hovering, Gideon had strained his eyes, then realized that Marius had been taken prisoner. His hide was far lighter than that of the demons and he seemed to be their only captive.

Linnea was safe, perhaps. But where was she? And where had the ship and its demon crew come from? It had the look, he'd thought, of a vessel from the Outer Darkness, a galley rowed by damned souls, but it was sailing toward the distant land of men.

His strong white wings beat powerfully as he rode warm currents of air, as strong in his element as Simeon was under the sea.

He dared not accompany the demon ship all the way into the harbor. He was not armored against arrows, and he would be shot at as soon as he was visible in the first light of day.

Far below the clouds opened and he caught another glimpse of the ship, making for port, the thin white lines flanking it made by the steady dipping of hundreds of oars. Demons moved about the decks, dark shapes against the lighter wood, and went about the endless tasks of sailing a man-o'-war. He dropped lower to get a better look. Of a sudden a demon lifted a hatch cover and looked into a pit, joined by another one. Directly below Gideon spied the centaur, not moving.

A creature paced the deck nearby, head downcast, but still— something about its head was different from the others.

He saw it turn and saw the spiraling goat's horns. Ravelle. Gideon heard a cry of warning from the lookout and wheeled away in the gloomy sky.

Far forward from the pit in which the centaur was imprisoned were the captain's quarters, rough-hewn and spare. In the center of the main cabin was a table. Ravelle and the captain sat on either side of it.

"My men say having a centaur aboard a ship is bad luck," the captain said gruffly.

"Why?" was the demon's careless reply. He was stalling the man.

"They think he is cursed. More than a man, less than a horse."

Ravelle laughed in a coarse way. "Then they have been looking at him closely."

"Yes, when Marius is taken out for exercise upon the deck. He is not at liberty but—"

"Who would not look?" the demon asked breezily.

The captain made a harrumphing noise, neither confirming nor denying the question. "Such beings no longer exist in the world of men. Except as marble statues, of course. There is one such in the harbor to which we sail."

"I look forward to comparing it to Marius."

The captain glowered at him. "Your tone is too light, my friend."

"My apologies," the demon said, adding after a few seconds of silence, "my sincere apologies."

"Hm. I look forward to the day when that creature is off my ship."

"Do you," the demon said conversationally. "Consider yourself fortunate that he remains a centaur."

"What? I don't take your meaning."

Ravelle nodded, as if that was to be expected. "At one time, he could change from a centaur to a man and back again."

"Ah," the captain said.

"If he could do that now, he could go among the sailors undetected."

"Not on my ship," said the captain. "The first mate or the bo'sun would winkle him out. Or the men would."

The demon shrugged. "Well, he is stuck as a centaur." He fingered the carved stone that hung about his neck without explaining it to the captain. "And in that form he is no more extra work for your men than a horse would be."

"But even so," the captain began, "they are not pleased with the presence of your sea-demons on board either. Always coming and going on mysterious errands, and muttering in a language no one can understand."

"Do they do the work assigned to them?"

"They have taken on more than that," the captain complained, spreading his big hands open on the table. "Some say they have taken over. They allow no one else up to the crow's-nest, for one thing."

"They must keep a good watch, captain. And demons do not sleep much."

The ship pitched and rolled in the heavy swells.

"And why is that?" the captain asked after a time. "What is it that they watch for?"

"Those who would follow us."

"Who is that? I have had to quash many strange rumors since we sailed for the Arcan Isles and back again."

"Such as?" The demon did his best to sound concerned.

"Some men were convinced that they were sailing to their deaths over the edge of the known world," the captain replied. "A promise of more gold was not enough to allay their fears."

"Your sailors look alive to me," Ravelle said nastily. "Swearing and slaving and buggering one another the same as always."

"They do not consider themselves slaves," the captain said with anger. "That word is reserved for the damned souls who are chained to the oars."

Ravelle nodded. "I stand corrected."

The captain leaned forward and interlaced his thick fingers on the table. "Tell me something, Ravelle. How did you manage to find so many?"

"I have access to a never-ending supply of the damned," the demon said, "because there is no end of sin in your world and even in the enchanted realm of Arcan." He looked idly about the cabin, not meeting the captain's eye as he continued. "Let us just say that they come my way. The Outer Darkness is crowded with the damned."

"I am sure that is so."

"They jump at the chance to serve in a galley, thinking that they will contrive an escape and live as before."

"Indeed."

The captain himself had escaped the Outer Darkness in exactly that way, but he saw no reason to inform Ravelle of it. A lesser demon held the rights to his immortal soul and that was that.

He turned to take a bottle down from a nearby shelf, lifting it free of the slats that kept it upright and uncorking it. He put the open bottle in the middle of the table with his hand wrapped around it and tipped it toward Ravelle.

The demon shook his head.

Shrugging, the captain treated himself to several swallows of whatever was inside. He exhaled a spirituous breath and a gleam entered Ravelle's eye.

With a snap of his clawed fingers, he caused a spark and set the captain's breath on fire. A blast of red flame scorched the table and ignited the spirit left in the bottle, which exploded.

Shards of glass embedded themselves in the wood of the cabin. Ravelle gave a low chuckle. "Why did you do that?" Seeming imperturbable, the captain wiped away the blood on his skin and picked at the glass embedded in his tattooed flesh.

"To amuse myself," Ravelle said. "And to let you know who is master of this ship."

The captain suppressed a shudder. "I fear my men are right. I will be glad enough when we sight the harbor."

"We all will."

More spirits went down the captain's throat before he spoke again. "Now then. Getting back to your demon sailors—"

"What about them?" There was again a noticeable edge in Ravelle's voice.

"It was bad enough I had to pick them up at the edge of the Outer Darkness what with that volcano spewing and all," the captain said. "But I will not bring them back there. The men will mutiny."

How fortunate that the volcano had belched fire as they'd passed it on the way to the Darkness, Ravelle reflected. Coincidence, of course, but even so. What fools men were. And how easy it was to frighten them.

Failing that, they could always be corrupted. Ravelle had paid the captain in gold, and he expected full service from him and every sailor on the ship. He would not tolerate disobedience, and the sea-demons had picked up what they needed to learn. The sailors, a low-born lot of criminals and drunks to his understanding, were no longer needed when all was said and done.

He had expected more from the captain, an intrepid and tough man. But Ravelle had marked him as an escapee from a slave ship by the invisible mark upon his forehead.

The mark of terror endured and survived, but never quite vanished. It was invisible to a mortal man, and the captain did not know he had it. But it was not invisible to a demon who traded in fear and shame. In his evil mind, better than gold for his purpose.

Ravelle looked straight at the captain, who quailed under his gaze. The demon's eyes were glowing red and in them the man saw his own death.

"So Ravelle has him." Simeon rose and paced the hall of his fortress. "We can do nothing. Every weapon we have is useless in the realm of men."

Gideon sat before the fire, allowing Rhiannon to rub and soothe his weary wings. "There must be something we can do."

Simeon, Lord of the Deep, shook his head, lost in thought.

"You did not see Linnea?" Rhiannon asked after a little time.

"No. But I had to fly away—the lookout spotted me only seconds after I saw Ravelle on deck. She may be on the ship. As for Marius, I know nothing of how he was captured or where."

"I suspect Ravelle captured Linnea first, and then used her to lure Marius. A centaur is naturally wary."

"We all should be. A small army of demons has come ashore at the Valley of the Great Death," Gideon said.

"What?" Simeon said incredulously. "How?"

"By ship, I think. The same ship that took Marius away."

"But my spies and my selkies knew nothing of it. Why did you not tell us of this first?"

Gideon glared at him. "One thing at a time, Simeon. I have been aloft for hours, while you sat in your fortress—"

Megaleen's gentle voice broke in. "The great lords of Arcan should not quarrel like boys."

Simeon said nothing.

"And there is much to be discovered." Rhiannon rose, giving Gideon a final caress. "We have no knowledge of where Marius and Linnea went during their time away from here. What did Lord Vane say, Gideon, when you flew to him?"

"The first time? He said that he had no idea where they were. I thought for a moment that he himself might have designs upon Linnea, but then—"

"Appalling," Simeon said forcefully. "I would not put it past him."

Gideon gave a sigh. "I am almost certain he is innocent of that sin. A fire sprite has beguiled him of late."

Rhiannon favored him with a look that said much about fire sprites—for the most part, that they were no better than they had to be.

"I think, though," Simeon said after some minutes, "that Lord Vane will prove a formidable ally against the demon. We cannot shut him out of our plans."

Gideon's wings gave an involuntary twitch. "I am done flying for the night."

"Very well. Then I will swim."

"The Isle of Fire is leagues away," Megaleen protested.

Simeon only nodded. "Please see to our guests, Megaleen." He turned and left the hall.

The tunnels that connected the Arcan archipelago were not the swiftest route. Walking as swiftly as he could swim, Simeon soon reached the strand, striding through the rounded pebbles that tumbled over and over with each incoming wave.

It had been too long since he'd swum so freely and strongly, as exhilarated as the seals he and his kind sprang from and no less adept in the water. The powerful undersea currents embraced his sleek body, parting to let him penetrate the depths of the ocean and at last casting him upon the grim shore of Lord Vane's fiery domain.

Simeon spat out a mouthful of water. Even still in the sea, it tasted not of wholesome saltiness but of brimstone.

He walked out of the waves, shuddering as the sulfurous water clung to his hide, shaking away the last of the foul-smelling drops. Ahead loomed the vast bulk of Vane's castle. By night the black stones of which it was built seemed even darker, as if they absorbed both moonlight and starlight into themselves.

He found Vane with the aid of a servant, a nervous little man who scuttled away as if he expected to be blown into his next incarnation by a furious upbraiding from the ill-tempered lord of fire.

Simeon hesitated at the door of Vane's private chambers, knocking loudly.

Vane bade him enter in a boisterous voice. It was wine or a woman, thought Simeon with an inward sigh, noting that it was the latter when he entered.

Hella's skin shimmered deep blue when she was introduced and a red blush stained her cheeks. She was stark naked and sitting next to Vane in front of the fire on an iron divan. Several of her kind, considerably smaller, were disporting themselves lewdly among the logs.

"You interrupted us." Vane chucked his beautiful but dangerously hot companion under her chin. "Too bad. Hella has been insatiable lately, wanting more and more. Why is that, my dear? Do you have something to prove or are you trying to distract me?"

Simeon wanted to turn around and get back into the ocean. Shamelessly clinging to Vane, Hellas was a vision of sensuality, her fire-edged curves a potent distraction.

"We were watching—oh, never mind," Vane said. "You don't

seem to be in the mood for it." He waved at the entangled sprites and they flew up the chimney. "What brings you here?"

"Marius has been found," said Simeon without delay or preamble. "But Linnea has not."

Was it his imagination or did Hella give her lord and master a guilty look? How very odd. Vane did not seem to notice it.

"Where was he?" Vane asked. Hella writhed into his lap, as if she was indeed trying to distract him.

"Gideon glimpsed him on the deck of a ship manned by demons, enchained—must we talk with her here, Vane?"

"She's only a sprite," he said cheerfully. "Here today, gone tomorrow."

Gone where, Simeon wanted to say, but didn't. Gideon had seemed to think that Vane would help them. As usual, the fire Lord was half-drunk and more interested in an ongoing seduction.

Vane was fondling her rather roughly and she seemed to like it. Which didn't stop him from carrying on a conversation at the same time. But Simeon knew which of them would win the war for his attention and she was blue. "And who was the captain of the ship, Simeon?" Vane asked, nipping at the sprite's ear. "Mmm. Ravelle?"

"He didn't know." Simeon felt like a fool and vowed to leave in the next instant. "He did see Ravelle on deck."

Lord Vane spread out on the divan, his fire girl licking at his neck. The unabashed display of sexuality caused Simeon the stirrings of arousal. How was it possible that Vane could think with his beautiful blue concubine squirming on his lap?

"Marius can smell a demon leagues away," Vane was saying, caressing an ass of blue flame absent-mindedly. "He never would have gone willingly or let himself be captured."

"What are you saying?"

Vane stroked Hella's hair until it gave off faint trails of smoke. "He would only fall into a trap with Linnea at the center of it. Beautiful, innocent Linnea—ow!"

He removed his bleeding hand from Hella's mouth and glanced at the bite marks. Then he grabbed her hair and held her head back while he glared severely at her.

Both men saw a flash of pure white fire in her eyes at the same instant.

"Now that is a color I have never seen in your eyes," Vane said curiously. "You don't like her name, do you? And you can't hide it. Do you know what happened to Linnea?"

There was another flash, whiter than white. Pure hate blazed in the sprite's eyes. The lords of Arcan exchanged a look.

Hella struggled silently, placing her slender blue hands on Vane's chest and pushing at him.

Simeon seemed visibly upset by what he was seeing. "Don't manhandle her, Vane—"

"When Hella is jealous, she takes it out on me—and she is lying to both of us."

"Leave me out of it."

Vane didn't let go. "You saw that she drew blood when she bit me. And it happened the second she heard Linnea's name. As I said, she can hide nothing."

"Even so." Simeon felt sorry for her but he always felt an instinctive wariness around fire spirits. They in turn stayed away from selkies.

"She knows something." Vane's grip on her hair tightened.

Simeon was shocked into shouting, "Don't!"

Vane looked at him with surprise. "She is only a sprite and I will handle her however I please."

Simeon's hand shot out and he forced the lord of fire to relinquish his grip, brushing against Hella's arm as he did. At the contact of his damp skin, Hella diminished and shrank.

"You'll put her out, you soggy bastard," Vane growled. "Don't touch her."

Hella edged away from him and looked pleadingly at Simeon.

Again he fought the feeling that her expression held a measure of guilt. "Very well."

"By the way, she can fly," Vane said. "She doesn't stay unless she wants to or I have a tight grip on her."

Simeon gave her a sympathetic look and Hella, drying out, grew to her full size again. With a movement supple and quick, she crossed one leg over the other and returned his look with a demure glance. Demure but . . . scorchingly hot.

"Don't be taken in by that shy smile," Vane warned him. "She is not to be trusted."

Hella drew back her hand to slap him and Vane caught her by the wrist. "You're not getting away this time," he said. "I don't care what he says."

With unashamed fury, the fire spirit gave in to her temper again and lived up to her hellish reputation. But Lord Vane prevailed. His eyes were glittering with excitement when he had nearly subdued her.

Hella howled silently. Simeon stared into the inside of her open mouth and the flicking tongue of flame inside it. Her adversary seemed unimpressed, but it took all of his great strength to hang onto her.

Biting, scratching, kicking Hella grabbed a hank of his long black hair and hung on until it burned in her hand, throwing the singed hair on the floor and going back for more.

Lord Vane didn't seem to care but the smell of burnt hair made Simeon feel sick. So the lord of fire thought nothing of brawling with a blue harlot. He, Simeon, very much doubted that Hella would give in, although she seemed to share Vane's love of fighting.

"Tell me where you went that night when Gideon came here," Vane panted. "You left me asleep on the bed and out the window you flew. He'd talked about Marius and Linnea—"

Again there was a white flash in her eyes. "There it is! For the third time you have given yourself away. You found Linnea—where is she now?"

Hella kicked at his groin but missed when he dodged her. She was so angry and overheated that Simeon was able to hear her silent voice.

Nowhere!

"You are lying, Hella," Vane growled. He got one supple arm behind her back. "Tell the truth or I will force you to lie between me and my friend. Two of us. I will make you hot and he will make you wet!"

For a fraction of a second, the bawdy suggestion stopped her and then the struggle began all over again.

"For the love of the God of All, stop, both of you!" Simeon shouted. But the fight intensified. He stared at the two of them, transfixed by what he saw. It was as if they had become transparent, physically and emotionally. They were utterly without self-consciousness, their heated intimacy a mind-altering mix of love and hate and unbridled sexuality.

Vane's clothes fell off his body in smoking shreds and Hella, who had been naked to begin with, glowed fiery red all over. Then Vane's hands began to move all over her, caressing and squeezing, making her his own, using pleasure to bend her to his will just as he had tried to dominate her by force.

Her lips parted and she sighed submissively. Pleasure seemed more effective.

"Tell me what happened," Vane said again. "You must. You crave this and you will have more, but I will have the truth from your beautiful red lips. Did you find Linnea on that fateful night?"

Yes . . . by chance . . .

Vane caressed her ardently, standing behind her. The lord of fire looked over her shoulder at Simeon. "Do you think she is telling the truth?"

"You have a hell of a way of forcing a confession from her, Vane! Must I watch?"

"I think she likes it when you do," he purred.

Simeon looked away all the same, loyal to his Megaleen and furiously angry with Vane. But in time he had the whole story from Hella—interspersed with distracting little moans. That she had been jealous. Had followed them. Had conjured a sleeping mist so she could look at her rival, then accidentally sparked a fire in grass that had ensnared her. She'd sparked more to free herself and then that brute Marius came running.

After that she didn't know what had happened. She entwined her lithe blue arms around Vane's neck and begged him to love her.

I gave you what you wanted. Now it is my turn.

Simeon excused himself and went outside the room to wait. The finale was swift and glorious. Not more than a few moments later, Lord Vane stepped outside, carelessly dressed and waving away the hot smoke that drifted out from the chamber after the lovemaking.

He clapped Simeon on the shoulder. "I am ready to leave."

"And Hella?"

Vane smirked. "She is no more than a gleam in my eye again. When she is satisfied, she is much less trouble. And infinitesimally tiny."

"Do you believe what she said?"

"I do. It is not easy to lie with such brevity and ingenuity simultaneously. Her actions fit her impulsive nature."

"But we know very little more than we did before, Vane."

The lord of fire did not seem dismayed by that fact. "Then we will find out more. I told Gideon I would help him."

Simeon looked at him with disgust. "For what it is worth. We have work to do and battles to fight. You are a randy bastard who thinks of nothing but sex."

"True enough. But do not underestimate me."

14

Linnea opened her eyes but could not focus them. The details of her strange surroundings eluded her.

She vaguely remembered falling asleep on the grass Marius had crushed to make them a bed, remembered waiting for him to return in the night, and then . . . nothing. Her hands touched something soft beneath her. Leaves by their shape, fur by their feel.

Had Marius made her another bower in the woods, gathering all this soft stuff together and brought to it? If only she could lift her head.

No. There was no sky above with drifting clouds or stars, but a ceiling of some thick, craggy wood. The sounds she heard were muted, though certainly there were birds about. Not far away. Not in here.

It came to her slowly that she was inside a tree. But what sort of tree it was and the reason why she was in it eluded her foggy brain. Linnea closed her eyes and thought backward into the dream she'd been having before her eyes opened.

That too eluded her, the odd images of the dream seeming to

vanish down twisted paths of an altered awareness. She tried to chase them mentally, seeing herself in the shape of an antelope and a dream lover in the guise of a centaur mounting her, fulfilling a nameless animal desire with human tenderness.

A poignant sadness filled her and twin tears trickled down her cheeks from under her closed lids.

Then a hideous being with spiraling horns shattered that image by stepping through it and his own replaced it. Leering. Bestial. A satyr of infinite power and evil. Seeming so close that she wanted to open her eyes and make it vanish, but she could not. The demon's glowing red eyes enspelled her again.

Linnea opened her mouth, gasping for breath. The pure air inside the tree she slept within filled her lungs and somehow it dissolved the frightening vision of the satyr.

Weakly, she brought a limp hand up to her chest and placed it over her racing heart. Her eyes opened slowly and this time she could see more clearly.

She was in an alcove off a main room inside a—yes, she was in a tree. Someone just out of sight was humming faintly. There was an odd, papery sound and then a thunk, as of a scroll being unrolled too rapidly, the spindle at its center hitting the floor.

Linnea thought and thought without wanting to move.

The last few days began to come back to her in bits and pieces—but were they only a few? She had no way of telling how long she had been sleeping and she felt too weak to get up.

But wherever she was now felt safe. It was almost as if the great tree breathed too—she had a sense of air flowing in a rhythm as deep and old as time. Then she heard footsteps, small footsteps that were quiet, as if the being who made them was walking on a forest floor.

Bright eyes in a deeply wrinkled face that seemed to be covered with bark peered in at her.

"So, Linnea. You have awakened at last."

She did remember who was greeting her. Vaguely. He certainly seemed to know her. She'd heard that it was possible to lose all memory of oneself, but she had not. "Good morning," she answered politely, hoping he would keep on talking and help her understand the particulars of her situation.

"I am Quercus, in case you do not remember me." He paused, letting that sink in. "Marius brought you here when you were overcome by a mist in the woods."

"Ah." She studied him, but not as calmly as he studied her. A rush of memories coursed through her mind. A journey. On foot. On horseback. On . . . Marius. Through woods. It seemed like a dream until all of it came back at once. Her body shook as if something taken violently from her had been instantly restored and not gently.

She had woken alone when Marius had left her in the night, feeling somewhat frightened, yet the lingering warmth of his massive body was still comforting her. And then—she frowned at the recollection—a blue flame had bedeviled her—and then . . . nothing.

That must have been the mist. It still was making her confused. But what had happened before that, including her first meeting with this strange but kind little being, had been preserved in memory. She reached up to touch the scar on her chest where Quercus had drawn out the demon's poison from the scratch.

The pouches under his eyes drew up as he looked at her narrowly. "That scratch does not hurt you, I hope."

"No."

"How do you feel?"

Linnea rubbed at her eyes. "Not very strong. But I think I will be, with more rest. Thank you for taking care of me again, Quercus."

He harrumphed. Had his skin not been made of bark, he would have blushed. "It was nothing."

"Not to me." Linnea looked and listened, perceiving no sigh of Marius. "Where is Marius?"

"Not here," Quercus said, a thread of annoyance in his voice. "He had too much to drink and galloped off into the night, vowing vengeance on Ravelle and all his kind."

Linnea struggled to sit up and managed it with the healer's swift assistance. He plumped up the pillows on the bower. "By himself?"

"There was no stopping him, alas. He was convinced that you would not recover by the time he finished the third bottle, and roaring for blood by the fourth." Quercus looked a little shamefaced. "It was my fault. I thought if he were tipsy from my elderflower wine I could persuade him to be cautious."

"It is his nature to take chances. And he loathes Ravelle."

The healer nodded. "With good reason. He was beside himself, thinking that he had put you in danger. You were limp in his arms, Linnea—he brought you up the stairs and plowed up my garden to make you the bower in which you lie."

Linnea shook her head upon the pillow. "I have no memory of it. Just the blue flame . . . and then the mist, drifting."

"Marius told me of the flame and I examined the burns, which are healing well. I have reason to believe the blue flame is a fire spirit, although I do not understand why one would seek to injure you."

"Could it have been Ravelle's imp?" She ran her fingertips over one of the burns on her shoulder. "They are not so strong as he and that has also healed."

"Possibly. I cannot be sure," Quercus sighed. "But Marius is obsessed with destroying Ravelle personally. I wanted to explain that there is more than one way to fight a demon, even a supreme one, but Marius would not listen."

Linnea nodded.

"For one thing, his malevolence can be turned back upon him, given the right spell. There is no reason for Marius to risk hide and hoof—" He stopped when he saw the tears brimming in Linnea's eyes.

"No, and I never asked him to. The other lords of Arcan were preparing to help," she whispered. "Is there no way to bring him back, Quercus?" She pushed off the covers and swung her legs out, standing on unsteady feet as if she was prepared to run after him herself.

"We might see him in my scrying pool. Although I would rather not use it—I still think that Ravelle has the power to spy on us all through it, though we are otherwise safe from demons here. However—" Quercus hesitated, moved by the beseeching look on her face. He stretched out a hand to her. "I may be able to keep him at bay. Come along. Perhaps I worry too much."

Linnea let herself be guided to the next room where the scrying pool was. Quercus seated her by it and waved his hand over the small pool, muttering a spell. All Linnea understood of it was Marius's name.

She watched in wonder as the surface of the water trembled within the stone basin that held it. After a while the pool became still and glassy. In it she could see only moving shadows.

"He is in a dark place," Quercus said, "a place of evil."

Linnea made out firelight in the background of a scene and saw it gleam on a length of heavy chain. Then a shadow moved in front of that as well.

"Is that Marius?" she whispered.

"I don't know." The image in the scrying pool shifted as Quercus waved his hand over it again.

Then she saw the sweeping curve of the centaur's back and someone's hand resting in the hollow where she'd ridden him.

A hideously familiar hand, with long claws.

"Ravelle," they said at the same time.

Quercus's face crumpled into sad lines. "So he has been captured. But where is he?"

The firelight she'd seen flew up into showers of sparks and a massive figure moved into view, demonlike but not Ravelle.

Quercus waved his hand over the water again and suddenly the entire scene became clear. The centaur was in a smithy.

He wore chains and shackles of crude make that were being struck off one by one as new ones were put on. Linnea wanted to weep when she saw Marius humbly bow his head as an iron collar was fitted around his neck. It was scrolled and bedizened as if made for show, but its cruel strength was clear enough when the blacksmith gave it a yank and made his captive stumble forward a few steps.

"What are they doing to him?" she asked.

"I suspect he will be paraded through the streets," Quercus said, a note of anger in his voice. He straightened as the image in the pool went entirely dark. "I have lost him."

"Is he in the land of men?" Linnea asked. "How came he there?"

Quercus shuddered. "By sea, I would guess. For one as rooted as I am, the thought is frightening."

"Not to me," she said. "I will go to him if I can—"

"He made me promise to keep you here, Linnea," Quercus replied. "Would you go against his will?" Quercus told the lie with a clear conscience. No, that promise had never been asked of him, but with what Quercus had learned in his hours of vigil over the unconscious woman in the leafy bower since Marius's thundering exit into the night, it was best if Linnea did stay.

"Yes. He is not here to gainsay me," she said with spirit.

"Well, no," Quercus said, a bit nonplussed. How difficult would it be to persuade her to say? He had not expected her to recover to this degree so soon. Still, the healer had new reason to insist that she remain safely within the branches of the old oak, though he was in doubt as to when and how to inform her of that reason. "But you are not strong enough to go a-journeying. Especially not over the seas that divide the Arcan Isles from the land of men."

"Who will help him if I do not?" Her tone was as passionate as it was determined.

"There is always a way," Quercus soothed.

"Then you must tell me of it. I will not rest until you do. And, Quercus—"

He gazed at her mildly, as if hoping to calm her down with a look alone. "Yes?"

"How long was I asleep, if that is what it was?"

"It was like sleep," he assured her. "You lay upon your bower for several days."

An anguished look flashed in her eyes. "So he has been gone that long?"

"Yes, my dear. I could not leave you nor would I follow him. I assumed somewhat foolishly that he was bashing around the island and would return."

"Did you not worry when he did not?"

Quercus considered his next words before saying them. "I was more worried for you. Marius has the strength of a horse and of a man combined, with a touch of the divine in him also."

"He is not indestructible, Quercus."

"No. And he puts himself in harm's way, as big and bold as he is. There is no telling what ordeal he has undergone or how Ravelle entrapped him."

"Yet he has survived," Linnea said softly.

Quercus frowned. "At what price? He hoped to slay the demon and he has failed. The Marius I know might wish he had died instead."

Linnea's eyes flashed. "Do not speak so!"

The healer seemed abashed. "Forgive me. I am thinking of when last I saw him. Before you awoke, well before. We quarreled, unfortunately."

"You did not tell me that."

"One thing at a time—" He broke off, looking at her worriedly. "He did what he did for love of you, Linnea."

"Oh?" she asked as if she very much wanted to believe it. Then, with a hint of womanly self-doubt, she added, "And not for his own glory? He is proud to a fault."

"More than that, impetuous. If only I had been able to stop him from rushing away!"

Linnea looked into the scrying pool. "Even his image is gone. Waiting here will be unbearable. I cannot live, not knowing what has happened to him."

"It is not only for ourselves that we live, Linnea," the healer began.

"Who else do I have without Marius?" she burst out. "My human mother is gone from this earth and my father, the Great White Stag, is distant, as was always his way." She dashed away her tears, looking fiercely at him.

Quercus hesitated. He was not at all sure he should tell her of his guess, though it was an informed one, on the subject of *who else.* "If you and Marius are destined to be together, then you will be," was all he said.

He indicated that she should come away from the blank pool, lest her tears fall into it and tempt the demon.

Weakness was Ravelle's wine.

Too distraught to talk, Linnea paced the floor of the room next to the one where Quercus kept his scrolls. He was in there now, patiently rerolling the one that had fallen to the floor earlier. It was concerned with fertility, gestation, and childbirth, judging from the illustrations she'd glanced at disappearing around the spindle.

Without saying anything more, he put it back up on a shelf and occupied himself with his studies.

She looked out the window and spotted Esau, preening himself vigorously. She went and called to him softly, and he looked up, eyes bright. Then he flew to her extended hand.

Linnea stroked him, wishing as she had before that the bird

could talk. She found him something to nibble at in the kitchen, then took him back to the window, setting him on the sill so he could eat.

Absently, she looked out. The forest was drenched in sunlight, dappled green and gold. Its beauty had been restored to purity again, hushed in a primeval way. Even without having learned of Ravelle's departure to the land of men, she would have thought that the Forest Isle was free of his evil influence.

How long it seemed since she had entered the forest at Midsummer, intent upon capturing its equine lord for her own private pleasure! If the revelers had marked her disappearance, none had come looking for her. She would not have been the first woman to go native on the island of forests and never return.

She smiled sadly, stroking the bird's black-and-white feathers. He closed his beady eyes and let her scratch the top of his head with delicate care.

Did he know where his master was? Linnea wished she could fly.

And then what, she asked herself. They did not even know exactly where the centaur was. She could not fight the demon by herself—oh, it didn't matter. She was not strong enough to do anything but abide here and Quercus would not let her leave.

How she longed to go to Marius's side, wherever he was in the land of men. She wanted to swing a sword with the best of them, sunder his iron bonds by magic, and escape . . . ah, there was no place left in the Arcan realm that was safe any longer.

Uncertain and distraught, Linnea nearly blamed herself for attracting the demon to the Forest Isle. If she had not run away, playing a foolish game . . . no, no, no. The fault was not with her but with the nature of evil in and of itself. No, from the beginning Marius had loved her well, treated her like his goddess, lingered with her most lovingly, rescued her from grave danger and put his own life in peril to do so.

Linnea heaved a heartbreaking sigh. She had to summon up the strength to go on, somehow, some way. As Quercus had said, she and the centaur would be together if it was meant to be. Feeling a little queasy of a sudden, she steadied herself with a hand to one side of the window and ceased her attentions to the magpie. Without opening his eyes, he gave a faint chirp of thanks and tucked his head down between his wings.

Evidently the spell she'd been under was not done with her yet. Her unsteadiness returned. Feeling her way along the wall, she went back to the alcove, settling herself upon the impossibly soft heap of lamb's-ear leaves. In a little while sleep overcame her again.

Quercus was expecting as much. He kept himself occupied as she moved about his tree home, and waited until he heard soft, steady breathing before he went to the alcove to look at her.

Her color was excellent, he thought, noting her rosy cheeks. Her continued sleepiness, nothing unusual, even though the effects of the mist had worn off. Her emotions had been heightened upon the shocking discovery of Marius's enchained state—that was also to be expected. Most likely the emotionality would continue.

Quercus studied her. Linnea sleeping was blessedly peaceful at the moment. How did the males of her species cope with changeable moods? Humans were excitable creatures. He would have to look it up. There was a scroll just come from the library at Alexandria which limned the workings of the brain in fascinating detail, and argued that it might be the seat of the soul.

When her eyes had opened, they had been large and lustrous, as was typical for a woman in her condition. And her breasts were newly plump, rising and falling with each breath she took. Below that, there was an ever so slight roundness to her belly. Marius's vigor and impetuousness were matched by—Quercus permitted himself a wry smile—his virility.

It did not require witchcraft or a scrying pool to ascertain that she was very likely pregnant.

Seeing that she was comfortable, he went back to his study. He did not take down the scroll on the matter to look at it again. He had committed its text and its drawings to memory as soon as he suspected that Linnea was with child, finding the process most interesting. His own kind reproduced by means of enormous acorns buried in the yielding earth.

He was not sure when to inform her of the fact and of course she would soon figure it out for herself. And she was bound to ask questions of Quercus, having, as the healer now knew, no mother to turn to.

One question in particular would require immediate reassurance and he had been curious about it himself: If she had conceived when Marius was in the form of a man, their offspring would be entirely human.

If Marius only knew . . . The old healer felt his heart clench in his chest at the thought of the centaur's plight. Even if he could get a message to him via Esau, it might be intercepted by the demon—and Ravelle would stop at nothing to get Linnea in his clutches.

Quercus had a thousand reasons to keep her safely here.

Yet the evil ones had never made it through the defenses with which Quercus surrounded his domain, of which the demon-trapping spiral stairs were the last. She was safe—he would see to it. He, as a healer, had taken a solemn vow eons ago to preserve all life.

For someone all too willing to risk everything, like Marius, the vow was almost impossible to keep, Quercus thought soberly.

No, Linnea and the child she carried were Quercus's first responsibility now. Newly awakened from a problematic spell, she did not seem to have the first inkling of her pregnancy. But she would. Until then, Quercus would keep his diagnosis to himself.

Linnea's sleep was fitful, besieged by more strange dreams whose intensity troubled her. She woke gasping, unable to remember much about them, besides that they made her feel deeply afraid. It was now late in the day and long golden shadows pierced the serenity of the forest surrounding the tree.

She rose and walked as softly as she could, wondering if Quercus was about. Yes. She heard the sounds she'd come to associate with him: the rattling of papyrus scrolls and his absentminded talking to himself as he read them. His voice was very low, lower than leaves rustling. Sometimes he muttered words she could understand, and sometimes exclaimed in Treeish.

She listened carefully without going to him. It dawned on her that he was planning Marius's eventual rescue. Linnea wanted to rush in and wrap her arms around him, but she stopped herself from breaking his scholarly concentration. His best idea might fly out of his head as swiftly as the magpie took off into the sky.

He would tell her in good time. Until then she would bide her time and find some way to occupy herself that would not disturb him.

Linnea glided over the smooth wood floors, not making a sound. She went again to the window, seeing this time the thick branch that sprang from the trunk beneath it. Her confinement and long sleep made her long to be out in the leaves where she could breathe and just think.

She leaned through the window's sides to see if it was possible to clamber out and walk upon the branch. It seemed so.

Would Quercus scold her for leaving the tree without telling him? He might. She hesitated. But she was not really leaving the tree, she reasoned, just going elsewhere upon it, never touching the ground.

She hoisted her kirtle and raised a leg to straddle the sill. In another few seconds, she was outside upon the branch, balancing with care. A good thing that she was barefoot and her wooziness had left her, she thought, looking down at the ground far below.

But if the magpie were to startle her—she glanced about for him. Esau was nowhere in sight at the moment.

Moving as gracefully as a ropewalker, she continued on to the fork in the branch. It was a cradle of deep moss on which she could sit and look up at the skies—some other creature, smaller than herself, had done so and left the impression of its body. In a few more steps she reached the fork and settled herself upon the moss. She wished she'd stolen a bit of food from Quercus's pantry, because her stomach was objecting to its emptiness. Linnea fought a slight feeling of nausea by breathing deeply.

Whatever ailment she had was nothing compared to Marius's woes. A fresh upwelling of tears filled her eyes and she hung her head, letting them fall onto the emerald moss like sad drops of dew.

15

Linnea sat on the branch like a bird whose wings had been clipped, lost in thought, looking about herself without seeing much. Then she saw, directly below her and half-hidden by leaves, a small pool of water in the fork of another large branch, its calm surface reflecting the untroubled sky above.

Hand over hand to steady herself, she moved like a caterpillar along the branch she was on to get a better look. Above the pool now, looking down into it, she saw the surface of the water darken and tremble as if a looming storm had appeared in the sky.

Yet the sun dappled the leaves about her and there was not even a hint of a breeze.

She looked again. Fleeting images of men and women and a city she had never seen came and went in the pool, appearing and dissolving in an instant, too swiftly to be clearly discerned.

It was a tree-born scrying pool, she thought with wonder. Her mother had told her of such. Such hidden pools, far above the earth where they could not be muddied, occurred not by the art of man or gods. They were brought into being by the ancient wisdom of the deep forest, and only the most venerable trees could create them.

Their scrying was the most powerful of all.

The moss around the small pool was thick and velvety, without a trace of disturbance. Around its pure water the individual filaments of the moss formed a mass of living green more precious to her eyes than emeralds.

Could it be that no one had ever looked into it? If so, that would mean that its magic was deep indeed. She might be able to see into the heart of the world, travel over seas and mountains, far from here to where Marius was, in spirit, at least. The old healer had mentioned nothing of this pool when they all had been looking into the one in his chambers. Indeed, he might know nothing at all of it. And he was too dignified to scramble around on tree branches, though he might have done in his youth.

But Linnea had no idea how long Quercus had lived inside the oak. She thought of him as she knew him, immersed in his studies and not much aware of the world outside, except for what he saw in the scrying pool in the stone basin in his chambers.

Never mind, she told herself. Look and look again, before the pool changes. Something told her that it would.

Linnea reached out for branches that would support her safely and swung down from the one above the pool. She landed with ease, thinking briefly that her bovidine surefootedness was as useful in a tree as it was upon the ground.

A small herd of deer passed below her, not looking up, racing away. A young buck and several does, she noticed. Then two small spotted fawns. Was their mother, the doe she had seen at the very beginning of her adventure upon the Forest Isle, among their number?

Linnea longed to tell her of what had happened since that day. She would bid her sister of the woods to run.

As if she had said the words out loud, the deer ran faster, too swiftly for her to tell if the one she'd seen just moments before her first encounter with Ravelle was among them. They soon vanished in the surrounding woods with a faint swishing of leaves and the occasional snap of a twig.

Linnea crouched by the pool, careful not to press a hand upon the velvety moss that surrounded it. But this close she noticed a subtle design in it, grown as the moss itself had grown, of runes and magic glyphs she could not read.

She looked into the pool again.

It showed a city, a port, to judge by the masts holding furled sails that thrust up behind the buildings. They were humble in height with few windows, but made of white stone, a dazzling contrast to the vivid blue of the sky. The vision in the pool moved through the streets, showing now a trudging beast of burden yoked to the cart it pulled, and then a group of gossiping women in flowing, sleeveless shifts tied at the waist.

They were all dark-haired, their locks bound with narrow ribbons in every color of the rainbow. A man walked by and chaffed them rudely, and the women laughed at him.

A pair of small children ran up to the women as swiftly as the fawns she'd seen, and pulled one away by the hand. She held a market basket, Linnea noticed.

An ordinary day in the land of men. Why was the pool showing her this? She willed it to find Marius and the sunny scene went dark.

Then she saw him. In chains as before, but not in a smithy. In a place where performers—slaves, dancers, fighters—were milling about. To one side was a stone door that led out to the stage of an amphitheatre.

Linnea concentrated. The vulgar roar of the crowd filling the tiers was just audible. She saw Marius's hide tense over his ribs and was instantly jealous when a lovely young dancer soothed him by stroking him.

If you cannot be there to comfort him, then be grateful that she is, Linnea scolded herself.

Could he not escape? To her, the centaur was close to all-powerful. But perhaps that was only in their world. In the land of men, enslaved by Ravelle's demonic art, he was not.

She looked through the distant door in the place the pool revealed and then she saw the lion.

It too was chained, with massive shackles upon its legs and a studded collar, wider than a man's hand was long, half-buried in its mane.

The lion growled and tried to rise up against the men on the stage who goaded it to greater fury. One dragged a spear along its prominent ribs like a boy dragging a stick against a fence. The difference was, he drew blood. The animal roared with pain. It had been starved, clearly, to make it more fierce, and beaten too.

So it would be a fight to the death between her Marius and this poor beast, Linnea thought frantically. He was dragged on stage, bashing at his handlers with shackled arms, blows they dodged easily.

He reared, striking out with his hooves—the chain between his front legs allowed him that freedom, to entertain the crowd. The lion shrank back.

With a hammer and chisel, a man ran out and struck off the shackles on the lion's front paws. Another urged Marius forward, dodging the killing force of his hooves as the centaur reared and wheeled.

Linnea wondered helplessly why did he not take the shape of a mere man again. He'd told her that the force of anger or passion could spur the change; and he'd been able to will it in their time together.

Ravelle's evil magic was preventing him, she supposed, brushing away the hot tears of fury that trickled down her face.

The battle between centaur and lion began, terrifying in its speed and fury. The crowd roared louder than either of them, filled with bloodlust. Stricken with shock, Linnea glanced away from the combatants briefly, looking with anger at the people in the amphitheatre. Had the race of men fallen so low and so far from their own beginnings in paradise that they reveled in the sight of pain?

Then she realized that she could not look at the centaur and the lion as before. The pool forced her gaze elsewhere, moving in view through the tiers. Now and then it stopped on a face that seemed ordinary, but . . .

In a few more seconds, its scrying power revealed the demons among the crowd. At first they seemed like ordinary men but as the eye of the seeing pool stayed on them, the sinister demon features and leathery skin appeared.

To a demon, they resembled Ravelle. None had his spiraling horns and none were as large, but they were in some way his brethren or his spawn.

Linnea shuddered. She, a demi-goddess of gentle birth in woodlands, had little knowledge of such things. Marius's heroic efforts had saved her, but his impatience with the deliberations of the other lords when it came to dealing with Ravelle had been his undoing.

Never should they have come back to the Isle of the Forest! If only she had not gone along with his wish to escape the convocation of the Arcan lords and come here.

To walk upon his land gave him strength—he was vulnerable in that way—and the echoing loveliness of the woods had called him home, its sweet call too strong to resist.

Yet the ominous things that lurked within it had changed everything. How wrong it all seemed now. The halcyon days and erotic nights of the Midsummer celebration had promised riches of the harvest, fruitfulness and fertility. This year the festival had reaped only evil.

She should have insisted on staying within Simeon's fortress, with Rhiannon and Megaleen to keep her company. The other women must be frantic with worry over her disappearance with Marius. She had no way to get a message to them.

As she had seen Marius do, she waved a hand over the pool in the fork of the venerable tree and said the words she remembered of his chants over the pool in the stone basin. The water turned inky black and she began to panic. Had she invited the wrath of some unknown god? The leaves around her shook and rattled. Linnea drew into herself. The ancient pool was not under her control.

Blithe to a fault, too eager to be alone with him again, she had given in to a false sense of safety, but things had begun to happen.

He'd rescued her again, brought her here, spurred to chase Ravelle once more. Because of her, he had run directly into a trap of which even Quercus had no knowledge.

The old healer hadn't known where he was. Heartless gods! It would be her task to tell him of what she had just seen—and Marius's victory.

Or death.

How would it end? Her falling tears disturbed the scrying surface, making circles that widened to the edge of the moss.

Still inky black, the pool would not show her the combat of the centaur and his maddened enemy, the lion. No, only the watchers came into view. Was she supposed to guess from their coarse shouts and twisted faces who was winning?

She could not.

The raucous demons among the crowd, visible to her but not the men and women they sat among, were screaming for blood, urging the raging lion to tear the centaur limb from limb and devour him.

No one dared to champion Marius, it seemed. And in the amphitheatre, he had no name. He was only a beast to them, like the lion, to be treated with cruelty.

She could only watch, mute, terrified, unable to help him and far, far away. Even if a magic eagle bore her away over the sea that separated them, the battle would be long over.

She concentrated fiercely on the images in the pool. Were he to win, she might find him somewhere in the land of men. She looked as they did, could disguise herself as a woman of the port city, with a flowing gown and ribbons in her hair. She would cut it all off were he to die. No matter where she was, she would grieve for him.

If he lost this battle, there would be no grave and no honor for one who'd fought so bravely. No, the mauled corpse would be fed to the jackals who prowled the edge of the city at night.

The scrying pool of the tree vouchsafed a knowledge that shattered the last of her innocence.

She, Linnea, was by no means an isolated victim of Ravelle. No, the legions of Outer Darkness had been summoned forth by him and the three remaining lords of Arcan Isles could not stop the malevolent army. Her near-rape by Ravelle had been only a harbinger of a rape of the world on both sides of the Arcan seas.

Beguiled by his masterful trickery, thinking of him as her lover, she'd been whipped and humiliated—and to her secret shame, found it pleasurable. How near she had been to becoming his creature, having his split hoof forever upon her neck as he slowly destroyed her mind.

After the terrifying encounter—it seemed suddenly vivid in her mind—she'd hated to think of what had happened to her, had told Marius only when the hurt of the demon's wicked deception had become too much to hide. She'd wanted to believe that she had only blundered, meeting evil by chance. But no.

Ravelle had not been idly roaming the forest upon that day, beset by obscene urges, looking to inflict his unholy lust on just anyone. If her guess was right, he had been stalking Marius even then.

The scrying pool had revealed a deeper and far more terrifying truth if she read what it showed aright: there would an end to all innocence and all hope. The demon surely hoped to rule the world of men, and the beings of the Arcan Islands.

He had started with Marius and not been able to finish.

The centaur's rescue of her and his swift vengeance had fired the great demon's blood with intemperate fury.

"Show me all!" she begged the pool.

Its surface afforded her one last glimpse of the combatants on the amphitheatre's stage. Blood poured down Marius's flanks from gashes made by the lion's claws. They were still shackled by their back legs, unable to escape, forced back into the fight by the men who goaded them on.

But he had one mighty arm around the lion's neck. Its tongue dangled from between long teeth that too had tasted Marius's flesh—blood dripped from them.

Strength for strength, they were matched. But who was winning? From the outside in, an impenetrable darkness seeped into the water until the centaur and lion were blacked out.

Her heart breaking, Linnea raised her hands to the heavens and screamed, sending frightened birds flying out from the leaves, calling brokenly, their cries echoing her own despair. Something above her, far above, swooped in circles.

She cringed, believing for a moment that she had called forth another demon or Ravelle himself. Linnea had nowhere to hide.

If she scrambled back into the tree, he would get Quercus too, she thought wildly. Let the damned one take her then. And let her die swiftly, she pleaded with the uncaring gods and goddesses.

She felt a heavy landing upon the branch she was clung to and tightened her grip upon it, pressing her cheek into the rough bark, feeling tears of fear stream into the crevices as she closed her eyes.

Linnea braced her body for the claws that would spike into her hair and lift her by it . . . but no.

A gentle hand touched her shoulder instead, shaking her lightly. "Linnea?' a familiar male voice asked.

She lifted her head and opened her eyes.

It was Gideon.

16

He raised her up and his long wings folded around her as she stood. "Are you all right, Linnea? It was only by chance that I heard your cry—but I was so glad. Rhiannon begged me to find you."

She sobbed without answering right away, giving in to her boundless misery, but comforted by his hold upon her, envying for just a second the woman who was privileged to enjoy such embraces for her lifetime.

Then, brokenly, keeping her voice low, Linnea told him what she knew of what had happened since their departure from Simeon's fortress and that she and Marius had taken shelter in the hollows of this tree. But she said nothing of the shy healer. She hoped, in fact, that Quercus would not hear them talking, for she wished passionately to escape. Her next task, a daunting one, was to persuade Gideon to fly her to Marius—where had he come from?

He was not that familiar with the Forest Isle, and this part of it was ancient and untrammeled.

How to explain? She wondered as he murmured words of

comfort if the other lords of Arcan were angry with her. Surely Megaleen would not be, but Simeon seemed to Linnea as chilly and remote as the sea that was his element and as for Vane—she chose not to dwell on the unpredictable lord of fire. She was new to their world, their ways, their laws—would they think she had endangered Marius? Gideon had said nothing of what had transpired in the time since they'd left and she scarcely wanted to know.

Now, every second counted.

"So that is what happened." He opened his wings and let her step away from him. "When we realized you were not coming back, I set out to look for you both on my own, from the air," he said, his voice as soft as hers. "He is alive. That is all I know for now. I spotted a ship upon the open sea and flew lower when a hatch was opened. Marius stood in chains, enclosed in a pit."

"A ship?" The pool had not shown her that. "Where did it sail?"

Gideon named the port city he'd seen in the distance over the sea, the same one the pool had revealed.

"There is an amphitheatre there," she began.

"Yes," Gideon interrupted her, "but how did you know? Have you been to that place?"

For answer she pointed to the scrying pool in the fork of the tree. "I saw it there. He fights for his life against a lion even as we speak. Unless the vision it showed me was a fever-dream. I have not been myself in the last several days."

"So you said." Gideon drew in his breath. "But that is a tree-born pool and its magic is as pure as its water. Whatever you saw in it was no dream."

"I thought not." She looked at Gideon, her eyes as luminous as the pool, as if something inside her made her soul glow. "We must go to him!" she pleaded with anxious fear in her eyes.

Gideon stroked the arms that she'd wrapped around herself when he'd released from the embrace of his wings. "I—I will try, Linnea," he said. "I am weary of flying in my every feather. The journey home took long against the winds. Simeon and Vane charged me to report to them and I was headed thence when I happened to see you below—"

"It is a sign that you have come to me," Linnea said. "A sign that you must help Marius before you do anything."

"Perhaps. The pool has provided you with more recent knowledge of him than I have to offer. We both should go before Simeon—but what else did you see?" he asked, looking down at her, swayed by the emotion in her beautiful eyes.

Swiftly she gave an account of the battle in the amphitheatre and how the pool had gone dark before the victor was declared. Gideon nodded soberly, rising again. "Then he was sold," he told Linnea, not sparing her that truth. "Rescuing him will not be easy."

"Must we leave him to the lion?" Her words were whispered but she wanted to scream them aloud.

"No, but we must think it through—"

"There is no time for that," she said with urgency.

Gideon's gentle touch calmed her but only for a second. "Look again into the pool, Linnea. Ask it for an answer. May I look with you?"

"The pool is not mine and it is as silent as a grave," she said heatedly.

"Yet it holds the deepest wisdom. I have heard that one can see the real nature of the beings that appear in tree-pools," the winged lord of the air said. "Through the clothes, through the skin, to the soul."

Linnea's sweet face looked deeply troubled. "The pool perceives the beings that have no souls," she said at last. "It made me look also among the spectators. Hidden beside the men and women of the city are demons in great numbers."

Gideon squatted on his haunches to look into the dark waters. "Are there?" he asked. "I see nothing at all now."

"Can we not go?" Linnea could not force him to fly with her. Why was he not alarmed by Marius's plight?

"You have not seen such contests of strength before, I think." His voice was more soothing than his hands, but she recoiled from both, consumed with fear for Marius. "Yes, one will be dragged as if dead from the stage, and one hailed as the victor but it is all a show. They will be brought back again for another contest."

"What?"

"I have been a spectator of such staged battles," he explained.

She shot him an appalled look, her hands on her hips. The queasy feeling that had troubled her before returned in full force. Linnea fought a strong urge to vomit.

"From high above as I flew, not in the tiers. Do not look at me that way—I did not make the world of men," he said defensively. "We of the Arcan Isles do not fight for entertainment, but—well, I watched once or twice. What of it?"

"Why do you blather on? Will you not rescue him?" She curled her fingers into her palms, outraged of a sudden.

"Linnea, I answered your question. And there is yet time. Just enough, I think."

She just barely kept herself from slapping him. Were she to give in to the impulse, she might knock him off the branch they both stood on. "Explain!"

"The answer is simple. There has not been a centaur seen in the port for a hundred years. They will not waste him by allowing him to be killed. Nor will they kill the lion."

"It is Marius I fear for. He has suffered grievously already." Linnea's temper flashed in her eyes. "So. Why do you delay and ask questions?"

"Because strange things are happening. I flew over a distant valley that opens into the sea around the forest isle. Demons are massing there too, by the thousand—"

"I do not care," she said softly. "There is only one demon

you should worry about and that one is the ruler of all the others. And there is only one man who concerns me: Marius."

Gideon could not deny the wisdom of the first part of her unexpected response, but it was her love for Marius that was beginning to sway him. So Linnea was ready to risk all for that. He had only known one other woman of such great-heartedness and she had given him his life back. Rhiannon's face came to him—yearning, tender, and vulnerable—and he almost said yes to Linnea.

But as far as Rhiannon, the love of his heart, she had told him in no uncertain terms that he was not to go a-roving these days. It was a promise he had sworn on his own wings to keep, and he had been gone from her side too long already. He said as calmly as he could, "Linnea, if you have been ill, then you should not hide yourself away in this ancient part of the isle or go to the land of men. I will take you back to Rhiannon so that she can care for you—"

"No!" she burst out. "Take me to the mainland and leave me there."

"The journey is long and fatiguing for someone strong, let alone you—"

"I cannot explain everything now. You must help me!" Her trembling lower lip, the tears that threatened to fall—she had him with both.

"How can I refuse?" Gideon held up his hands in a placating gesture. "If I can carry Rhiannon, I can carry you. But not a centaur."

"That is all I ask."

Gideon doubted that. "Will you battle the lion and all the spectators in the amphitheatre to free him? Do you think you can lead him out of danger all by yourself? Can I not meet again with the lords of Arcan to formulate a plan—"

"Gideon, please!" she beseeched him. "Must I beg you to help me? If I had wings of my own—" She took a few steps backward, away from him, and lost her balance. The ground rushed up at her with sickening speed until Gideon's arms caught her.

He held her close to his powerful body and swooped up to the top of the tree. She was breathless, afraid to speak, seeing both reluctance and weariness etched in his face. His huge wings beat with steady purpose as he headed over the forest.

Neither saw the flash of black-and-white as the magpie flew up after them. Flying with all his might, Gideon swiftly outpaced little Esau, who fluttered and sank in slow circles back into the highest leaves of the old oak.

He hopped down, down, from branch to branch and went in at the window of Quercus's chamber. The old healer did not look up, absorbed in a scroll.

If the bird had been able to make sense of the illustrations, he would have known that it was about trees and rocks—not that he would have cared. The magpie hopped upon the papyrus, right under Quercus's barky nose.

"Yes, Esau, what is it?" he asked absently in Treeish. He asked the question again in Mag when the bird cawed with frustration.

The bird answered at length, causing Quercus to scramble out of his chair and rush to the window. He peered this way and that, searching the clouds above for long minutes, then came back dejectedly to his scroll.

"They are long gone and it will be a perilous journey," he told the bird, an edge of fear in his calm voice. "From what I have seen, she loves him well. Her bond with Marius is stronger than the fear of death. Alas, I cannot follow."

Esau hopped upon the scroll, his eyes bright and his head cocked.

"I know, I know," Quercus said. "You can." He studied the bird as if thinking of a plan. "But you will have to make Linnea understand you somehow. When and if you get to the land of men."

The bird spoke again.

"What's that? Oh, you are very sure of yourself, Esau. Did Ravelle not scare you enough?"

At the mention of the demon's name, the bird waggled its tail as if about to eliminate.

"Not on the scroll," Quercus said hastily, pushing the bird gently off it. "Not anywhere inside my house, if you please."

Esau fluttered to the window, turned around, stuck his nether parts well out in the air and let go a stinking blast.

"Eloquent in its way," Quercus said. "I share your opinion of demons, if not your ability to do that out of a window."

The magpie fluttered back and walked on the table again.

"So. You cannot read but I will tell you that the scroll you stroll upon concerns the immortal souls of trees and rocks. I will derive a spell from it and you will fly with it over the sea. The magic involved is powerful and very old," Quercus went on, "and it will protect and guide you as a tree-dwelling creature."

Esaue nodded.

"You must get it to her safely and in good time. She will have one chance to use it. No thieving along the way and none of your mischief, do you understand?"

Esau nodded in assent. He watched as the old healer dipped a pen in oak-gall ink and inscribed runes upon a slip of paper. Then Quercus cast sand upon it from a small box to dry the ink, then brushed it away, looking over the written-out spell with thoughtful care. "Yes, it is correct." He rolled it up and tied it with a thin red ribbon around the magpie's neck.

The journey through the air to the port seemed interminable and took most of Gideon's remaining strength. His wings were shaking when he landed with her in his arms. She had buried her face in his chest for most of the way, clinging to him with her own waning strength, terrified to look down, disoriented and queasy.

He had said nothing. The wind on high was strong and a hint of moisture in it prophesied a storm to come.

The sky was overcast when he touched down in a deserted quarter. The gossiping women, the children tugging at them, the poor beast drawing the cart—all were gone and there was no sign of life. Still, Linnea marveled silently at how accurate the pool's reflection of the port city had been. The white stone of the buildings no longer dazzled, turned to gray by the clouds overhead.

"Where is the amphitheatre?" she asked, looking around.

"Around that corner and down a long street. You cannot see it from here, but I saw it when I flew over."

Linnea nodded, smoothing her windblown hair and gown. "I am ready for anything the Fates have in mind."

"Have you gone mad, Linnea?" he asked softly. "I am beginning to be sorry I gave in and brought you hence, but—"

"But what?"

"You reminded of someone to whom I can never say no."

She waited for him to say who that was, but he didn't. "I should not leave you. There is nothing you can do on your own to help Marius."

"I can try," she said with bravado. "If he dies, then I will die with him." She felt a flash of guilt when she remembered the old healer's odd words on that subject. *It is not only for ourselves that we live, Linnea.*

Gideon shook his head. His utter exhaustion was evident. "Shall I tell the others that those were your final words to me?"

"Tell them nothing for now," she said. "Give me your solemn promise."

Reluctantly, he did.

"I would not have them blame you for obeying me. They will come if they can, when they can. But stay with me a little longer," she said. "I will find food for you. You cannot make the return trip if you are weak. If something happened to *you*, they would blame me for that and rightly so."

"No. I must go," he said in a low voice. "Rhiannon is waiting. And so are the others."

It was clear to her which of them mattered most to Gideon. She was touched by his devotion. "I see." She turned to walk away, then stopped when his hand touched her shoulder.

"Leaving you is wrong, very wrong," he said, a troubled look in the depths of his eyes. "If anything happens—ah, me. I want you to know why I must force myself to go back without you."

"Tell me quickly," she said. She was eager to begin her mission and find Marius, encouraged by Gideon's assurance that the centaur was most likely alive. Still and all, even her rampageous lover might not survive another battle with a dangerous beast.

"Rhiannon is with child," he blurted out. "We had not told anyone of it, but if not for that, I would stay with you and fight with you. But I cannot risk the little life she carries for someone else's. I am all she has, Linnea."

She stood stock-still, gazing into his eyes, burning with manly tears. A flutter deep in her own womb was her first response to his joyous news. Then Linnea patted his cheek. "I am happy for you. Rhiannon is blessed. Give her my love. Now go, and may the goddess speed your wings."

He reached for her hand and pressed a kiss to it. "I will look for you in the tree pool if I can find that old oak again," he whispered.

"Thank you," Linnea said simply. "For everything." Then she turned and walked away.

17

Two days later...

The lords of Arcan—minus the chief subject of conversation, Marius—sat gathered at Simeon's table, their countenances stern. Even Lord Vane was paying attention to the solemn discussion of the danger that threatened them all. Gideon had returned from aerial reconnaissance.

"The demons are still swarming in the Valley of the Great Death," he said, "but they have gone no further. It was an effort to stay out of sight of their sentries, but I managed."

"I wonder why they stay," Vane mused.

"Because they are leaderless, as far as I can tell." Gideon blew out a breath, still tired from his flight. "They mill about and fight in the open, without tents or shelter. I think that without Ravelle there is no one in charge."

"And your source has him still in the land of men?" Vane asked.

"Yes, in the port city."

"Their restlessness could be dangerous," Simeon said thoughtfully. "I posted selkies close to shore who said the same thing, Vane. The demons have nothing to do but quarrel, yet they do not leave the valley or enter the water."

Vane frowned. "Then they are waiting for Ravelle to return. Let us hope they do not get too bored and decide to loot and pillage."

Gideon gave him an irritated look. "Hope? Is that all we can do?"

Vane slammed his hand down on the table. "It seems so. Unless we can destroy them all and quickly. We still have not done anything but watch and wait."

"For good reason. One of our number has been captured and taken to the land of men, and his lady has vanished. That is a problem that has not been solved. Rash action may cost the lives of both Linnea and Marius," Simeon said.

Gideon said nothing in response, keeping his vow to Linnea. He wondered how she fared, saying a silent prayer for her as he looked at the other men. "Marius would tell us to carry on without him and to be strong, I know that."

"Here on our islands we are strong," Simeon replied, "but there, across the wide seas, we will be outnumbered by a hundred thousand, should Ravelle turn the ranks of mere men against us. And there is no counting the number of demons and the like in the Outer Darkness."

Vane only shrugged. "I have no doubt that demons have infiltrated humankind. Evil is always attractive and eternally tempting. Not to mention power. The two combined are highly seductive."

"You would know, o lord of fire," Gideon said dryly.

"Yes." Vane grinned. "The prospect of battling so many does not daunt me."

"Your arrogance may be the death of you," Simeon commented.

"I don't think so. And I have come up with plans while you two were talking."

"I am almost afraid to ask what they are," Simeon said, sinking his head in his hands. "It is a good thing Rhiannon and Megaleen are not here to listen."

"They would have taken up swords and shields long ago," Vane said indulgently, "if you two would let them. Women have a hidden ferocity and are quite capable of vengeance. To say nothing of hatred."

"They don't like you, that is certain," Gideon pointed out.

"Too high-born for my taste, both of them. But," he coughed and dodged the glares of the other two, "they are certainly spoken for. No matter. I am never without female companionship."

"Which brings us to Hella," Gideon said to Simeon. "Who attacked Linnea in a fit of jealousy. What to make of it, I cannot say."

Vane gave him a bored look. "It was fun making Hella talk, wasn't it?"

"Shut up, Vane." Simeon gave the lord of fire a hard look. "Can you not control a mere sprite?"

"Hella is impossible to control. At least she was able to verify that Linnea was alive and with Marius on his island—is still alive, as far as we know," he corrected himself.

"Whereabouts unknown. Can Hella help us with that?" Simeon asked.

"She might," Vane said. "She moves more quickly than any living thing. And," he added cheerfully, "she is prepared to make amends for her mischief." He leaned back in his chair. "Do you want to hear what I want to do?"

"No. But get on with it," Simeon said with a sigh.

"To begin," Vane said with satisfaction, pleased to be the center of attention, "I propose sending every single one of the demons in the valley back to the Outer Darkness without hand-to-hand fighting or other pointless heroics."

"How will you do that?" Gideon wanted to know.

"With my usual incendiary ingenuity," Vane said. He took a

small scroll from his tunic and let it unroll upon the table until the spindle end of it came loose and hit Simeon. The lord of the deep picked it up and toyed with it as Vane flattened the scroll.

On it was a sketch of a catapult of monstrous size and other machines of war. He jabbed a finger at the catapult. "Using this, we send a fireball into the valley. The dry trees will ignite and do the rest."

Simeon and Gideon looked over the plans in silence for some time, reading the scrawled formulas for Arcan fire and volcanic explosives.

"If it will rid us of so foul a plague as demons, then we should use it," Simeon said. "But I cannot help thinking of the original conflagration that destroyed the valley. The blast that started it came from your volcano, Vane."

"What of it? That was eons ago. I had not been banished to my island."

Simeon rolled the scroll and shoved it back to him. "The valley is a place of spirits. Do we dare disturb them?"

"Its dead lie unburied," Vane pointed out casually, as if it didn't matter.

"Yes. And if we use this killing machine you have drawn, their innocent bones will be mingled with those of demons. When the risen dead of Arcan are called before Mica, the God of us all at the final judging, he will not be able to tell the good from the bad."

"Mica is a swear word, nothing more, and that is superstitious nonsense," Vane growled.

"Not to the beings of our various realms. When this battle is over, we will have to answer to them," Simeon pointed out.

"We will have to answer to them if the demons go any farther than where they are nor," Gideon said. "The encampment in the valley is Ravelle's advance guard and the forest isle is particularly vulnerable. The spirits of the innocent dead will forgive us for protecting the living. No one good goes there,

Simeon," the winged lord of air remonstrated. "It is a place of ill omen."

The depths of Simeon's eyes flashed with dark light. "That is true. It seems that *we* must go, however. There is no telling what dark force we will unleash. But are we agreed?" He looked around at the other lords. The shadows of the fire flickered on their faces. Gideon's face showed his uneasiness; Vane's, only gleeful eagerness.

Simeon rose and left the table, looking straight ahead. He did not want to look in the sea-glass mirror at himself.

The overcast sky boded a storm of great strength when they gathered again a few days later, well above the valley. Gideon's dawn reconnoitering had told them that the demons were huddled for the warmth in the lowest and narrowest part of it.

The dark, leathery-skinned backs looked more than ever like a disgusting swarm of insects, heaving and shifting. Faint but harsh cries floated up to where they were.

Vane's soldiers and servants had built the catapult in pieces overnight and brought it all here. The last pegs were being driven in. His fire-master, a strange, singed-looking creature who ran on two legs but seemed otherwise inhuman, was stirring a concoction of boiling pitch that reeked of noxious chemicals. Other of the inhabitants of his island were preparing the great ball that would be saturated with the vile mixture and thrown.

Vane strode about, overseeing the process.

"Death and devastation come naturally to you," Simeon said, observing the process. He seemed deeply uncomfortable, out of his element, and his eyes showed a trace of fear.

"Someone has to be good at it," Vane said. "You are lucky it is me, for I am far from entirely evil."

Simeon shrugged and looked again at the soldiers and servants. "It is not for me to say, perhaps."

"I would use the word energetic to describe myself. And excitable. But not evil. I do like to set things on fire, though." He took a small sack from his pocket and drew out a flint and a piece of metal, striking sparks that flew off into the gloomy air.

One landed on his callused knuckle and Lord Vane blew on it gently. "Come, Hella."

The fire sprite was soon straddling his thumb and then, growing larger, jumped down to the ground. Simeon gave her an uneasy look. She didn't glance his way keeping her eyes on her master.

"It is time, Hella. You are to run down that side of the valley and then up the other, setting fires everywhere you can. There are nothing but dead trees in it—the valley is a tinderbox and we want the demons in it to keep to as small an area as possible."

She nodded, running lightly to where he pointed and beginning with a twisted snag of white wood. It blazed up swiftly, followed in rapid succession by many more.

There were cries from the demons, who, as Vane had predicted, moved together for safety. Simeon watched dispassionately as the fireball was loaded. It happened almost too swiftly to imagine.

With a creak of timber and the groan of tautening ropes, the ball was loaded, soaked with the volatile mixture, and set on fire with a touch from the returned sprite's slender blue finger.

A nice touch, Simeon thought, as it was hurled into the air. In another second the whole valley exploded in towering, red-hot flames. There would be hell to pay for what they had done soon enough unless they could kill Ravelle. And they were no closer to finding Marius or Linnea.

Far away in the land of men, Ravelle felt the blast in his bones. A death blow had been dealt to his kindred, he knew it at once, for they were truly bone of his bones, all made from a particle of his indestructible flesh. The ones who'd disembarked at the Forest Isle had been the best of the first litters, descended from Ravelle himself and a pack of jackal-women that roamed the outer darkness. They were violent and fearless, a new breed entirely, young, strong demons who ate their enemies raw. But they were only the advance guard. Here, in the land of men, more were breeding. Demon spawn, once born, grew full-size in a matter of days. Their human mothers were not required to nurse them—their breasts would be torn to pieces by needle-sharp teeth if they did. No, they only had to mate again and grow more in their wombs for Ravelle's army.

And more.

Whoever had slaughtered the demons in the valley would pay for it—and it would not be difficult to single out the culprits. He had planted any number of spies among the forest folk, paving the way for his conquest of Marius's verdant isle.

Its erstwhile ruler stood chained in a nearby stall, watching him with rolling eyes. Nary a scream or even a whicker. The centaur's mouth was sealed with pitch.

Ravelle turned his attention back to the owner of the amphitheatre. "You say you will not pit him against another lion?"

"He kills them too quickly," the man complained. "With his wounds and all. His hide has been ripped open more times than I can count and yet he vanquishes each one."

Ravelle disliked him for telling the truth. He disliked humans, if he were to tell the truth himself, hated coming down to their level, finding sport in molesting the women and scorching the hides of the stupider men until they all ran from him. But he would get his way. Each and every one of them would end up in hell—his hell. "The crowds must love it."

The man scowled. "They want to see him die. He appears to be unkillable."

Ravelle pondered that unpleasant news without speaking.

"Take him back," the man said. He took out a sack of leather and poured jingling gold coins in the center of the table. "Sell him to a mill. He can die in harness for all I care. Maybe I could sell tickets to that."

Ravelle gave him a narrow look. "Very well. I do not care how he dies. I only want to humiliate him before it happens."

"You're a strange one."

The demon took the man by the throat and lifted him from his chair, setting him down when he heard a gurgle coming from his throat. "Yes," he said, collecting the coins. "I am. You will say nothing of this to anyone."

"N-no," the man wheezed.

Ravelle lifted a claw and slit his throat anyway.

Marius was manhandled into a cart with high sides and a roof, from which he could see nothing. The wounds in his hide were festering, which did not stop the hostlers from jabbing them again to get him to move.

His shackles clanked as he kicked hopelessly at them. They had been, he realized after a time, imbued with a binding magic forged into the molten iron by the demon blacksmith. He could not break them.

He rested his aching head against the planks of the cart as it began to move, jolting along the streets of the port until he was forced to stand up straight. Better for him to do so.

Ravelle had not succeeded in obliterating Marius's pride. Fighting lions bent on tearing out his throat had revived him in a strange way. He was prepared to go down fighting, if it came to that.

Where were they taking him? Ravelle had said something to the man at the table before he'd killed him, but Marius hadn't heard it. Too many flies buzzing in his ears, which rang anyway. His head had hit the stone stage of the amphitheatre when he'd fallen in the last battle.

If not for the thought of Linnea, he would have been happy enough to die.

The cart came to a juddering halt and he prayed as he often did that Quercus was keeping her safely hidden. Then an eye pressed itself to a knothole in the side of the cart and looked at him. Dully, shutting off the constant pain in his body and head, he looked at it.

A lustrous eye, it was. With long, feminine lashes.

Linnea whispered to him, "I am here, Marius."

He trembled all over, dumbstruck. And terrified for her. *Go away*, he tried to whisper. Ravelle's pitch held fast. His lips did not move and his dry tongue heaved inside his mouth.

She disappeared. Was she safely away?

When the hostlers backed him out, he saw nothing on either side of the cart but the glaring white stone of the houses and a flash of a bird, black and white, just before he was led into the mill.

So Esau was with her. How had they come to the land of men?

His mind racing with confusion, Marius allowed himself to be yoked in the circular yard inside. He was led beside two immense millstones, one atop the other, grinding, ever grinding. The blind oxen doing the work were taken off and he, put on without the massive stones stopping. He hardly cared. The fleeting sight of her brought him the wild joy of knowing that he could die, having seen her.

But it was not to last, that joy. His next glimpse of a living being made the centaur want to stop but the momentum of the grinding stones prevented it. His legs were still shackled, front and back, permitting him a measured stride but nothing else. The heavy yoke fastened to the wooden structure through which the stones turned prevented him from rearing.

Ravelle stepped back as Marius stepped forward, extending a claw. Dangling from it was the amulet. He held it in front of Marius, stepping back on cloven hooves so the centaur could see what he was about to do. Then he dropped the amulet to the stone floor of the mill and put his hoof upon it. The crack echoed through the mill.

"So," he sneered, "you will die a beast. I wish I had more time to enjoy your torment here. The monotony will make you go mad in the end. Around and around and around. Beaten and—"

Marius interrupted him, making an unintelligible noise in his throat that almost burst his sealed mouth open.

"Let me finish, will you? Beaten and blind." Ravelle gestured to a man to stop the millstones, but it took three revolutions before they did. It was almost with tenderness that he sealed Marius's eyes shut, very quickly. "There. In a little while Linnea will be brought in. She too will be yoked but to other gigantic stones hard by." He gestured to them but the centaur could no longer see. "She will witness your torment with every revolution of her wheel and you will be able to hear hers. A fitting revenge, I think."

The centaur's nostrils flared. He smelled her. She was nigh.

"Trying to find her?" Ravelle asked. He gestured for the stones to begin their ceaseless grinding once more and the centaur stumbled under the yoke. "We have captured her," he lied, "but she is still under interrogation. Linnea will be dragged in only when she is close to death."

Above him on a beam Linnea heard the centaur struggle to breathe. She dashed away her useless tears and unrolled the spell that Quercus had sent with Esau, along with—the old healer could not help himself—an explanation. It was now or never. She chanted the spell soundlessly.

The ancient words stirred the souls of trees and rocks in their natural form and more so after they had been cut and shaped by the hands of men. Its enchantment brought both back to what they once had been. She clung to the wide beam, feeling it vibrate. The supporting timbers vibrated too and the centaur felt it through his hooves. A low, booming sound reverberated through the mill and the man in charge of the wheels made them stop.

The great stones began to slide, the top one off the bottom, the moving weight of both cracking the giant pole at their center. Ravelle looked frantically around but the men of the mill had run outside, fearing an earthquake, screaming a warning.

Marius's muscles tensed and bulged as he braced himself against the collapsing wood of the complicated yoke, snapping its heavy timbers. He scraped his mouth against the gritty millstone nearest him and unsealed his lips, roaring with inchoate rage. Ravelle stood aghast as the centaur charged directly at him, finding him by smell.

He went down under Marius's slashing hooves, crying for mercy. Unseen in the dust near the demon, the pieces of the cracked amulet joined to become whole once more. It was forgotten in the melee. Again the centaur reared but came down to the side of the demon's head when he heard Linnea's soft gasp.

"Where are you?" he screamed, still blind, his wounded sides streaming blood from his mighty efforts to be free.

The sight broke her heart and steeled her resolve. There was a chance—the barest chance—that they might yet escape. She crept backward on the beam and down the timber that supported it, making an effort not to be seen by Ravelle.

He was struggling to his feet and he spied her instantly. Badly injured, he staggered toward, bloody froth dripping from his slack lips. The centaur made straight for him, guided by instinct and a hatred so feral that he was a true force of nature, a maddened beast bent on vengeance.

Head down, he slammed into Ravelle and threw him against the shifting stones with tremendous force. The top stone tipped and the demon slid off, barely alive. Linnea watched with horror as the massive stone came upright, wobbling.

Marius galloped around the obstacle, not seeing the precarious tilt of the stone. She gasped, calling to him over the demon's shrieks and curses. He did not hear. Again he charged toward the foul odor that clung to Ravelle, broadsiding the wounded demon as he staggered away, sending him straight through the hole in the center of the stone.

There Ravelle stuck, screaming for help.

Tipping, the gigantic stone wobbled and she ran to Marius, shoving him out of the way of the millstone and grabbing his mane to mount him. She clung fiercely to him, kicking his sides, riding him out the door to the astonishment of the people who'd gathered in the streets, expecting an earthquake.

Not five seconds later, they scattered in all directions as the rolling millstone burst through the wall of the mill, Ravelle still stuck in its center, his neck whiplashed as his head banged against the stone with every revolution. It gained speed on the steep lane that led to the harbor, rolling and rolling until the demon's horrified howls became faint, rolling into the sea, rolling along the stone road that the sea had swallowed with the first town centuries ago. Deep underwater, it slowed and finally fell over in a ruined temple.

Sand rose in obscuring clouds around the stone and its passenger, smothering the cruel ruler of the Outer Darkness once and for all.

Linnea could only guess at that. For a time, she watched the spot in the sea where the stone had finally stopped, finding it by the rising discoloration in the water. She shaded her eyes to see the billows of sand . . . and then, black whorls of demon blood.

Beneath her, she felt Marius's hide twitch from the flies that had come to suck at his wounds and she slid off, tending to him at once, brushing off the disgusting flies, leading him to water and giving him it in her upraised, cupped hands.

"My love, my love," she murmured, filled with desperate fear. "I am here at last."

Marius took great gulps of the water before he spoke. "Eyes," he rasped. "Can't see." He rubbed at them but she pulled his hands away.

"He did the same to me once," she said. "Wait. If he is dead, then his magic will dissolve. Just wait a little."

Marius lifted his face to the sun. Its warm rays did the rest. Tears came from under his eyelids, and then they slowly opened. The centaur blinked and beheld the most beautiful sight in all creation.

The woman he loved, her face lit with joy.

"Linnea . . ." he said softly. They were lost in an embrace. Neither saw the magpie flutter down into the ruins of the mill a little distance away.

Curious as always, Esau picked up a glittering stone from the rubble, and dropped it. It was only mica and he would have to carry it back. He hopped to another spot. There he saw something that he vaguely remembered: a small piece of smooth stone, carved in the shape of a horse. The magpie picked it up in his beak, then flew up in the air, where he spied Marius and Linnea.

The centaur looked rather the worse for wear, but he did have Linnea to take care of him. Esau decided to give him the small stone as a gift to cheer him up rather than fly back to the Arcan Islands with it.

Epilogue

Esau had delivered the wedding invitations and all of Arcan had responded, it seemed. They waited but the bride was nowhere to be seen as yet. Simeon and Gideon were chaffing a side-stepping Marius, whose mane and tail were woven with flowers sacred to the nuptial rites of the forest folk.

"Stop," Megaleen chided them. "You are supposed to stand by the groom, and remember what he forgets, not make him nervous. Do you have the rings, Simeon?"

"Yes." Simeon showed them in his palm.

Megaleen gave him a stern look and went off to join the women. A tiny baby girl peeked out from the gossamer sling around Rhiannon, who was helping Linnea to dress. A shift of pleated white linen adorned with colored ribbons flowed over her swelling belly, and the bride rested her bouquet upon it.

"How fares the babe within?" Megaleen asked. "And the blushing bride?"

"Both well," Linnea laughed.

"This is a happy day in Arcan," Rhiannon said, straightening. They moved to take their places to the left and right of Linnea, and led her with graceful steps through the crowd to her waiting groom.

It was Quercus who joined them in holy union, rambling on a bit about the meaning of it all, which gave Lord Vane a chance to conceal his late arrival and slip in to the back row of guests.

"Where there is true understanding, there is true happiness. And that is the basis for enduring love," Quercus finished. Murmurs of gentle assent ran through the hushed crowd. "They are as one!" he cried. "Rejoice!"

Marius leaned down and kissed his bride. "For forever and a day," he whispered.

"Yes," Linnea whispered back, joy shining bright as the sun about her.

The Chanku chronicles continue
with WOLF TALES VII!

Turn the page for a preview!

On sale now!

1

_____

Night was all around him, and the darkness complete, but he sensed he wasn't alone. It was unbelievably dark, considering his terrific night vision. He wondered, for a moment only, if he might be in one of the many limestone caverns nearby, but that didn't feel right. He thought of turning around, to see if he could see who or what waited behind him, but he couldn't move.

He tried to scream. His lungs expanded and his vocal chords strained, but he made no sound.

Why?

Impossible.

The voice in his head sounded smug. His own voice. _Well, of course. Anton Cheval knows everything._

Bastard.

Well, crap. Was it possible to curse oneself?

Okay . . . so if I know it all, why the fuck are my arms trapped? Why is my heart pounding? Why can't I move. Why?

He fought whatever held him but fear exploded. Alive, a twisting, clutching thing, and it made its own horrible sound. His sounds. Heart pounding, blood rushing in his ears, the loud *whoosh, whoosh, whoosh* drowning everything.

Telling him nothing.

Keisha screamed.

My love! I can't move! His heart thundered, muscles strained. *Nothing. Not a damned thing. I'm sorry ... so damned sorry. I can't help you. ...*

Scalding tears filled his eyes. They slid down his face. Hot, wet trails of frustration.

Lily cried. The terrifying sound ripped through him. The heartrending cries of an infant, of *his* child! He fought harder, battled through the cloying darkness, struggled to reach out with arms like lead, tried to run with feet trapped in thick, grasping mud.

The screams grew louder, more frantic. He ran blindly, free now, but the very air surrounding him was impenetrable. Gelatinous, thick, clinging stuff. Someone had his family. Someone was stealing his mate, taking his child, taking everything that mattered.

Everyone he loved.

Gasping, Anton struggled harder, cried frantically for Keisha. Called out to Lily, but he couldn't run and he couldn't see and his world was ending.

It ... was ... all ... ending. ...

"Anton? Wake up! You're dreaming. You're having a nightmare."

He blinked, shocked into awareness, surprised out of cloying madness by the gentle glow of sunlight filtering through the window blinds. It seemed so much at odds with the frantic pounding of his heart. He took a deep breath, relieved yet unbelieving, to see the lovely face of his mate peering down at him.

He reached for her, ran trembling fingers along her silken cheek. "You're okay? Lily's okay?"

Keisha laughed. "We're fine. I was already awake or you would have scared me half to death, shouting like that. What were you dreaming?"

He shook his head. His body sagged back against the mattress as he realized his loved ones were safe. For now.

"It was nothing. I don't remember what it was."

But he did remember and he blocked his thoughts, hiding them away from Keisha. He remembered all too clearly the dream that had awakened him, and it was much too threatening.

It was the same dream he'd had, in one form or another, all this past week.

Someone wanted his mate and his child. Someone evil.

He was used to being a target. As the most powerful of the Chanku shapeshifters of the three known packs in existence, Anton was well aware of the risk of capture. There were those in the medical world who wanted his kind for study. Others in the government had hoped to create a secret army, breeding more Chanku to train and use for some unknown yet nefarious purpose. His race maintained secrecy as best they could, but enough humans knew the Chanku existed to make the threat of disclosure all too real.

It was one thing to worry about his own safety. Another altogether to worry about those he loved. He'd been entirely alone for so long. Then, in such a short span of time he, Stefan, and Alexandra had formed a pack. His life mate, Keisha Rialto, had joined them, and Keisha had given him the ultimate gift of love, their daughter Lily Milina. Just as Stefan and Xandi had produced little Alex.

Anton had never understood the strength of the family bond. Now he knew it all too well. Knew how powerful it was, how all consuming.

Finally, he understood the meaning of unconditional love.

Even more, he understood the fear of losing what he'd not had before—that deep, immeasurable love of family. It weakened him, made him vulnerable. At the same time, the love of his packmates, of his child and his one true mate, made him more powerful than he'd ever been.

His abilities as a wizard had grown exponentially. He'd developed skills over the past couple of years beyond anything he'd dreamed of, among them a more powerful sense of fore-knowledge, an ability to sense what was to come.

The problem was figuring out if he was merely projecting his own neurotic fears into what should have been restful sleep, or if he was having a valid premonition?

His premonitions had been frighteningly accurate, yet he'd had dreams just as frightening that were nothing more than dreams.

The secret lay in determining which was which.

His thoughts slipped back to the trip they'd all taken to Tia Mason and Lucien Stone's wedding in San Francisco, and the hijacking that had almost succeeded in ending their lives.

He'd worried about that flight for days. Had put his unease aside, assuming the graphic dreams were merely those of an overly concerned mate and Keisha's advanced pregnancy.

Then he'd come so close to losing her. So close to never knowing Lily, to never again holding his beloved Keisha in his arms.

Anton wrapped his fingers loosely around the back of Keisha's neck. He wondered if she felt his tremors. It took only a small amount of pressure to bring her close, to touch his lips to hers.

Lily slept on. The morning sun caressed Keisha's dark skin with golden fire as Anton slowly kissed her full lips, nuzzled the tender skin beneath her right ear. He twisted his fingers in the silken strands curling against her throat and drew her close.

She arched against him, her body supple and sleek in spite of the extra pounds she carried since giving birth. Her full breasts, heavy with milk for their daughter, drew Anton. He ran his tongue across one turgid nipple, tracing the taut edge of darkened areola.

Keisha moaned and lifted her hips, pressed her mound against his burgeoning erection. The sleek brush of her pubic hair tickled the underside of his penis where he was most sensitive and forced his shaft up against his belly.

He reared back and slipped his cock down between her slick folds, sliding over her clit with his entire length. Raising up again, he dragged himself slowly back and then surged forth at the same measured pace, sensing her growing arousal with the increased heat and friction.

Keisha moaned. She spread her thighs and arched against him. With his hips maintaining a slow but steady rhythm, Anton's tongue lightly circled the darker edge at the base of her nipple. He pressed his lips around the swollen tip and flicked the sensitive nub with his tongue.

"Ah," she breathed, laughing softly. "Be careful, my love. I'm really sensitive and my breasts are so full they ache. Lily's not fed for almost four hours. We could end up with a very big mess."

He chuckled and gently ran his tongue around the taut curve beneath her right breast, then the left, careful now to avoid her tender nipples. Keisha's fingers clutched at the tangled bedding beside her hips and he felt the rush of slick fluids between her legs. The knowledge that she was so ready for him sent a new surge of blood through his loins. His engorged cock, already aching and hard, grew even harder, stretched even longer.

Her desire was a potent aphrodisiac; the evidence that she needed him every bit as much as he needed her. Raising his buttocks, Anton carefully positioned the sensitive head of his cock between her slick folds. He held still for a moment, savoring the heat and moisture, the soft clasp that teased him. Then he thrust forward, slowly entering her tight passage.

Amazing, he thought, how this rippling channel that clasped him so warmly could be the same passage their daughter had taken when she entered their lives. The same passage his seed had traveled almost a year ago.

Keisha enclosed him within her heat and sheathed him like a warm, wet glove, holding him tightly, drawing him forward.

Anton sighed. Nothing in his world felt better than this. *Nothing.*

Keisha raised her hips, inviting him deeper. Tiny whimpers escaped her parted lips when the head of Anton's shaft touched the hard mouth of her cervix. He held himself there, immobile, relishing the enduring warmth of his beloved mate, the tiny sounds she made that told him she was lost in desire, caught completely in sensation.

He was caught as well, preternaturally aware of her halting breaths, her beating heart, her desperately needy cries.

Then she shuddered beneath him and her thoughts grabbed his, sharing the pressure of his cock deep inside, sharing the ache in her breasts and the urgent yearning of her body for the friction that would take her so quickly over the edge.

She wanted. She needed. She must have more of him. More of his heat, more of the fullness, the thick girth and filling length of his cock. She wanted the pain that so quickly leapt into pleasure when the flared crown of his glans pressed against her cervix. The pressure inside when he filled her, then slowly retreated, only to fill her once again.

Anton began to move, thrusting deep and slow, driving the solid length of his cock over her swollen clitoris with each deliberate penetration. Her growing arousal fed him, her need increased his own. He felt the rhythmic clenching of her powerful vaginal muscles as Keisha reached for her climax. She arched her back, pressing him even deeper and he drove into her harder, faster.

Keisha cried out. Her fingers clutched his sides and her nails scored his back while Anton raced her to the next orgasm.

She won, shuddering beneath him once more. Her long legs wrapped tightly around his hips. Her heels dug into the hard muscles at the backs of his thighs and she strained against his lean torso.

Clinging to him, Keisha met him thrust for thrust. Anton wrapped his arms around her and reared back, carrying her with him. When he sat on his heels and felt the tight clasp of her vaginal walls holding him close, pulling him deep, their minds and bodies linked. Their thoughts blended into a single tortured flash of fire and light, and still he held on, still his hips thrust hard and fast against his mate . . . and his arousal grew, hot and demanding.

Anton groaned, caught on the precipice of climax. He buried his face in the silken curve of Keisha's throat. He was enveloped in her scent, her warmth, the salty dampness of her skin. He existed only in the firm clasp of her rippling sheath, the rhythmic plunge of his hips as he drove into her warmth.

Then Keisha nipped his shoulder. The stinging pain from her sharp teeth sent him flying over the edge.

A white-hot flash of pure, indefinable power rolled from spine to balls to rock-hard cock. Burning a trail of pleasure so closely linked to pain, it coiled and struck him like a bolt of lightning. His body surged forward. He felt the hot blast of his seed and the familiar touch of Keisha's mind to his.

Lungs bursting, lights flashing behind his tightly closed eyes, he cried out with his release. Still holding his mate in his arms, Anton's hips continued their steady thrusting into her welcoming body. His heart opened to her love. His mind, all his thoughts and fears, were now an open book.

He could never hold a secret from his mate. No matter how

hard he tried, in this she would always have power over him. Taking his seed into her body, she took his fears and his love into her heart. They fell together, collapsing against the thick comforter and tumbled sheets, their bodies still linked, their thoughts as one.

Keisha brushed the sweat-tangled hair away from Anton's face and kissed him softly on the mouth. Her tongue circled his lips and tangled with his for a brief moment, easing him down from such a mind-blowing climax. Her taste was ambrosia to him, the food of the gods, and it was his alone this morning.

Just as his thoughts, his dreams and all his fears, were hers.

Keisha's lips moved once more against his mouth. She sighed, a soft sound of exasperation and love. "It was a dream, my love. When will you learn to share your worries? You have to learn to tell me your concerns, not hide them from me. We're mates. You're not meant to carry these unnecessary burdens alone. No one will ever take me from you. No one will take Lily. We are yours and you will always keep us safe." Her fingers combed through his long hair. Her beautiful amber eyes glistened with tears. "We will keep each other safe," she said, and kissed him once again.

That she would try to shoulder his fears made him feel small and vulnerable, but her thoughts laughed at his foolish notion. Keisha shook her head. Once again she kissed his mouth. Lily stirred in her crib. Keisha raised her head and smiled at their daughter. "I'm going to miss her being so close to us at night."

He'd heard this argument before. "I know, but it's time she moved to her own room."

"I know, but she's so tiny."

"She's Chanku. She has an old soul."

Keisha laughed, and he knew he'd won this battle, at least for now. Anton rolled to his back, carrying Keisha with him. She raised up with her forearms crossed on his chest and her heavy breasts warm and damp against him.

He felt her turgid nipples where they met his chest, the press of her large breasts, solid with the weight of milk for her daughter. She kissed the end of his nose, teasing.

"I feel you getting hard inside me again, but Lily is waking up and my breasts are about to burst. Worry about that, not about something that's merely a bad dream."

He kissed her lips and smiled. The mental link had quietly slipped away. He could worry in peace, now that Keisha was out of his head. "Yes, ma'am. Now take care of our daughter before I decide you've not been loved nearly enough this morning."

Laughing quietly, Keisha slipped her body free of his and headed to the bathroom to wash away the remnants of their lovemaking. He watched her walk, lost in the slow sway of her rounded hips and the deep indentation tracing the sensual curve of her spine. She was so perfect, so trusting. So unwilling to admit to danger, even though she had once endured the worst possible abuse.

He would never let anyone harm her again. Not ever.

She was his world. There was no life without her, and once again, he worried.